Diana ha   **desirable**   **thought.**

'Diana?' he said, using her Christian name for the first time.

She looked up at him. 'Neville?' she replied, and her voice had a question in it, too.

He was going to say—what was he going to say? He had never been in this situation before. He was drowning in her eyes, and in the little lift at each corner of her mouth as though she were about to smile, and he, God help him, was in a worse case than ever. He was losing his mind and about to run mad, for all he wanted was to have her under him, here and now. The mere sight of her had been enough to rouse him. This was new territory, and like all new territory must be explored carefully, but he had never felt less careful in all his life.

Paula Marshall, married with three children, has had a varied life. She began her career in a large library and ended it as a senior academic in charge of history in a polytechnic. She has travelled widely, has been a swimming coach, and has appeared on *University Challenge* and *Mastermind*. She has always wanted to write, and likes her novels to be full of adventure and humour.

Recent titles by the same author:

AN UNCONVENTIONAL HEIRESS
THE BLACK SHEEP'S BRIDE*
MAID OF HONOUR*

*part of the *Elizabethan Season* quartet

THE DARING DUCHESS

Paula Marshall

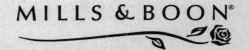

MILLS & BOON and MILLS & BOON with the Rose Device are registered trademarks of the publisher.

First published in Great Britain 2004
Harlequin Mills & Boon Limited,
Eton House, 18-24 Paradise Road, Richmond, Surrey TW9 1SR

© Paula Marshall 2004

ISBN 0 263 83984 2

Set in Times Roman 10¼ on 11½ pt.
04-1104-95563

Printed and bound in Spain
by Litografía Rosés S.A., Barcelona

Author Note

I like to make my novels as accurate about life in the past as possible. In case some of you think that Neville and Diana's adventures are based on my invention, I have written the following notes which I hope will interest you.

The belief that sex with a virgin would cure venereal disease goes a long way back in history. It may, in fact, be a misreading of the truth that if you were clean yourself and slept with a virgin you would not be infected! Whether or not that was its origin, the belief was certainly held and exploited by brothelkeepers like the one in my novel. They could command a large fee from wealthy patrons.

In our own time we have seen that sexual sleaze can ruin governments as well as individuals once it becomes public knowledge. The fear of revolution, so strong in Britain after 1789, lasted well into the nineteenth century, and every effort was made to suppress the emergence of potentially ruinous scandals. Marie Antoinette's reputation was ruined by such scandals about her, the most notorious being that of the diamond necklace. That they were all false saved neither herself nor her husband.

Captain Knighton's conspiracy to overthrow the government is based on the career of Captain Arthur Thistlewood, who helped to organise the Spa Fields Riots which were designed to overthrow the then government by seizing the Bank of England and The Tower. They failed, but in 1820 Thistlewood tried again by promoting what came to be known as The Cato Street Conspiracy. He planned to kidnap members of the Cabinet when they met at a private dinner party. Through an informer the police learned of it and arrested the conspirators, who were tried for treason. Thistlewood and several of the other leaders were hanged.

The conduct of the duel and the rest of my background of low-life London and its streets is as accurate as I could make it.

I hope that you enjoy not only my lovers but also my recreation of the past.

Paula Marshall

Prologue

1817

Diana Rothwell, now the Dowager Duchess of Medbourne, was a widow who had never truly been a wife. She had become a Dowager at the early age of twenty-four, and had also insisted on being present when her eighty-year-old husband was lowered into the crypt in the family chapel, which stood in the grounds of Medbourne Castle in Nottinghamshire.

This, of course, was against all the rules of etiquette, which stated that no woman of quality was ever to be present at the funeral service of any member of her family. She was dressed in her ordinary outdoor clothing, too, not in the compulsory black and the widow's cap that mourning decreed she ought to wear for a full year.

What the shocked spectators did not know was that, as usual, Diana was obeying the wishes of her dead husband, Charles. He had not only left her the majority of his entire fortune, including Medbourne Castle and the many acres that he had owned since he was the last of the Rothwells, there being no heir, but also a long letter setting out his wishes for her future.

Present in the chapel were all of the senior servants and a

number of men who had been friends and neighbours of the dead man and whom he had invited to the will reading, which would follow the ceremony. They were, although they had not yet been informed of it, all to be rewarded by being left either money or some memento of what had been long friendships or, in the case of the servants, long service. The quality's wives, obeying the demands of etiquette, were in the Great Hall of the Castle, waiting for the men to return. They were happily passing the time by busily deploring their hostess's behaviour and her appearance.

'Neither proper nor *comme il faut*,' they agreed to a woman, 'but then, who would have expected anything else from her? Neither was it proper that a man of the Duke's age should have married a girl of seventeen, young enough to be his granddaughter.'

'And she never gave him any heirs, either,' sniffed several of them.

'Helped him with his experiments, too.'

Heads were collectively shaken, and shaken even further when they later learned that the Duke had left her virtually everything—other than the titbits which had gone their, and their husbands', way.

Diana thought nothing of this nor of them. On his deathbed the Duke had handed her a letter.

'You have been as good a wife as any husband could expect,' he said. 'As soon as I have died, read my letter and take careful note of my wishes for your future. On no account wait until after my funeral to find out what I have written.'

Obedient as always, Diana had read the letter with mounting surprise, not to say shock.

'My dearest child,' he had begun, 'for that is what you have always been. The child I could never have, since I am barren through impotence. Child and pupil, too, who loved an old man who could not offer you what was rightfully yours, a true marriage and children. I therefore cheated not only you, but your family, and you never reproached me once.

'I also know that you only married me because I bribed your poverty-stricken parents so that they gladly handed you over to an old man. Fortunately I have not wasted all your youth and, now that I am gone, would wish you to enjoy yourself in the great world that has hitherto been denied to you.

'I am sure that you do not entirely regret the years that we spent together when you proved to me something which I had always suspected: that a young woman could be as well educated and trained as a young man and perform as brilliantly. Were you a man, you would have achieved a double first at my old University. To that end you were my experiment and royally you have proved my belief to be correct.

'Now it is time that you amused yourself. You are not to mourn for me in public. You are also to attend my funeral, but not in widow's weeds. You are not to spend a year in black and further months in lilac, but you are to go out into society straight away and do all those things of which I robbed you of when you married me—even though I gave you other treasures instead.

'These are my last commandments to you and I hope that you will carry them out. I know that you will always remember the years we spent studying together and that you will benefit from them. Beware of fortune hunters and if you do marry again I trust you to find someone worthy of you so that I may rest in peace.'

Diana had put the letter down, her eyes brimming with tears. Yes, he had known, he had always known, that there had been times when she regretted the life she might have had—and now she would have it with his blessing. Let the polite world think of her as it would, she would carry out his last instructions to the letter. The one thing which that world would never know was what a bluestocking she was, able to

cut and thrust in debate as well as any lawyer, that she was
something of a natural philosopher, and in the last two years
of her husband's life had run his estates for him.

He had added a Post Scriptum that amused her. 'I have
asked the Widow Marchmont, a distant relative of yours, to
introduce you to the great world as soon as possible and she
has so agreed. Do not shock her too much—but you have my
permission to shock her a little.'

His last sentence had made Diana smile through her tears.
Mrs Marchmont had arrived at the Castle early that morning.
She had immediately begged Diana not to attend her husband's funeral service—and Diana's refusal of her request had
been her first shock. Otherwise she seemed to be one of those
four-square sensible women who are the pillars of any com-
munity in which they live.

The funeral service was over at last and the assembled company streamed back into the Castle, to eat, to drink, to listen
to the will reading—and to express their shock at the last
sentence in the will, which commanded his widow to go out
into the world and enjoy herself. Intended, no doubt, Diana
thought, to reinforce what he had written in his last letter to
her.

Yes, she would do as he wished: her last tribute to him.

Chapter One

1819

Sir Neville Fortescue later thought that his whole life changed after he accidentally overheard two of his supposed friends talking about him at Lady Leominster's ball.

'Fortescue,' Frank Hollis proclaimed to Henry Latimer. 'Oh, no, I shouldn't trouble to ask Fortescue to make up the party for the Coal Hole. He's not a bad fellow, reliable and respectable, but dull, damned dull. Never put a foot wrong in his life. Virtue its own reward and all that. It bores me just to think of him, never mind doing the hobnob bit. He can neither hob nor nob.'

'Slow and steady often wins the race, you know.'

'Depends on what race you're running in. He's spent five years in Parliament and he's not left the starting gate yet. No, let's forget him and talk of better things. What do you think of his cousin Alford's latest ladybird? Now there's a fellow who knows how to live. Let's ask him to join us.'

The speakers moved away, leaving Sir Neville Fortescue MP to reflect glumly that listeners never heard any good of themselves. Not that what they had said had been particularly bad, rather that it was the wrong kind of good for him to be dismissed as merely a priggish bore. Even though he had no great opinion of Frank Hollis's ability to judge anyone correctly, his careless remarks stung him to the degree that he found himself in a simmering rage at being judged at all.

It would not have been so bad had he not, earlier that day, called on Harriet Beauchamp whom he rather thought would be a useful wife, and proposed to her. His widowed mother, who occasionally acted as his hostess, was constantly nagging at him over his failure to marry.

'A man in your position needs a wife,' she frequently told him, and when he had mentioned to her that he had decided to ask Harriet to marry him, she had been overjoyed.

Well, Harriet was a pretty little woman, if a touch frivolous, but he and his mother both agreed that she would undoubtedly make him a very creditable wife, even if his mother would have preferred him to pop the question to Diana Rothwell, the Duke of Medbourne's enormously wealthy young widow who had descended on society last year. It was this that had made him suddenly decide that if he had to marry, Harriet would be a more suitable Lady Fortescue than Diana, the daring Dowager, who was as frank as any man and had the wit of the devil. She was, he was sure, the very last woman he would choose for a wife. He needed someone quiet and comfortable, whose conduct would always be proper.

Alas, he had done and said all those things which a man ought to do when proposing to a pretty young thing after speaking to her papa. To which Harriet had said, outwardly sorrowful, but inwardly pleased that her papa would support her in her refusal of him as he supported her in everything, 'Oh, Neville, dear, I like having you as a friend, but I could never be your wife.'

Neville, trapped on his knees, and having never thought for a moment that she would refuse him, exclaimed, a trifle indignantly, 'Why ever not?'

Harriet looked down at him, and decided to tell him the

truth. 'When I marry I want to have some excitement in my life. You are so sure to do the correct thing at all times that I fear that our marriage would never have any.'

He rose, reflecting that the tight breeches which were the current fashion, made prolonged kneeling painful, and replied a trifle stiffly, 'I thought that most young ladies preferred a husband they could depend on.'

'True, but you are so dependable that it makes you a trifle dull,' she informed him tactlessly, 'and I could not bear a dull married life. I am sure that you will find some nice but proper young lady who would make you a far better wife than me. You will still remain my friend, I hope. I am certain that if I ever needed any help you would always offer me the most excellent advice.'

Neville's first instinct was to say, rather savagely, 'On the contrary, I think that you ought to go to a good lawyer for that,' but, as usual, he came out with something safe, but banal. 'I'm sorry that you have seen fit to refuse me, Harriet, but rest assured that I shall always wish you well.'

'There, I knew that you would not take offence at my refusal. You are much too good for that.'

The something wild that lived inside Neville, but which he usually managed to suppress, had him on the verge of seizing hold of Harriet, and giving her a savage and prolonged kiss, before he retreated, snarling at her, 'Was that exciting enough for you? Or do you wish me to go further?'

Of course he did no such thing. He had spent his whole life trying to be the opposite of his drunken and rake-hell father who had died in the arms of a lady of easy virtue. Only the fact that Neville's grandfather had, on her marriage, tied up his mother's inheritance so that her husband could not pillage it had prevented them both from being reduced to penury after his death.

It was just as well that his mother was spending the summer with her widowed sister in Surrey, for were she at home he would have had the painful duty of facing her reproaches for failing to convince Harriet that he would make her a good husband. Never mind that he did not particularly want to marry her—that had never entered his mother's consideration.

Harriet, he thought, driving away from his failure on the field of amorous battle, would be well served for her folly in wanting an exciting marriage if she ended up marrying someone like his father, Sir Carlton Fortescue, Baronet, and was then compelled to live in the misery that Sir Carlton had inflicted on both his wife and his son.

What he had not bargained for was that on the very same day, while attending the Leominsters' ball, he should overhear a pair of rakes describing him in language very similar to that which Harriet had used.

Was he so dull? Was it wrong to be virtuous and dull? Was it possible for one to be virtuous and exciting? Why was it that he should feel so offended by the sad fact that a pair of fellows whom he had thought were his friends were able to dismiss him so cavalierly? Was it possible that he might enjoy being a little less dull, still avoid the excesses of his father, but not appear to be the kind of prig whom the two men had laughed at and Harriet had dismissed?

It was useless. He was what he was, the first Fortescue for two hundred years to live a good life and not be a byword in both town and country for his escapades. He had become an MP in his mid-twenties and had always tried to fulfil his Parliamentary duties carefully and honestly—which was more than most of them could claim.

Neville walked back into the ballroom. He would take his leave of Lady Leominster, go home to try to forget what he had just heard and continue his orderly life no matter what others thought of him.

On the way to her, however, someone clapped a hand on his shoulder exclaiming, 'The very man! Come and enjoy yourself for once, my dear Neville, by joining the party I'm assembling to move on to the Coal Hole when we've finished doing the pretty here. But before that, allow me to introduce you to Duchess Diana, who for some unknown reason claims that she is positively dying to meet you!'

It was his cousin, George, Lord Alford, with whom he had, earlier, been compared—to his own detriment. He winced a little. George was everything he was not: flashily handsome, dressed to kill, and determined to enjoy every moment of his life, whether he was with fast women, fast horses, betting in dubious gaming hells or racing his fast curricle to Brighton to win a bet. If Neville were a betting man, which he wasn't, he would have bet that George was running through his inheritance at the same speed as one of his better horses.

He had absolutely no wish to accompany him either to the Coal Hole or to be introduced to the Daring Duchess, as Diana had been nicknamed. From all he had heard of her she was as irresponsible as George: the very last woman he wanted either as a mistress or a wife.

'Now I really do doubt that, George—the Duchess Diana bit, I mean, and, no, I don't wish to oblige you on either count. I'm for home and my bed.'

George Alford began to laugh. 'You could oblige me, old fellow, if you would. I've bet Frank Hollis that I could persuade you to join us and I stand to lose a tidy sum if you refuse me.'

Neville stared at him, remembering only too well Frank's unkind remarks about him. 'Frank Hollis, eh?' he said at last. 'In that case I will join you—but not for long.'

'And Duchess Di, too. He also bet that you wouldn't agree to meet her.'

'Did he, indeed? Yes, you may take me to her, but I don't promise to enjoy myself at either rendezvous.'

'That's no matter. I'd like to see Frank's face when you make your bow to the lady and when you join us on the stroke of midnight to depart for pastures new.'

Reluctantly, Neville allowed himself to be led by George to where Diana was holding court in one corner of the room, surrounded by admirers.

She had come upon the town with all the éclat and passion that Lady Caroline Lamb had once displayed. True, she was not so carelessly silly as Lady Caro, since she would have passed for a bluestocking had she cared to reveal that interesting fact. Instead, she frequently demonstrated that she not only had the power to charm all around her by her beauty, but that she was also able to enliven even the dullest function by her wit and originality of mind.

She played whist and chess as well as any man, her performance on the piano was masterly and it was whispered that she spoke three foreign languages. What was more, she had created a sensation in Hyde Park when she drove there in a curricle with two spirited horses that a man would have been proud to control and handled them perfectly.

Not only that, once, when out for a walk with the elderly cousin who was her chaperon, she had come upon a man brutally thrashing a dog. She had immediately demanded that he desist; when he refused, she had set about him with her parasol, calling on a passing gentleman—to whom, of course, she had never been introduced—to assist her in overcoming the man so that she might rescue the dog.

Fortunately, the gentleman proved to be more than that. He was Lord Vaux, a peer of impeccable lineage, fortune and behaviour, who promptly did as she bid him, before handing the fellow over to a passing constable. He then insisted on escorting both the ladies and the dog to Diana's home off Piccadilly. Two days later he proposed to her, but was refused.

He was not the only one who sought her hand—but she refused them all, both high and low, steady and rakish. It seemed that the catch of the season was determined not to be caught. Bets were laid at Watier's as to how many fellows would propose to her before the season was over. It was said that the count had already reached twenty and included Prince Adalbert of Eckstein Halsbach, a cousin of the Princess of Wales, and Neville was determined not to be added to the list, since she was exactly the kind of woman whom he most disliked.

Nevertheless, facing her while George introduced him, he was also, again reluctantly, aware that she was possessed of a rare beauty. He had seldom seen such glossily gorgeous raven hair, such heavenly blue eyes and such a shapely mouth, which seemed to have been especially designed for kissing.

Her toilette surprised him a little because it was so simple; her dress was a plain white, adorned with silk snowdrops, and her fan was small, not some great thing with which to strike at and tease a man. Most surprising of all, she wore no jewellery.

He was a little shocked by his immediate reaction to her when he took her delicate hand and bowed over it, saying, 'A pleasure to meet you, Duchess.' To his eternal surprise, he really meant what he was saying.

She was equally gallant, responding with, 'And a pleasure to meet you, Sir Neville. I had been told that you are an extremely serious gentleman who might find such a flyaway creature as myself beneath your interest or consideration.'

Flyaway, indeed! Without any real evidence to the contrary he thought that the lady was misnaming herself. There was a hint of the formidable about her, an attribute that many women in the *ton* had never possessed, or even aspired to. And why did he think that? This was a question that he put to himself later—and could not answer.

He tried not to appear too overset by saying, 'I have heard nothing but praise of you, and I am indebted to my cousin George for persuading me to be introduced to you.'

'So you needed persuading! That disappoints me a little.'

'Is that because,' Neville replied, 'you expect everyone to wish to be introduced to you as soon as possible?'

He was a little worried that he might have said something overtly critical to her, which might cause offence, but the lady was of sterner stuff than that.

'Indeed not. It is rather that when one is the latest unmarried and wealthy creature to come upon the town, every Tom, Dick and Harry thinks that they have the right to be introduced to her as soon as possible. It is refreshing to find someone who is a little reluctant to meet me—which is the impression that your cousin George left me with when we spoke of you.'

By now they had moved through the crowd to the edge of the ballroom floor—or rather, Diana had skilfully urged him in that direction—so that he felt compelled to add when the band struck up the music for a quadrille, 'If your programme is not already filled, Duchess, I would be honoured to escort you on to the floor. I have to add that I have not danced much of late so you must excuse me if I am occasionally clumsy.'

'Well, I was, much earlier, engaged to dance it with a gentleman who has later asked to be excused as he had received a message of some urgency begging him to return home at once, so I shall be very happy to stand up with you,' and she offered him her hand.

'Excellent.' Neville bowed and they joined three couples who were busy making up a set, leaving behind them George Alford, his mouth agape, never having seen his strait-laced cousin on the dance floor before—and with the beauty of the season, too! He resolved to roast Neville until he was done to a turn when they were on the way to the Coal Hole since, of all things, that upright old Neville should be so struck by the Daring Duchess was the oddest.

He was nearly as surprised as his cousin was. Neville was too busy trying to keep up with the dance to explain to himself why he had allowed George to introduce him to the lady at all, and why he was so immediately struck by her, while she stepped through the dance with all the grace and elegance of a prima ballerina.

What neither of them knew was that Diana was nearly as favourably surprised by Sir Neville Fortescue as he was by her. She had heard him spoken of as a dull dog who, in Frank Hollis's words, 'never deigned to join in the fun, his nose always stuck in some giant tome or other'.

She had pictured him as short and ill-dressed: a stoop-shouldered bookworm, blinking at her through thick-glassed spectacles. Instead he was tall, athletic and, although not conventionally handsome after the fashion of Lord Byron, had a strong face, full of character. His chestnut hair, his green eyes and his stern mouth pleased her rather than otherwise. Nothing about him reeked of high fashion—he was, she thought, very much his own man.

The first time that she passed him in the dance she murmured, 'Why have I never met you before?'

The second time, he replied, 'I don't go out into society very often.'

To which her riposte on the third was, 'I think that is society's loss.'

When they passed again he countered that with, 'But my gain, perhaps?'

'Your gain?' she said, eyebrows raised. 'I'm not sure.'

Frank Hollis, watching them, his jaw dropped in surprise, muttered to George Alford, 'Is that really old Nev dancing— and with Duchess Di of all people? I thought that he never danced, just sat there, watching everyone, with a superior expression on his phiz.'

George laughed at him, rather than laugh at himself for having misjudged his cousin a little. 'Oh, it's Nev who's her latest victim. He took one look at her and practically dragged her on to the dance floor. What's more, he can dance as well, if not better than the rest of us: he just didn't care to before.'

'Oh, that's Duchess Di all over,' Frank grinned. 'She has this strong effect on every man she meets. But who'd have thought she'd have caught Nev in her snares. Just goes to show, don't it. Best turn-up of the year, and no mistake.'

Still turning and twisting to the music, Diana and Neville continued to address each other in what Diana thought afterwards was the oddest conversation that she had ever engaged in on a dance floor. Well into it, she said, daringly, 'I would like to meet you again, Sir Neville, where we might pursue some of your notions more seriously. The dance floor is fit only for idle, if flattering, conversation, I fear.'

To which, to his profound astonishment, Neville found himself saying, 'Oh, if that is what is seemly, may I say how much I appreciate your toilette. No frills, no furbelows, no flashy jewellery, just your own good self, which needs no unnecessary adornment.'

He was no more surprised than Diana herself. The slight mockery with which he had spoken pleased her more than a little. She had grown tired of grovelling flattery, addressed to her fortune more than to herself. One thing was plain to her, Sir Neville Fortescue was quite different from every other man she had met since she had arrived in London. For both of them the dance seemed to be over in a flash—time had somehow turned in on itself—and they had hardly bowed to one another at the beginning than they were bowing to one another at the end.

Neville escorted her off the dance floor, and after he had thanked her and shown her to her seat, moved away a little. He had no wish to monopolise her; more to the point, though, was that she disturbed him, and he was not sure why.

He was immediately accosted by a grinning George who exclaimed, 'You old devil, you! I thought that you never danced, claimed that you didn't want to be introduced to Duchess Di, and once you had been, before I could propose myself for the quadrille, you had annexed her and were leading her out on to the floor to the manner born.'

Neville found himself glaring at the talkative fool. 'If you can't hold your tongue, George, I'll not come with you to the Coal Hole and then you'll lose the other half of your bet. What I do, or care not to do, is my business, not yours.'

He had never before spoken so aggressively to George with the result that his cousin was now staring at him and muttering, 'I can't allow you to do that, I'm pretty short of cash these days, so I'll not roast you further, but you must admit that you're not a bit like yourself tonight, Nev.'

'Perhaps not, perhaps I'm a little tired of being myself. If you will excuse me, I'll retire to the supper room until midnight.'

George was still staring at him when he moved off, and was piqued even further when Duchess Di called him to her side to say, 'Why have you never introduced me to your cousin before? He's not a bit like his reputation, is he? I can't imagine what everyone can be thinking of. He can be quite the gallant can't he?'

Neville quite the gallant! Whatever next! The world must be coming to an end. What on earth had Nev been saying for Duchess Di to come out with that?

Diana herself was not sure what it was about Sir Neville Fortescue that so exercised her. She must meet him again soon to try to discover whether she had taken leave of her senses— or found them.

Neville, in much the same predicament, caught up with George and the others when they were leaving. Frank Hollis, who had begun to think that Neville was crying off, and thus that he had won his bet with George, looked most dejected when he walked rapidly towards them.

'Thought you'd changed your mind,' he muttered.

Nev glared at him again. It was not something that he normally did, but he seemed to have been doing rather a lot of it at Lady Leominster's ball. The good lady herself had carolled at him when he took his leave. 'So glad that you have seen fit to come out of your grotto tonight. Your mama will be pleased when she hears of it and the Duchess is such a dear girl, isn't she—even if she is a little wild? It's time a man of sense such as yourself took an interest in her after she has been besieged by every fashionable nodcock in town!'

The world and his wife, Neville thought savagely—again— seemed to be taking an undue interest in him and his affairs these days, but he offered her ladyship a polite smile and went to join George's party. He could think of nothing that he would less like to do after a long day than move on to the Coal Hole, which was situated in a cellar and proved to be as crowded, smoky, noisy and smelly as he had feared, but he had made a promise to George to go with him, and he always kept his promises. Another dull and boring trait of his, was yet another of his unspoken conclusions.

Perhaps it was because he was not half-cut that he found the whole excursion so dismal. Perhaps if he started to drink as hard as the others he would find all the women there pretty, all the men witty, all the songs melodious, all their lyrics poetic, and the surroundings as pleasing to the eye rather than, as they were at present while he was completely sober, absolutely hideous.

It might make an interesting experiment if he were to drink rather more than he ought to. So when George called for yet another round, and after that, still another and another, he determinedly joined in until he found himself on his way to being fuddled, but still as unappreciative of everything about him as he had been when he was sober.

'Time to go home,' he announced a little later—although no one took any notice of him. George was already under the table and Frank Hollis and Bobus Ventress were not far from joining him, so he slipped away unnoticed, lest by continuing to drink he joined them, too. Once outside the night air revived him a little and he walked briskly along until he saw an empty cab coming towards him. It took him all the way home to Fortescue House—and bed, but not to sleep. Duchess Diana's face came between him and that.

Chapter Two

'I thought that you were rather *épris* with Sir Neville Fortescue last night, and that it was no bad thing if you were.'

Diana looked over her book at her companion and chaperon, Isabella Marchmont, who was busy stitching away at a cover for a hassock to be used in church.

'Why do you think that?'

'Because he's more steady than most of those who have been chasing you since we came to London. The majority of them are rakes and wastrels of the first water—and poor as church mice into the bargain.'

'Not seduced by my charms, but by my money, you mean?'

'If you like.'

Diana put her book down. It was one of the Reverend William Paley's more difficult theological works and, while she was interested in what he had to say, it was hardly the most exciting of reading.

'I found him…' she hesitated '…quite intriguing, for want of a better word, and most unlike his reputation as a dull prig. Nor did he seem to me to be a rogue or fortune hunter solely after my money, but that could have been a ploy to deceive me.'

'There is that, my dear. You would be wise to be careful.'

'Oh, I will be, you may be sure.'

She did not tell Isabella that the name of every man who had approached her and shown a burning desire to marry her had been referred to her lawyers. In each case they immediately ordered an ex-Bow Street Runner who worked for them to investigate his financial position and report back. Later in the afternoon she would drive to their offices and ask them to check on Sir Neville Fortescue's situation for her. It was not that she believed that behind his apparent rectitude his pockets were to let, but it was always better to be safe than sorry.

The expression on her face hardened when she thought of the reason why she was being so hard-headed, so apparently callous. In her first days in the *ton* she had trusted a man, only to discover, quite by accident, that he had been deceiving her grossly. Never again, she had vowed, never again would she be taken in by a handsome face and a charming manner, for he had quite convinced her that he loved her for herself alone and only a lucky chance had revealed to her what a cheat he was. After that she had determined she would never take anything, or anyone, for granted, but would remain as wary as the veriest miser who was guarding his money from thieves and swindlers.

No, she would have Sir Neville investigated as a matter of course, and until the lawyers' verdict on him arrived, she would go carefully with him—however much she might be attracted to him. In the deep watches of the night after she had met him at the Leominsters' ball, she had come to understand that, for the first time since she had dismissed Henry Latimer, Sir Neville Fortescue had pierced the hard shell of indifference to the opposite sex that lay behind her seemingly free and easy manner.

Neville was as exercised by Diana as she was by him. He could not get her out of his mind. Her piquant face would rise

up before him even when, on the following morning, he was
going over the estate books with his agent—and that was
something which had never happened before.

Seated at his desk, two days later, he was still not free of
her, or of the unkind verdict delivered on him at the Leominsters' ball, when a timid knock sounded on the door.

To his cry of 'Enter', it was young Lemuel Banks, one of
his footmen, who came in.

'Yes, what is it, Banks?' he asked, a little impatiently for
him.

Lem hesitated for a moment, so that Neville said, brusque
again, 'Well, what is it, man?'

His servant's hesitation had been caused by his master
seeming to be most unlike himself. He had never known him
to be so short with him before. All of the Fortescue servants
compared him favourably with the other employers of whom
their peers gossiped when they went to the local inn.

'It is this, Sir Neville,' he began at last. 'I have been walking out with a maidservant, Belinda Jesson, who works in the
kitchens at Medbourne House. I called there three days ago—
as we had arranged—to take her for a walk in the Park.

'The housekeeper told me that she had gone on an errand
for the cook on the previous afternoon—but had never returned. They wondered if she had run off with some young
man, but if she did, she had left all her possessions behind
her. Besides, I told them that I was the only young man she
had ever walked out with, and I knew nothing about her disappearance.

'The thing is, sir, one of the Duchess's servants called this
afternoon and asked for the housekeeper to release me so that
the Duchess might speak to me about Belinda's disappearance. It seems that her housekeeper had just learned that another servant girl on Lady Jersey's kitchen staff had disappeared in the same fashion. It was only then that our

housekeeper recalled that last winter, when you were in the country, one of the girls on our staff had apparently wilfully run away—and that she had left all her possessions behind her, too.'

He ground to a halt for a moment.

'She allowed me to visit Medbourne House where I was interviewed by the Duchess, who has decided to investigate the matter herself. She was most severe in her questioning of me, but seemed satisfied that I knew nothing of how and why poor Belinda had disappeared. She sent me away with a note for you, which I hereby deliver.'

Neville took the proffered letter from him. He remembered that Lem had always taken very seriously the lessons that the children of his staff were given at a dame's school near his country home, and that he had already told the butler that he wished to better himself. Neville had heard educated clerks give a worse explanation of some matter or other than the one that Lem had just offered to him.

He read it rapidly. The Duchess had written briefly and to the point: 'To Sir Neville Fortescue. Your footman has convinced me that something very strange has happened to two young girls, one from your household staff and one from mine. I would be exceedingly grateful if you would see fit to call on me tomorrow, after nuncheon, so that we might speak of it.'

She had appended no postscript of any kind, nor had she referred to their meeting at Lady Leominster's ball, merely signing herself as 'Diana Medbourne'.

Neville refolded the letter, sat down at his desk and began to write her an answer. When he had finished he looked sternly at the waiting Lem.

'You will deliver this message to the Duchess immediately. It tells her that I will pay her a visit tomorrow—as she requests—at two of the clock. You must say nothing to any-one—not even the housekeeper—about what has passed be-

tween the three of us. This may all be a great fuss about
nothing—indeed, I hope it is. But I owe a duty of care to
those who work for me, and I am sorry that our housekeeper
did not speak to me, or to my mother, of the runaway girl. If
more than one has disappeared rather mysteriously, then
something must be done.'

He was not certain quite what that something might be, but
he felt that he needed to reassure Lem, who was such a good
fellow. He would visit the Duchess immediately, if only to
settle things once and for all.

Lem's face brightened considerably. 'Thank you, sir. If I
may say so, it is what I expected of you.'

Well, that was something, after all the dismissive remarks
that he had heard about himself recently. Perhaps being dull
and reliable was not such a bad a thing after all!

The only fly in the ointment was that he would have to
meet Diana Medbourne again. She had had a most unsettling
effect on him and the last thing he wanted was to become
heavily engaged with a woman who possessed such an equiv-
ocal reputation.

Diana read Sir Neville Fortescue's letter with some interest.
Not only would she have the pleasure of meeting him again,
but she also had the oddest feeling that there was more to this
business of missing girls then met the eye and that she needed
the help of someone discreet. Sir Neville possessed the reputation for being exactly that—their whole world was agreed
on it.

She had refused to join Isabella on a visit to some friends,
pleading tiredness and waited for him in her drawing room
with the splendid Richard Wilson landscape over the hearth.
She was sure, now that she had met him, that he would arrive
pat upon the hour of two of the clock—the time that he had
stipulated—and so he did.

When he entered he seemed, somewhat surprisingly, to be a little more handsome than she had remembered him being from their first meeting. His clothes were still simple, but perfectly tailored. Everything about him combined to present to the world the picture of a man who did not aspire to the dandy set, but was determined to give an impression of perfect respectability—and dependability.

'Duchess,' he murmured, bowing when she rose to greet him. 'I have come at your request. How may I help you?'

'First,' she said, 'we must sit, and perhaps deplore a little the fact that we are alone together in private, for although I am now a widow I am told I am sufficiently young enough to require a chaperon to be present. However, since Miss Marchmont is absent, I hope that, given the delicate nature of the problem that we are about to discuss, you will forgive this breach of etiquette. We could scarcely have discussed it before her.'

There, that should mollify him, and so it did. Neville, who had felt somewhat disquieted on finding the lady on her own, gave her a small smile, and replied, as she had hoped, 'Certainly, I am quite prepared to breach etiquette in the unusual circumstances of this case.'

'Excellent.' And she motioned him to an armchair opposite to her. His matter-of-fact manner pleased her all over again. She found his conversation, from which flowery sentences devoted to her charm and many of her other attributes were all missing, to be most refreshing. Many of the men she had met since she had arrived in society felt it necessary either to flatter her unctuously, or else to give her the impression that she overwhelmed them, but not, as she had already discovered, this one.

In this she was most mistaken. Sir Neville Fortescue was not only overwhelmed, he was almost, but not quite, struck dumb by meeting her in private. Only his habit of behaving in the most matter-of-fact manner was preventing him from being as openly moonstruck as most of the men to whom she had been introduced.

Now that they were alone, away from the distractions of the ballroom, he was even more free to admire everything about her. He had all the time in the world to appreciate such easy charm, such *savoir faire,* such a kissable mouth and such a delightfully sylph-like figure… The impression that Diana was making on him with hardly a word spoken was so strong that his body was behaving in the most disgraceful way. So disgraceful, indeed, that wearing the tight breeches which fashion demanded of him was becoming painful.

What, he wondered, while conversing apparently sensibly with her, could be the matter with him? He could only conclude that it must be the lengthy period of continence, which he had suffered recently, that was doing the damage. Except that, if that were true, why had he not been similarly overcome when he had been courting Harriet Beauchamp?

He had met her many times and he—and his wretched body—had always been able to behave with the utmost propriety. He had never had to reprimand himself—or it—for indulging in such carnal thoughts. But he knew, he knew what was wrong: Diana Medbourne was, for him, the living and breathing image of temptation and he was lusting after her as though he were a green boy again, scarcely able to control himself.

This definitely would not do. How could he admire such an unconventional creature? But there it was and there seemed to be nothing that he could do about it. Old habit prevailed, however. Words flowed from him, almost without him bidding them, and, since she was nodding her agreement with his apparently sage advice, his outward state must be giving her no indication of what was happening to his inward one— to say nothing of his body.

When he had finished speaking, his face and manner still grave, giving no sign of his physical and mental turbulence, she told him, 'An admirable summing up of the situation, Sir Neville. Yes, it is quite plain that there is something very suspicious about the disappearance of these young women. Your suggestion that you should approach the local magistrate and ask him for the matter to be investigated is an excellent one.

'I would have gone to him at once, were it not for my sex. If they have been kidnapped, I fear it must be for some reason of which I, as a woman of quality, ought not to know, or to speak of. You understand me, I'm sure.'

Yes, he quite understood her. She knew, as well as he did, that it was possible that pretty Belinda and the other two girls might have been spirited away in order to be taken to some house of ill fame where they would be used for immoral purposes. By her speech, the Duchess was as clever as she was beautiful. Could it be that it was the combination of cleverness and beauty which was disturbing him so much?

His mother had remarked, a little disapprovingly, that the lady was known to be wild. 'Just imagine, she invited that dreadful, immoral, radical revolutionary William Godwin to dine with her: a man whose first wife wrote that foolish book on the rights of women!'

There was, though, nothing wild in her behaviour towards him today. On the contrary, she was all that was ladylike. A spirit lamp that stood on a side-table had just boiled water for the silver teapot, which was waiting for tea from a mahogany-and-silver caddy to be spooned into it.

Diana rose, said, 'You will partake, Sir Neville, I am sure.'

She did not wait for an answer, but brewed the tea, waved the milk jug at him and, when he nodded agreement—being by now, almost too far gone to speak—she poured him a cup and came over to hand him that, and a small bowl of sugar.

Her intoxicating scent, a mixture of what was essentially Diana and the subtle perfume that she was wearing, almost did for Neville. His hands shook when he took the cup from her. He tried to drink his tea slowly and by doing so revert to the man that he, like society, thought himself to be: staid, decorous and steady—almost sexless.

His nervousness surprised Diana. She had heard that he was a man supremely in control of himself, but he was not giving her that impression. She had noticed his shaking hands when he had taken the cup from her and she had wondered whether he was sickening for something.

Neville was in a state in which he had never been before, where on the one hand he was eager to be away from her so that he might become again the man he had always been, and yet at the same time was equally desperate to remain with her. He pulled out his hunter and looked at it in an attempt to restore himself to his original state.

When he thought that he had succeeded, his treacherous tongue almost gave him away. He began in fine form by saying, 'I fear that I must leave before your cousin returns to find us—' And only at the last minute prevented himself from coming out with *'in flagrante delicto,'* a phrase commonly used to describe the act of love. He murmured instead the more decorous, 'Breaching the code of behaviour to which we all subscribe.'

Diana, for no reason at all—or so she thought—displayed a little of her fabled wildness by replying with a naughty grin, 'A code greatly spoken about in public as unbreakable, it is true, although in private it might be quite another thing—as I am sure you already know.'

Was that a hint? Did she want him to stay so that they might enjoy themselves? No, that could not be. Instead Neville gave her a pained smile before saying, 'It is rather late for me to visit the magistrate today and ask him for his help. I shall make it my business to approach him early tomorrow morning. I will, of course, inform you straight away of what his advice was.'

By thinking of cold water and snowy weather while she

agreed with him again, he succeeded in subduing his errant body a little so that he was able, fairly painlessly, to rise and take his leave of her.

The problem of what had happened to puritanic Sir Neville Fortescue occupied his mind all the way home. He had heard of a *coup de foudre* when confronted with a pretty woman, but he had never believed in it until he had walked into Duchess Diana's drawing room and had felt such an intense desire to have her on her back beneath him. Certainly neither his charming Marie, his one-time and only mistress, nor any other woman, had ever had such an immediately powerful effect on him before.

Once this wretched business was over, he would have as little as possible to do with her lest lust—for that was what it must be—should turn him into a man like his father.

'So you received Sir Neville Fortescue on his own!' wailed Isabella Marchmont. 'How could you do such a mad thing? Where would your reputation be if the world found out? You would be ruined, quite ruined!'

Diana replied, naughty again, 'Well, I don't propose to tell the world of this afternoon's meeting with him, and I hope that you don't, too, so why should it ever find out? Besides, it was necessary for me to meet him in private for a reason that I cannot tell you.'

'But think of the servants,' Isabella wailed again, 'they are sure to talk. It was from my maid that I learned of your folly.'

'May I assure you that Sir Neville behaved with perfect decorum?'

'You may—but nobody will believe you.'

'So his reputation as a man of extreme integrity and known good behaviour means nothing?'

'But he still remains a man.' Isabella's wailing was louder than ever. 'And we all know what men are. Deceivers ever.'

'Nevertheless, I spoke the truth when I said that we were

as well behaved as if we were at a curate's tea party. Would
you be shocked if I told you that I rather wished his behaviour
had not been quite so decorous? I found it—what shall I
say?—yes, a little disappointing and not very flattering.'

'Oh, you are impossible, my dear—and one day you will
go too far!'

'No doubt—but not yet, I hope. Say nothing if the rumours
begin to fly and they will die of their own accord. I shall take
good care to see Sir Neville as little as possible once the
problem over which he came to visit me has been resolved.'

'In the meantime,' Isabella told her severely, 'you might
consider encouraging some of the many men who have expressed admiration for you.'

'Or my money,' replied Diana drily.

'Oh, you are always so…so determined to see the bad in
everyone. Myself, I like Lord Alford very much. He is most
handsome, charming, as well as being attentive in a pleasant
fashion.'

'His pockets are to let,' said Diana dismissively, 'and the
rumour is that he lives a wild life, which will neither fill his
pockets nor, in the long run, improve his looks.'

'Well, you seem determined to refuse to allow rumour to
be true about yourself, while believing it in Lord Alford's
case.'

This was shrewd of her relative, and left Diana with little
to say other than, 'A hit, a palpable hit, Isabella,' as though
they had been fencing with foils rather than with words. The
truth was that it was not rumour which had informed her of
Alford being penniless, but her lawyers' helpful investigator.

This answer restored Miss Marchmont's good humour, so
much so that she privately decided to ask Diana's distant relative, Lord Marchmont, to visit London soon in order to give
her wilful charge some much-needed good advice.

Sir Stanford Markham JP was only too happy to receive
Sir Neville Fortescue—of whom he had heard nothing but

good—immediately, his being about his business so early in the morning seeming to bear his reputation out. He was not so happy, however, as to offer him any assistance in solving the mystery of the missing servant girls after Neville had told him his story.

'You see,' he explained, 'with crime so prevalent in the capital these days it would not be fair to expect either the Bow Street Runners, or the constabulary, such as it is, to waste time on something that might have an innocent explanation. These girls might have decided to run away for a number of reasons: they could have possibly discovered that life as a whore—to put it bluntly—in a house of ill fame would pay better than scrubbing floors, and be much easier.'

'If I had come here,' Neville asked bluntly, 'with a tale about some ladies of quality having disappeared in a similar fashion, would you have given me a different answer?'

'Of course.' Sir Stanford beamed, pleased to see that his visitor was a man of the world who quite understood that while it would be one thing to spend time and trouble looking for *them,* worrying about the fate of servant girls was quite another thing.

'You offer me a strange concept of justice for all,' replied Neville, trying to keep his temper, and not offend the self-satisfied man before him.

'Oh, but, as I am sure you must understand, common sense must prevail.'

'Well, my common sense tells me,' retorted Neville, 'that if this mystery is to be solved then I must look elsewhere than to your good self for assistance. Perhaps you might be able to tell me where I might find it?'

Sir Stanford was quite untroubled. 'You could visit Bow Street and talk to the Runners there yourself, but I suspect that they will give you the same advice as I have done, which is that they will not waste their time on this matter. There are

more important causes which you—as an MP—could undertake to pursue.'

Neville said coldly, 'Allow me to choose my own course
of action in this, or any other of my affairs. My duty at the
moment is to Miss Belinda Jesson, and to Master Lemuel
Banks with whom she was walking out when she disappeared.
He is a most worthy young man.'

He picked up his hat, ignored the glass of Madeira that Sir
Stanford had poured for him as soon as this interview had
begun, and paused only to bow in the JP's direction before
he left. 'I bid you good day, sir, I have work to do.'

All the way to Bow Street Neville was seething with rage
over Sir Stanford's offhand decision not to waste his time
trying to find the missing girls. Doubtless the Runners at Bow
Street would tell him the same thing, but he could at least
endeavour to persuade them to take Belinda's disappearance
more seriously.

Alas, after waiting for some time, he was admitted into the
presence of a stocky man, Wally Smith by name, who bore
the appearance of having once been a prizefighter.

This time he was offered no Madeira, just a blunt statement
of, 'Very sorry to keep you waiting, Sir Neville, but we are
so busy that it is difficult to find time to see anyone who visits
us at short notice.'

This was the same song that Sir Stanford had been singing—and doubtless the man's answer was going to be the
same. It was not expressed quite so elegantly, but the gist of
it was similar. The Runners were already overworked and
could not spare a man to assist Sir Neville.

'Is there no one, then, who can help me?' Neville asked at
last.

Smith smiled, rather ruefully, 'I can give you the name and
address of a man who was once one of us. He left by his own
wish, but he still undertakes for money those matters that the

Runners might feel to be time-wasting and fruitless to pursue. I can't, of course, promise that he will help you, but it might be worthwhile to visit him.'

'Then that will have to do.'

'His name is Jackson,' said Smith. Picking up a piece of paper, he began to write. 'And this is his address.' He handed the paper to Neville, saying, 'I wish you luck and I regret not being able to assist you myself. I should warn you that you may be on a wild goose chase. People disappear every day in London.'

Jackson's home, or office—Neville was not sure which until he reached it—was up a flight of stairs in a respectable villa in Chelsea. He apparently rented the whole of the first floor. A smiling landlady informed him that Mr Jackson was at home, but she would need to ask her visitor his name and his business before she allowed him to see Mr Jackson.

Privately, after hearing that he was Sir Neville Fortescue, she was sure that Mr Jackson would consent to be interviewed, but she did not say so.

More and more Neville was beginning to think that he had embarked on a wild goose chase. He pulled out his watch and looked at the time: it was long past his usual hour for dinner, he had breakfasted early and eaten no nuncheon. Left to himself he would have gone home after his unsuccessful interview at Bow Street, but he had promised both Lem and the Duchess that he would do his best to try to find out what had happened to the girls, and he could not rest until he had done his utmost.

The landlady reappeared. 'Mr Jackson will see you. He is in the front room, whose door is immediately on the right of the first-floor landing.'

Jackson proved to be quite a different person from either Sir Stanford or the burly Wally Smith. He was red-haired, wiry in body, and would not immediately be taken for a hard-bitten officer of the law. But there was something about his strong face that impressed Neville. His room was partly a drawing room and partly an office. He sat at a battered desk and came immediately to the point. 'What is your business with me, Sir Neville?'

Neville told his story for the third time that day. Jackson listened to him gravely, nodding his head now and then.

'I have already,' Neville ended, 'attempted to interest both Sir Stanford Markham JP and the Bow Street Runners in this sorry tale, but they refused to help me. The Runners, however, were good enough to give me your name. That is why I am here, in the hope that you might feel able to interest yourself in the fate of three poor young servant girls.'

Jackson nodded again. 'Yes,' he said. 'I have just finished an investigation for a senior government official and am, at the moment, free. I will assist you to the best of my powers. I agree with your belief that the girls have been kidnapped for use in a brothel, but we cannot be sure to which house they have been taken.

'What I do know is that some man, believed to be a member of the best society, has been assisting at least one Madame to acquire girls after this fashion; for ready money, of course, he being short of tin in consequence of his wild life. To find them, though, might be difficult. Now, if you would be so good as to tell me your story all over again, I shall not only question you, but also make notes of anything that seems to me to be significant—although it might not have done to you.

'For example, did the girls know one another? Are you sure that your man Banks is telling you the whole truth?'

He paused, dipped his pen in an inkwell and said, quite curtly, as befitted a man who had just successfully completed an investigation for Lord Liverpool, the Prime Minister, 'Please begin, Sir Neville—and take your time.'

In all, Neville spent nearly two hours with Jackson. Half-way through there came a knock at the door, and the landlady entered with a tray containing two cups of coffee and a plate of biscuits.

'I've taken the liberty, Mr Jackson, of bringing you your usual evening drink, and adding a cup for your visitor.'

Jackson looked at Neville. 'You will drink coffee with me, Sir Neville?'

Neville, who was beginning to feel massively hungry, felt that coffee and biscuits would be better than nothing. He agreed that he would, and ate and drank gratefully, in the intervals of further discussion.

At the end, Jackson gave Neville a hard look before saying, 'I will undertake this commission provided that you leave it completely in my hands. As soon as I have any information that would be of use to you I will send a messenger boy to your home. I don't think that you ought to be seen visiting me again. We will meet in some tavern or coffee house where we are unlikely to be recognised.'

Neville suddenly grasped that Jackson knew more about this business than he was admitting.

He was also wondering whether his dismissal by both Sir Stanford and the Runners was because for some reason they wished him to give up his search. On the other hand, Smith had recommended him to Jackson—but Jackson had no formal connection with government institutions so anything he did could not reflect back on the Runners—or Sir Stanford.

If anything, this heightened Neville's determination to pursue this matter to a successful conclusion. He would say nothing of these suspicions to Duchess Diana, because that was all that they were—suspicions—but he would bear them in mind.

While he was being driven home—in yet another hackney cab, because he did not wish any of his servants to know where he was going, or why—Neville decided that he would not call on Diana at her home. He was sure that she would be at Lady Jersey's reception later that evening, to which he had received an invitation.

He would seek her out there and tell her of his day's somewhat unsatisfactory experiences. He had originally decided not to attend the reception. He could not quite admit to himself his pleasure at the prospect of meeting Duchess Diana again. No, indeed, he was solely going there in order to satisfy his stern mistress, duty.

Diana dressed herself with care for Lady Jersey's ball. She forsook her usual virgin white for a delicate pale-green ensemble and put on some of the famed Medbourne jewellery, choosing the least ostentatious pieces from her collection. Her earrings, her tiara and her necklace were not the notorious Medbourne emeralds, brought from South America by a roving ancestor who had travelled there early in the eighteenth century, but were composed of seed pearls instead—much to Isabella Marchmont's disgust.

'You owe it to your husband's family to wear its most prized possessions, my dear. People will think that you are ashamed of them.'

'When I am old and raddled I shall wear every one of them, because they'll be needed then. While I am young, however, I shall depend solely on my youth, which is a woman's most prized possession. Alas, that it lasts such a short time and turns our earlier blessing into a curse when it is gone.'

'You are too fanciful, my dear,' was her companion's answer to that. 'Youth, as well as age, needs to be adorned.'

Neville did not think so when he saw her. He thought that in a crowd of women of all ages, hung about with precious stones of every colour, Diana stood out precisely because of the simplicity of her appearance. This was merely another aspect of her cleverness, he supposed.

He did not immediately rush to her side because his cousin Alford was with her and he would wait until the crowd around her had lessened a little. He noted, with some amusement, the fuss that Sally Jersey made of him.

'To what do we owe the honour of your appearance, Sir Neville?' she carolled at him. 'Did you know that you have been nicknamed The Hermit?'

So that was why Lady Leominster had teased him about leaving his grotto. Most daringly he answered Sally with a quip of his own, saying, 'I assure you, Lady Jersey, that to call me a hermit is as untrue as nicknaming you Silence.'

His daring lay in the fact that Sally Jersey, who was notoriously talkative had been christened Silence by the *haut ton* as a knowing joke. Far from being cross with him she allowed herself to be amused. 'Oh, you are wittier than I was given to understand, but in payment for that sally, you may tell me whether you are here because you wish to meet the Duchess of Medbourne again. Gossip tells me that the man who never dances with anyone danced with her at Lady Leo-minster's.'

Her smile at him was a knowing one, and he liked the way in which she had leaned upon the word sally which was, of course, the name by which her intimate friends knew her. What he did not like was that rumour had already linked him with the Duchess. What would the gossiping peeress have said to him if she had known that he had met her in private? He trembled to think and decided to go as carefully as he could.

'Oh, I have come to see all the pretty women tonight,' he told her.

He didn't deceive Silence. She struck him gently on the shoulder with her fan. 'Come, come, that is the tale you are telling everyone, I suppose, but we both know better, don't we?'

Neville made no answer, simply smiled at her and took his leave since the reception line was beginning to lengthen and his time with her was up.

The lady had done everything but wink at him, and if gossip about him and Diana was so rife then he must bide his

time and approach her later. He wondered if she had looked
for him as he was looking for her. Perhaps not. It would be
surprising if her feelings toward him were more particular
than those she had for any other man.

He was wrong. Diana had looked round the ballroom several times before she saw him standing unobtrusively behind
a group of mamas looking after their eligible daughters. Unobtrusively so far as the majority of the guests were concerned—but Diana was suddenly aware that she would always
be able to find him easily, even in the most crowded room.
Surprisingly she remembered everything about him, including
his chestnut hair and his green eyes, which the Medbourne
emeralds would certainly enhance—if men ever wore such
jewellery, that was.

Diana's impatience grew when Neville made no effort to
come over to her, particularly because convention dictated
that there was no way in which she could go to him on her
own. She contemplated playing the part of the Daring Duchess again who despised and defied all conventions, and would
therefore defy this one. She decided, however, as Neville had
done, that she must not draw attention to their newborn, and
strange, temporary alliance.

This preoccupation with Neville Fortescue was making it
very difficult for her to give her full attention to George Alford, who was clinging to her like a very leech, laughing and
gossiping away in his most charming mode—to the gratifi-
cation of Isabella if not to Diana.

He was telling her, with great enthusiasm, of a proposed
trip down the Thames in pleasure boats, at the end of which
all his guests would picnic upon the spot where the view from
its banks seemed most desirably picturesque. 'Do say that you
and Miss Marchmont will honour me by joining us,' he ended.

Of course she would have to say yes. She did not particularly want to spend an afternoon with George and his rowdy
friends, but the look of happy expectation on Isabella's face

was enough to make her change her mind. Isabella's life was supposedly devoted to pleasing her, and for once she would please Isabella instead.

'Oh, indeed,' she replied. 'We should be delighted to accompany you, would we not, Isabella?'

'Provided, of course, that the weather is fine,' Isabella added.

'Good gracious,' replied George who had been fearful that Diana would refuse this, as she had refused other similar excursions, 'it would not dare to be otherwise when two such stars of society had consented to venture out in it.'

Several more minutes of such inane conversation were slowly driving Diana mad, but fortunately George recollected that he had agreed to meet one of his friends in the adjoining drawing room at twelve of the clock, and he made his adieux with such grovelling delight, promising to be back with them soon, that he might have been on stage at Drury Lane in a satire on the folly of High Life.

As fortunately, an old friend of Isabella's had come along to engage her in reminiscent conversation about their long-gone youth, and it was at this point that Diana saw Neville making his way towards her.

Unfortunately she also sure that one of her more importunate and middle-aged suitors, Prince Adalbert of Eckstein Halsbach, was making a beeline for her. Desperate to avoid the unwanted advances that he insisted on making however much she discouraged him, she decided that to walk casually in Neville's direction would not be breaching society's code overmuch.

They met near an alcove in which a statue of Antinous, the favourite of the Roman Emperor Hadrian, stood.

'Lady Diana.' Neville smiled, with an elegant bow. 'It is a pleasure to meet you. I had hoped that you would be present tonight.'

'Oh, I made a point of coming, Sir Neville. One meets such interesting persons at Lady Jersey's functions.'

Anyone watching them would have thought them to be engaged in retailing the usual vacuous nothings, very like quid-nuncs, or gossips exchanging the latest news and rumours. Instead, Neville remarked idly, 'I understand that Lady Jersey has a collection of precious porcelain in the room beyond this alcove. I wonder if you would care to admire it with me.'

'Charmed,' exclaimed Diana with a flirt of her fan. 'I am longing to learn more about porcelain,' something which she had just discovered at the very moment that Neville had made his proposal to examine it.

When they reached the room where a few couples were already inspecting the beautiful pieces displayed in breakfront glass cases, Neville began a learned disquisition on them in a rather louder voice than usual so that those present would know that their visit and their conversation were innocent. They had inspected about half of the collection, while he knowingly admired Meissen and compared it with Wedgwood and the many pieces from China, before they were left alone in the room. Whereupon, without a pause, he started to tell her of the varying fortunes of his day.

'So we are not yet any further on,' he finished, 'except that Jackson struck me as a hunter who, once he had trapped his fox, would never let go of him—even, though, in this case he might not find a human offender, but, hopefully, a few facts.'

'Don't you think it rather odd that Sir Stanford was so unwilling to pursue the matter?' Diana asked, causing Neville to admire her shrewdness yet again, before he answered her.

'He was careful to explain to me that, had they been young ladies of good society, his decision would have been very different.'

'Now that,' said Diana, 'was exceedingly naughty of him. Servant girls ought surely be protected by the law as much as I am.'

'And so I thought,' replied Neville, admiring her all over again for her humanity, as well as for her beauty, 'and I told him as much.'

She was beginning to exercise a power over him that surprised him by the passion it was rousing in him. He had always prided himself on his self-control where women were concerned, but with Diana, even while he was talking about such an unexciting subject as porcelain, he was always on the verge of losing it. He dare not think what it might do to his hard-won self-control if he ever danced the waltz with her.

It was at this juncture that another party entered and, fortunately for him, Neville was constrained to return to his impromptu lecture at the point where he had left it off, after quietly assuring Diana that he had every intention of pursuing the whole business of the missing girls to the bitter end.

It was a good thing that he did not know exactly how difficult and bitter that end might be, but even so his resolution had been made and he would not turn aside from it.

Diana, for her part, was as impressed by Neville's feelings for others more lowly than himself as he had been by hers, and it was with some regret that they agreed to part lest their continuing association look too particular. Once he had escorted her back to where Isabella was waiting for her, her companion could hardly wait for him to leave before she began to reproach Diana for first approaching Sir Neville on her own and then disappearing with him.

'Whatever will people think of you,' she ended, 'if you continue to defy convention?'

Diana's answer was to exclaim with as innocent an expression as she could assume, 'Oh, surely, Isabella, no one can possibly think it wrong of me to accompany Sir Neville to Lady Jersey's Chinese room, a public place, where I learned from him some very interesting facts not only of the history of porcelain itself, but also of how it is made. I am not surprised that the Wedgwoods accumulated a fortune, having seen so many superb examples of their work!'

George Alford accosted Neville as soon as he had left Diana and immediately attacked him for making off with her, ending with, 'Do I have to believe, Nev, that I have a rival in you for the affections of the fair Diana?'

'If you mean by that do I like talking to her on subjects of mutual interest, then the answer must be yes.'

'You know perfectly well what I mean. Are your intentions towards her serious?'

Neville, stung by this inquisition, retorted, 'Are yours? Do you have anything to offer her other than your hand and a mountain of debt?'

If a mouse, running along the floor, had upped and bitten him, George could not have been more shocked. This unpleasant riposte was not what one expected from quiet old Nev, known for his diplomacy and his forbearance, not for such cutting sarcasm.

'Well, I do have a peerage, and a stately home to offer her.'

'Your country house is in ruins and your town one is in little better state. You are entertained by many in London, but you never entertain yourself.'

'I'll have you know that I have arranged a boating trip up the Thames for some of my friends—a jaunt that Duchess Di has promised to attend.'

'That is exactly what I mean,' was Neville's final shot. 'Your entertaining is all on the cheap. Furthermore, you have no right to quiz me on my feelings for the Duchess, they are no business of yours. And now you must excuse me, I have promised to meet an old friend of mine tonight: he has just come up from the country.' He gave George the smallest bow that gentleman had ever received and walked off, leaving his cousin staring after him.

Whatever had got into quiet old Nev to make him such a

surly curmudgeon? George had hoped to go round to Fortescue House in the morning and try to touch him for a loan—but he would have to think twice about that with Nev in his present mood. On the other hand, all his creditors were beginning to dun him at once, so he might have to risk receiving a dusty answer.

Come to think of it, his cousin looked more the dandy tonight than he had ever seen him. He was even sporting a fashionably tied cravat. Was it Duchess Di who was having this effect on him? George, with expectations of his own concerning the lady, truly hoped not.

He thus made it his business to return to Diana's side immediately. He found her in the supper room with that silly old maid beside her. George was not aware that Isabella was extremely taken by his handsome face and his perfect turn-out. He was always kind to the old trout because a companion was a useful ally if a fellow was wooing her charge—not that he thought that Duchess Di took much notice of Isabella and her advice.

Diana did not consider George Alford's company was a good exchange for Neville's when she found herself compelled to listen to George while eating and drinking the various delicacies laid out on tables and carried by obsequious footmen. She again let her mind drift whilst George was talking. She thought happily of her few pleasant moments with Neville in the roomful of beautiful china.

While they had been alone together he had behaved like a perfect gentleman the whole time, which was more than could be said of most of the men she had met in society. Also unlike other men, Neville was interested in a large number of different things. He certainly seemed to know a great deal about porcelain.

Without thinking she must have said this last sentence aloud because George, puzzled, looked hard at her and asked, 'Who's that who knows a great deal about porcelain?'

Diana flushed. 'Why, your cousin, Sir Neville Fortescue. Did you know that some of the Jerseys' collection once belonged to Catherine the Great?'

George laughed derisively. 'Oh, is *that* what he was talking about when he was with you? I hope that you weren't too bored. Poor old Neville knows a great deal about everything—for what that's worth.'

Diana's answer was rather sharp. 'It must be useful for him in his duties as an MP, and is surely better than knowing nothing about anything.'

'But it also makes him damned dull, you must admit.'

This time Diana, ready to make a hot defence of Neville, stopped herself abruptly. To do so might jeopardise their joint wish that they should not appear to be too friendly with one another. She had promised not to draw unwanted attention to them, so she desisted.

George took her silence for agreement with his verdict on Neville and began to feel a great deal happier about his chances with her. Of course, once he had popped the question and she had agreed to marry him, there would still be the lawyers to square, but his three-centuries-old title must stand for something, whatever his cousin had just implied.

All in all, a good night's work.

For different reasons Neville was thinking the same thing. Best of all, he had seen Diana again and he was daring enough to think that she enjoyed being with him. She had made some perceptive remarks about the Jerseys' porcelain, which pleased him greatly. All that time he had spent in the Potteries when he was a boy, listening to his old great-uncle prosing away at great length while they walked around his factory, had not been wasted after all.

He was still thinking about her while he was in the Entrance Hall waiting for his carriage to be brought round when Lord Burnside came up to him. They had once sat together on a

Parliamentary committee and he had not come across him since then.

Burnside beamed at him as though they were old friends, which surprised Neville a little. 'Happy to see you, Fortescue,' he said. 'I had hoped to have a word with you tonight, but earlier on I missed you in the crush. I wanted to tell you how much I liked your speech in the House last week about the sad plight of the framework knitters and the rural labourers in the Midland counties. I had thought, after his most moving defence of them in the Lords some years ago, that Byron would continue to strive for their betterment, but alas, it was not to be. I agree with you that if we are not careful we might yet see revolution taking place in this beautiful country of ours.'

Since Burnside was one of those for whose opinion Neville had great respect, he flushed with pleasure and bowed his thanks.

'That is most kind of you, m'lord. I'm afraid I blotted my copybook with the great men in the Commons because none of them has much sympathy with the sufferings of the many who work for us. My own belief is that unless we try to make their lives a little easier we may yet, as you have just suggested, bring down on ourselves some of the anarchy that prevailed in France after 1789.'

'Bravely said and it does you honour. You realise, I hope, that your stand might prevent you from finding the preferment that your abilities would almost certainly command if you kept quiet.'

'To do so, m'lord, would be at the expense of what I consider to be my duty.'

The expression on Lord Burnside's face as he listened to that statement baffled Neville a little. It was one of pleasure. All that he said, however, was, 'I see that you understand the risks that you run, Fortescue. I can only wish that there were more like you and that we had more time to speak together.

Unfortunately I must bid you goodnight for I see that my carriage is here. Remain true to yourself—it is one of the best things that a man can do.'

Neville stared after him. Now what had brought that on? He scarcely knew Burnside and, what was more, was not accustomed to such heartfelt praise. He shrugged his shoulders. One way and another his life these days was taking some odd turns, what with his new friendship with Duchess Diana and their mutual involvement in the strange affair of the missing servant girls. He hoped that it would not be too long before Jackson had some information for him.

Chapter Three

A few days later, just when Neville had begun to give up hope, he received by the promised messenger boy a short note from Jackson.

'I have some useful information for you. Meet me at two of the clock this afternoon at the Turk's Head coffee house in Bruton Street. J.'

At last! He had seen Diana the night before at the Cowpers' ball—he had never attended so many in all the years he had been visiting London. He had claimed her for a dance early on—not a waltz, that would have been too much of a temptation—and had told her that, as yet, he had no news for her.

She turned her glorious eyes on him. 'That is a pity; it seems to me that every day that goes by makes the state of these poor girls more parlous.'

'I have to trust Jackson,' Neville said, trying to keep his mind on their joint venture—which was difficult, since being with her so often was only serving to rouse him more and more each time he met her. Her very common sense excited him, partly because he was aware that when she was with others she assumed her mask of frivolity: the clever young woman who lived behind it emerged only for him.

Now, shabbily dressed as though he were a humble city

clerk, he was on his way to meet Jackson. He knew of the Turk's Head, but had never visited it; it was not a place which the *ton* frequented, being rather seedy, and they were unlikely to be recognised there. He entered to discover Jackson sitting in a side booth. He had a cup of coffee in front of him and, on seeing Neville, called for one for him. While they were waiting for it he made approving noises about Neville's disguise.

'I thought this would be better than a tavern. Not so much noise, and these booths are pretty private,' were his final words.

He began his report after Neville's coffee arrived with something of a disclaimer, by saying, 'This business is going to be more difficult than I thought. It began easily enough when one of my informants told that that there are two houses that supply virgins for those who want them. More than that, the girls they use are not always there by choice since pretty women—with no family in London—are hard to find.

'After that I came up against a brick wall. He refused to give me the names of those who arrange the kidnappings, or their clients, saying that it was more than his life was worth. But one thing I can tell you. There is no doubt that some great men are involved in this filthy business and, from the little he did say, I am certain that some hard-up members of high society tell the Madames and their minders where the girls are to be found—for money, of course.

'The other brick wall is that I have been asking around at the legal end and it is quite plain to me that my suspicions are correct—that this is why Sir Stanford and the official Runners would not help you.

'That is why information is hard to come by. There is another problem, too. Some of these houses are also used as a blind by those who plot against the present government in the hope of starting a revolution like that in France. No one would expect them to meet in such houses—so we now have two reasons why everything to do with them is kept so secret.

'If the Home Secretary's agents know where would-be traitors were present, they can keep an eye on them, but if they are frightened away by constables raiding the houses to rescue girls held against their will, who knows where they might vanish to instead?'

'You say that they look for virgins—why is that? Is it anything to do with the belief that to lie with a virgin cures one of venereal disease?'

Jackson nodded. 'That—and for other reasons. I have written down the name of the two houses where the girls may be found on a piece of paper, which I will give you—I don't wish to be heard using them. What happens next is up to you. If I can help you, I will, but we must be careful not to run into danger.'

Neville took the piece of paper that Jackson slid across the table. 'I shall not pay you for your services here, but later. If I need further help, I will send for you. In the meantime I shall drink my coffee.'

Jackson raised his cup and then said abruptly, 'I think that I see someone I know, but perhaps I am wrong. I think that we should leave as soon as possible.'

'With that I am in full agreement,' replied Neville, who was feeling more and more uneasy the longer they remained in such a public place.

George Alford had woken up that morning with an aching head and some bitter regrets. He had allowed himself to be persuaded by some of his rowdier friends into joining them on a visit to one of the gaming hells off the Haymarket where, they had told him, his run of bad luck was sure to change. It had indeed changed—but only for the worse. He had lost a great deal of ready money, something which he could not really afford to do since he was in the toils of someone whom he had thought to be a friend.

There was nothing for it but to try to touch cousin Neville for all that he could get from him. He must surely have recovered his usual kind and cool temper by now. It took George some time to feel well enough to crawl out of bed and it was mid-afternoon before he reached Fortescue House.

Alas, when he finally arrived there the butler told him that Sir Neville was out on some important business and was not expected back soon. He would, of course, inform his master of Lord Alford's visit when he did return. It was just his bad luck to find Nev absent from home, so George trudged off, since he was unable to afford a hansom cab for a second time that day.

Walking made his bad head, the result of last night's desperate drinking, hurt even more. George had never asked himself why these hells provided as much free drink as a customer could take, or he might have grasped that a half-cut man's condition made his judgement at cards poor and thus tipped the odds even further in favour of the house.

Instead, he cursed his errant noddle and made for a street near to his own lodgings, where he knew that there was a disreputable coffee house, the Turk's Head, which would be prepared to give him tick—or so it had always done in the past.

Unfortunately, when he finally staggered to his favourite table the waiter apologetically informed him that the proprietor was no longer prepared to allow him a drink until he had paid off his previous debt, which was considerable and far beyond what small amount of tin he had with him. On hearing this unhappy news, George looked around him in horror. Was there anyone present from whom he might cadge the price of a cup of coffee?

He could see no one, until suddenly his eye alighted on none other than Nev, dressed even more plainly than usual—

like a city clerk, in fact. He was not, however, alone. Seated across from him was a wily fellow whom he immediately recognised as Jackson, an ex-Bow Street Runner, whom he had last seen when another friend of his, Louis Frankland, had been in deep trouble over a swindle he had been running. He had been lucky enough not to be hanged, having been transported to Australia instead with no possibility of ever returning.

What in the world could old Nev be doing with Jackson? The butler had said he was out on business—but what business could he be doing with a Bow Street Runner, dressed as he was like a city clerk? George had his own reasons for trying to find out what it could possibly be.

He walked over and clapped his hand on Nev's shoulder, drawling, 'Never thought I'd find you here, old fellow. Your butler allowed that you were out on business.'

Neville, shocked at being cornered in a place that he and Jackson had thought was safe from discovery, swung round and said, 'Oh, I *am* on business, George. Parliamentary business, very confidential, I assure you.'

He thought that George would not expect him to tell such a thundering lie, and so it proved. George put a finger by his nose, and said, 'Understood, dear boy, and mum's the word. I wonder if I could touch you for a cup of coffee. I'm a bit short of the ready—came out without my purse.'

'Of course,' Neville said, 'my pleasure.' Lying again. 'Do sit down—you don't mind Lord Alford joining us, do you, Mr Jackson?'

'Not at all,' replied Jackson wondering how a cousin of Sir Neville Fortescue's could be so short of cash that he hadn't got the price of a cup of coffee on him. 'Our business is over anyway.'

Neville, cursing his luck that it was George, of all people, who had come upon him, waved at a passing waiter and ordered another cup for himself and Jackson, and a first one for

George, who had now sat down and was watching Jackson warily. What Parliamentary business could Nev conceivably have with *him?*

'Correct me if I'm wrong,' he said, 'but aren't you a Bow Street Runner, Mr Jackson? I'm sure that I met you when you were engaged in that sad business with Louis Frankland.'

'Not any more,' Jackson said, 'I've retired into private life. Isn't that so, Sir Neville?'

'Oh, yes, indeed.' Neville would have agreed to anything in order not to arouse George's suspicions that something odd was going on. His cousin was so loose-mouthed, as well as loose-moraled, that he had no wish for him to learn anything of the real nature of the business which he was engaged in with Jackson. George's one cup turned into three, but by then Jackson had made his excuses and left them, and he and George engaged in the kind of conversation that took no effort and meant nothing, until Neville rose and announced that he ought to be going home.

George caught him by the sleeve. 'Look, Nev, I don't like to ask you, but could you see your way to lending me a few hundred guineas? I'm in a bad way at the moment, and I'd be most awfully grateful.'

As Neville looked hard at his cousin and the friend of his youth, sadness overtook him. Very soon now his fast life would begin to take its toll of him. Which would be worse, to lend him money—or to refuse to? He put his hand in his pocket and pulled out a few guineas, saying, 'Do I have to remind you, George, that you haven't paid back the few hundred guineas you've borrowed from me three times before? If I thought that it would do you any good, I'd be happy to help you, but I know that if I do, you'll probably lose it all in some gaming house tonight and be as hard up again tomorrow.

'In the meantime, here's enough to buy you a cab home, with some left over.'

George reddened. 'You always were a sanctimonious bastard, Nev, even when we were boys. I'll take your guineas and thank you for the coffee, and try not to trouble you again.'

It was Neville's turn to put a hand on his cousin's shoulder. 'Would it really be too hard for you to reform your way of life, George? Otherwise you'll end in the Marshalsea, banged up for debt, if you don't change your ways.'

'Much you'd care,' returned George savagely. 'I'll not trouble you again.' And he walked briskly off, stuffing Neville's guineas into his pocket. He'd see him in hell before he ever asked for his help again, that was certain.

He'd forgotten how many times he'd said this before.

Neville watched him go uneasily. George was determined to stay on the primrose path to ruin. He knew all the symptoms—he'd seen them in his father's behaviour, and had also seen that nobody and nothing could ever help him.

He tried not to worry about his cousin and only succeeded when he had reached home, and divested himself of his clerk's clothing—without the help of his valet—and began to go over his meeting with Jackson. George was a lost cause, but it was just possible that the missing servant girls were not.

In the middle of his musings, his secretary, Charles Portal, came in. He had been working in the library, looking up some old Board of Agriculture reports in order to make notes on them as evidence for a possible speech in the House of Commons. Neville had invented this task to keep him out of the way while he engaged in his secret meeting with Jackson.

He handed Neville a pile of papers. 'I hope they will assist you in your work, Sir Neville.'

'Oh, indeed, I am sure that they will,' returned Neville glibly. He could not, for the life of him, think of anything useful to do with them, but worse than that, he was beginning to feel dismayed at the ease with which he had recently taken to lying and deceit. 'In the meantime,' he added, 'take a little time off as a reward for hard work. Oh, and ask the butler to send Lemuel Banks in to see me. I have received a letter from his father, asking me whether he is working well in his new post in London.'

This last was not a lie. Lem was the only child of his father's old age. John Banks had been a carpenter before he retired to a cottage on Neville's estate, and since Lem had shown no aptitude for his father's craft, he had become a footman instead.

Portal bowed his way out and not long afterwards Lem arrived, looking worried. 'You asked to see me, sir.'

'Yes, and I am sure that you know why.'

Lem's face lit up. 'You have some news for me? About Belinda, I hope.'

Neville was sober. 'I'm sorry to disappoint you, Lem. She has not yet been found, but I have had some information that may help us in our search. It seems that she, and the others, may have been taken to one of two houses of ill fame, but I am afraid that the law will not help us to release them.'

'Is there nothing we can do, sir?' faltered Lem at last. 'And does this mean that I shall never see Belinda again?'

'I have thought of a way out of this impasse,' Neville confessed, 'but before I tell you of it, I must ask you a question and you must answer me as truthfully as you can. My plan, which I must admit is a reckless one, might put you in danger of being arrested—should we fail, that is. Are you prepared to risk that?'

'By we, sir, do you mean that I would be joining you in this?'

Neville had always thought that Lem was cleverer than his lowly position in the Fortescue household might suggest, and now he was being given further evidence of it.

'That is a good question, and, yes, if we carry out my plan we should be working together on our own. No one, and I repeat, no one must know of what we are about to do. It will require the utmost secrecy, for I have been told that even though the authorities know of what is going on, and that it is against the law, they intend to do nothing to stop it.'

'Damn them!' exclaimed Lem. 'Damn them for leaving my Belinda to suffer. Of course I will help you and, of course, I shall say nothing.'

'You are quite sure, Lem, that you are prepared to run the risk of arrest and punishment?'

'I will do anything, anything, to try to save Belinda. I will obey any order you give me in the hope that I might see her safe again.'

Neville thought sadly that Belinda might already have been sold to some rich and diseased roué, but there was always the hope that so far she had remained untouched.

'Excellent,' he said. 'Now, I shall tell the butler and the housekeeper that I am giving you leave to go home to see your father who is ailing. In fact, however, I shall send you to my house in Chelsea where you will wait for me to join you before we try to carry out our errand of mercy. You will not remain there long, for the sooner we try to free her the better. Now, let me tell you how I hope to achieve this happy outcome. Sit down and listen carefully to me.'

For the next half-hour Neville told his faithful servant of his intentions, ending with, 'Remember, you must say nothing to anyone of what we are about to do. Not even a hint. Can I trust you to keep quiet? If I can't I must think of another way to free Belinda.'

'Sir, I would do anything, anything at all, to save my Belinda. I do not talk a great deal as it is—which some of the other servants do not like. They call me standoffish. Believe me, until I leave I shall be more standoffish than ever. It won't be difficult.'

He did not tell his master that he preferred to read an improving book rather than engage in idle gossip. He was pleased to remember there was a library in the house to which he was being sent.

So that was that, Neville thought, when Lem had gone. If this venture succeeded, he must reward him for his willingness to risk everything for his sweetheart.

There was still Diana to be consulted, although, of course, he would tell her nothing of the dangerous enterprise to which he was now committed, only that he had received certain information which would help him to rescue the missing girls, seeing that the law would do nothing. The afternoon was too far advanced for him to visit her, but he had received an invitation from Lady Devereux to a ridotto—an evening of music and dancing—to be held this very night. Diana was an accomplished pianist and would be sure to be taking part. He might be able to find an opportunity to talk to her there—or arrange to meet her the following day.

After eating an impromptu meal, he rang for his valet and, to that gentleman's delight, ordered him to lay out the most dandified clothing he possessed so that he might put on a good show at the ridotto. He had never before been in such a state of excitement at the prospect of attending a society function. He was not sure whether it was because he was about to meet Diana again, or whether it was the knowledge that he was going to commit himself to an adventure which no one who knew staid Sir Neville Fortescue would have dreamed that he would even consider, let alone take part in.

'So, Isabella informs me that you are, at last, entertaining the notion that you might marry. Now while that piece of news makes me feel happy, I am a little worried that she seems to be very partial to George Alford's suit. The man is a skimble-skamble bankrupt, and I am compelled to believe that she has been seduced by a pretty face.'

Lord Marchmont, who had just arrived in London and had

made it his first duty to visit one of his few living relatives, was giving Diana the benefit of his advice.

She began to laugh. She had always liked Lord Marchmont, who was principally distinguished by his no-nonsense attitude to life. 'You may rest assured that I am not being seduced by his pretty face, which, by the by, is likely to become less and less pretty as a result of his dissipated life.'

'Excellent. I have always known that you possessed more than your share of common sense. She also tells me that Sir Neville Fortescue has been showing an interest in you. Now, while I have heard nothing but good of him, there are two things about him that might disqualify him as a possible husband for you. You, my girl, are extremely lively, and Fortescue is extremely staid—which might not result in a marriage made in heaven. The other consideration is that he is not many generations away from trade. You deserve to marry a peer of impeccable lineage, seeing that yours and your late husband's go back to the Norman Conquest.'

Her eyes shining, Diana's riposte was one that he might have expected. 'Now, Uncle, we all go back to the Norman Conquest, only some few of us are fortunate enough to be able to list our ancestors, while most cannot. As for trade, I thought that the Fortescue baronetcy was an old one.'

'I might have known that you would offer me a witty answer. As for the Fortescue baronetcy, Sir Neville's grandfather was born John Smith. After he had made his fortune in trade he married the daughter of the then bankrupt Sir Carlton Fortescue and when Sir Carlton died of drink, changed his name to Fortescue, and a kind monarch not only allowed him to do so, but awarded him the baronetcy in order to keep the family tradition alive.

'Alas, the tradition that John Smith's subsequent descendant chose to follow was that of Fortescue dissipation, so ended up bankrupt, too. The present baronet is only wealthy because his mother's parents tied up her money at the marriage settlement so that her husband, Sir Carlton, could not touch it. When he died Sir Neville inherited it and his mother received a suitable dower.'

Diana's reply was a thoughtful one. 'Sir Neville shows no sign of following in the family tradition, being distinguished by his steadiness—you yourself called him dull a moment ago. Is not that better than being dissipated?'

Lord Marchmont shrugged. 'Who knows how long his good behaviour will last? He is still young.'

There was no answer to that which Diana could usefully make. She could not believe that the man she was coming to know would lapse into dissipation, but her word alone would not satisfy Lord Marchmont. He went on to list a number of eligible young men, some peers, and some the heirs to great titles, whom he would be happy to see Diana marry. The only trouble was that she had met many of them and they had not attracted her.

Until she had met Neville she had resigned herself either to not marrying at all, or to marrying someone who would at least be her good friend, even if passionate love was absent. Was she being a fool to think that Neville would be a passionate lover? Most people would think she was, but whenever they met there was a certain look about him that was beginning to convince her that he might be the man for whom she had been looking—whatever 'most people' thought of him.

She wondered how his enquiry into the disappearance of the three servant girls was going. Tonight she had promised not only to attend the Devereux's ridotto, but also—at Lady Devereux's special request—to play two pieces by Beethoven. Perhaps he might be there too, in which case they could have a few quiet words together. The thought pleased her and she ran upstairs, after ringing for her maid. She must be sure to look her best if he were going to be present.

Chapter Four

'Oh, there you are, Nev, thought that you never came to this sort of thing.'

There was a touch of the jeer in Frank Hollis's remark that piqued Neville somewhat. His answer was a cold one, surprising Frank, who always thought of Neville as an amiable dullard who never bit back.

'Then you thought wrongly, Hollis. I like music and Lady Devereux's choice of it at her ridottos is always excellent.'

With that Neville wandered away, to see if he could find Diana, whom he had already heard was present. He had not long to look. She was holding court at the far end of the salon where chairs had been laid out in front of not only a pianoforte—one of Broadwood's, of course—but also the instruments needed for the playing of a quartet.

For some reason that Neville refused to understand, the sight of her surrounded by men angered him—especially since one of them was Henry Latimer, a one-time friend of his whom he rarely saw these days, although he was generally popular with everyone else in the *ton*. He decided to join the little group in order to protect her—from what he was not sure.

By the time he had reached them, Latimer had managed by

some means to cut out the other men, who began to wander away. Neville's senses, which had never been more acute, told him that Diana was not happy at being thus isolated. He was not quite sure how he knew this. Afterwards, he thought it might have been something in her posture or the expression on her face, but whatever it was he decided to rescue her. How, he couldn't think, but rescue her he would.

Luck was with him. Diana, in an effort to escape Latimer's encroaching attentions without being overtly rude to him, turned her head and saw Neville coming.

Thank God for the sight of his sober face! He might not be as classically handsome as Henry Latimer, but his pleasantly sensible appearance had a reassuring element in it—and was she deluded or was there a hidden strength in him far removed from Henry Latimer's easy charm? Unlike Henry he was certainly not about to persecute her with the kind of unpleasant innuendos which were that gentleman's stock in trade.

'Sir Neville!' she exclaimed. 'I had hoped to see you here, but someone told me that you rarely attended such entertainments.'

This mild statement, uttered while Henry was in full flow, had the desired effect of infuriating him and pleasing Neville.

'Oh,' he drawled, 'you are indeed fortunate, Duchess, that Sir Neville has gone against his usual grain. Otherwise, in order to speak to him, you might have found it necessary to frequent the British Museum, or the Inns of Court where he usually spends his spare time.'

Neville opened his mouth to say something, anything, in reply to such a sneering comment, but Diana forestalled him. 'If that is so then I am doubly fortunate for I, too, would wish to visit the British Museum, but have no knowledge of how I might do so. Perhaps, Sir Neville, you could write me a letter of introduction?'

'With pleasure, Duchess,' he replied. 'As to why I am here,

I was taught the pianoforte when I was much younger and consequently musical evenings give me much pleasure. I am told that you are to perform tonight. May I ask the title of your piece?'

'To echo you, Sir Neville, I must, with pleasure, inform you that I am to play two short bagatelles by Beethoven. They are minor pieces, of course, but they still manage to display his remarkable genius to the full.'

'Splendid,' replied Neville, giving no sign that Diana's presence was having its usual effect on him. 'I have not heard them before so I will await your performance with great interest. His concertos would, I fear, be too long for a society ridotto.'

'Exactly, which is why I chose the bagatelles. We are also to hear one of Haydn's shorter quartets.'

This enthusiastic conversation about music left Henry Latimer hanging in mid-air for he knew nothing about music and did not wish to remedy his ignorance. He had come to the ridotto to see and be seen.

Diana turned her attention to him. 'I fear that we are boring you,' she said sweetly, 'and, since I am shortly to play the first piece, I must leave you both at once in order to discover who is going to turn the pages of my score for me. Although I am able to perform without it in private, in public I prefer to have an assistant present—I find that it gives me confidence.'

'I think,' Henry Latimer remarked nastily to Neville when she had left them, 'that, contrary to what she has just said, the Duchess possesses almost too much confidence.'

Neville, wistfully watching her walk away from him, raised his eyebrows. 'Really? I find her frankness most touching in a world where everyone is busily saying what they don't mean.'

Since the second half of Neville's sentence was an accurate description of Henry's usual behaviour it was, perhaps, fortunate that Henry was too lost in self-conceit these days to grasp that it was meant as a comment on his own conduct.

'There is that,' he conceded. 'You must know, though, that it is not always wise to tell the truth. Imagine what life would be like if we did.'

So the ass hadn't realised that he had been one of his targets! Neville laughed to himself. He rarely said anything unkind and he could only wonder what jealousy was doing to him to provoke him into such unusual behaviour. For jealousy it was: the sight of Latimer fawning on Diana had almost undone him.

He really must learn to control himself, which he did by trying to think about anything but her—which was an impossibility. He endured exchanging a few more inanities with Latimer before walking away to find a seat where he would not only be able to hear every note that she played, but which would also give him a splendid view of her while she entertained the company.

So much for not thinking about her!

As he might have expected, Diana's performance of the Beethoven bagatelles was most accomplished for someone who was only an amateur. She showed no signs of needing the page turner and the applause for her was genuine and prolonged. After the concert was over and the spectators and performers all adjourned to the supper room she was surrounded by admirers and any hope that they might have had a private word together seemed to have disappeared.

He must find another occasion to tell her of his news. Several people spoke to him—they all expressed surprise at his presence, so to escape them he wandered away down a corridor that was also a picture gallery and past a room from which the noise of roistering men came through an open door.

Curious, he walked in, to discover that there were no women present, only a group of men enjoying themselves, having found a sanctuary away from concerts and the neces-

sity to behave decorously. Neville wondered whether his hosts
knew of what was happening, but rather doubted it. Most of
those present had already been half-cut when they had arrived
and what they had drunk at supper had served to add to their
present abandoned state. They must have searched the house
to find a suitable oasis.

He was about to leave, when he heard Henry Latimer
speaking. He had his back to Neville and was declaiming
before a small audience, many of whom had certainly not
been invited, which included his cousin George and Frank
Hollis. He heard his own name mentioned and curiosity
stopped him from walking away.

They say that listeners never hear any good of themselves
and on this second occasion, as on the first, it seemed to
Neville to be a universal truth.

'Fortescue is here tonight,' Latimer drawled. 'Isn't this exactly the sort of dead bore at which he might be expected to
be present? What I didn't expect was that he and Duchess
Diana would begin an earnest tohu-bohu about music, and
there was I thinking that she was only fit to talk about bed
and board and high jinks generally. Small jinks are all she'll
get with Fortescue.'

The drunken and abandoned state of those present was confirmed when this unpleasant sally was greeted with laughter
and applause. Frank Hollis appeared to be particularly
amused.

George laughed too, then added, 'But he must enjoy himself behind the scenes, you know, because I caught him at the
Turk's Head this afternoon, dressed like a junior clerk and in
the company of a fellow who claimed to be an ex-Bow Street
Runner.'

'Was he, indeed?' drawled Henry. 'And what are we to
make of that?'

Someone shouted an answer that was drowned in laughter.
Neville debated for a moment and then withdrew from the

unpleasant scene, believing that discretion was the better part of valour. He also thought that to go in and defend Duchess Diana's honour, or his own, before such an offensive mob might do both of them more harm than good.

He did begin to wonder, though, why Latimer should have demonstrated such an intense dislike of him from the very first moment he had arrived—after all, they had been friends once. On his way to the supper room to try to find Diana he was stopped by his host, Jack, Lord Devereux, a man noted for his fine sense of honour. He had met him when on Parliamentary business and had discovered that he, too, was worried by the harsh and repressive way in which the government was treating starving working men who had lost their livelihood.

'Happy to see you,' Jack said, 'which is more than I can say for some of the many unwanted and uninvited guests who are here tonight. God alone knows how they managed to get in—but it's something from which we are all beginning to suffer.'

Neville debated for a moment before saying, 'I suppose it's not the done thing to peach on them, but are you aware that a group of them are misbehaving themselves in one of the rooms off the picture gallery?'

Jack's eyebrows rose and he suddenly looked as formidable as he was supposed to be. 'And here I was thinking that they had had the good sense to go home. Exactly which room were they in?'

'The one with a lion's head above the door. I particularly noticed it.'

'Good, I'll go and roust them out—with a couple of footmen in tow. Tell them they can stay if they behave themselves.'

He thanked Neville but did not ask him for any of their names, and Neville later discovered they had begun to misbehave themselves in earnest after he had left to the degree that many of them were exiled from Devereux House forever.

Unfortunately, it seemed that Henry Latimer must have left before Frank's party arrived and that he was not as drunk as the rest for Neville saw him, looking sober, in the supper room just after he had made his adieux to his hostess. His sobriety made his nastiness about Diana seem even worse.

He was in the entrance hall when he heard rapid footsteps behind him. He swung round to find that it was Diana following him.

'Sir Neville,' she exclaimed breathlessly, 'I'm so pleased that I've caught you. Do you know where there's anywhere where we can speak alone? I've left Isabella with a crowd of other gossips busy tearing everyone's character to pieces. I daren't stay long, though.'

'Nor need you,' he told her briskly. 'The library is along this corridor and I'm sure that neither Jack nor Cass would mind us meeting there. This way.' And he led her a few yards down yet another corridor into an airy and spacious room crammed to the ceiling with books.

He offered her a chair from one of the tables; when she waved a hand at him, saying, 'Do please seat yourself', he pulled out another one and sat opposite to her. To their shared amusement they both began talking at once, and then they said together, 'You first,' which brought on another burst of laughter.

Finally Diana said, 'I have a little to tell you, and I wondered if you have any news for me.'

Neville nodded, then said, 'Ladies first,' and waited for her to begin.

Diana found something soothing in his presence. He listened to her quietly, giving her his full attention.

'One of my footmen told the housekeeper that he remembered that, shortly before Belinda disappeared, she was very fearful because she believed that she was being followed. She had only lately come up from the country and he thought that she was confused by the busy nature of London life. The thing was, the man she described was well-dressed and she saw him more than once, but otherwise he did nothing wrong and never tried to accost her, so it seemed that she might have been imagining things. Perhaps she wasn't.

'It doesn't seem very helpful, but I thought that you ought to know of it.'

Neville thought for a moment of how to tell Diana of his dreadful news without distressing her overmuch.

He said at last in as neutral a voice as he could summon up, 'What you have just told me is very useful because it seems to confirm something that I learned only this morning.' He proceeded to tell her of Jackson's news, in particular that some of those involved were penniless men in good society who were paid for their services.

Diana thought for a moment before saying, 'Which might mean that Belinda *was* being followed by a well-dressed man for evil purposes.'

'True, but, of course, we have no proof of that.'

'So, what do we do next?'

Neville leaned forward and said earnestly, looking into her beautiful eyes, 'You, Duchess, for the moment must do nothing. It is I who must act, although at the moment I am not quite sure what to do next, only that something must be done. I don't suppose we shall be able to rescue anyone but Belinda, and perhaps not even her, but we must try to stop this evil trade. What troubles me is that neither the magistrates nor the police wish to act—which might indicate that some powerful people are involved.'

'I don't like feeling helpless,' retorted Diana, a mutinous expression on her face.

'But you must not put yourself at risk,' said Neville, simultaneously admiring her spirit and at the same time wanting to protect her from harm. 'If powerful people *are* involved, then it might be dangerous to do anything that would draw attention to us. For the moment, allow me to continue my investigations as secretly as possible. I will inform you of anything I discover and ask for your assistance should I need it.

'Now we must separate before anyone notices that we have disappeared. I will leave Devereux House at once. You may stay here for a few moments and then return to the main rooms, claiming that you lost your way before asking Miss Marchmont to have your carriage called to take you home.'

Neville rose. He did not want to leave her. Diana had never looked so desirable as she did now, lost in thought.

'Diana?' he said, using her Christian name for the first time.

She looked up at him. 'Neville?' she replied and her voice had a question in it, too.

He was going to say—what was he going to say? He had never been in this situation before. He was drowning in her eyes and in the little lift at each corner of her mouth as though she were about to smile, and he, God help him, was in worse case than ever before. He was losing his mind and about to run mad—all he wanted was to have her under him, here and now. The mere sight of her had been enough to rouse him. This was new territory and, like all new territory, must be explored carefully—but he had never felt less careful in all his life.

'Nothing,' he said desperately, 'only that you must be cautious. Say nothing to anyone about what is exercising us for I have the strongest feeling that there is more to it than the disappearance of servant girls, but what that more can be, I have no notion.'

'And you take care, too,' replied Diana, sure that what he had just said was important, but was not what he had been on the point of saying when he had looked at her in that odd fashion.

Odd, because she had thought that there was hunger in it,

and, being very perceptive, although her experience of life outside the study and the library was small, she was instinctively aware that they had crossed some border in their relationship with each other and that there was no going back.

And, yes, he was an odd creature. Something was telling her that beneath his outward calm banked fires raged, and that these fires were not only to do with her, but were also challenging all his own previous beliefs about how his life should be organised.

Was it to Charles, her dead husband, that she owed these strange insights? He had spent many hours telling her of the various ways in which men and women behaved and of the tricks they used to deceive not only others, but themselves.

All this ran through her mind while Sir Neville Fortescue was busy taking his leave, and after he had gone she wondered whether he had been trying to read her as she had read him—or thought she had read him...

Well, if he believed that she was going to allow him to conduct this tricky business on his own he was very much mistaken! Belinda had been in her charge, she was responsible for her and she must play her part in trying to recover her—if that were possible.

What action that might entail she did not know, but she would think of something, if only by asking herself what Charles would have done. He was her invisible mentor and her guide and, whenever she was confronted with a problem, she still asked herself what action he would have taken.

Neville was making his way to the house in Chelsea in which Lem was now living. He was discovering in himself a strange desire for action of the most physical kind. In the last few days, every rule by which he had lived his life from childhood onwards no longer seemed enough for him since they could afford him no guidance in what to do next.

It occurred to him that he had never before thought to ask

for advice from Lem—indeed, would probably have scorned the notion that a member of the servant class could give him instruction in anything. Now, however, he was beginning to understand that Lem and his kind often possessed a knowing and down-to-earth common sense that was quite alien to George Alford and Frank Hollis.

No doubt he was showing his own lack of common sense by sending his carriage home and finishing his journey on foot despite the lateness of the hour and he had no sooner experienced this unwelcome thought when he fancied that he was being followed. Yes, it was probably stupid of him to walk alone late at night in any part of London but he had felt the need to be in the open, beneath the stars.

He looked behind him when he reached the square off which his temporary home was situated, but could see no one. He could only conclude that probably the sense of something wrong, which had haunted him ever since he had visited Sir Stanford Markham, was giving him these untoward thoughts. He would be seeing ghosts and starting at moonbeams next.

He was wrong; it was not a ghost or a moonbeam that struck him to the pavement, but a man, a large man, who bent down to haul his dazed self upright and to hiss into his face, 'Listen, cully, keep to your own kind and don't meddle with the affairs of those who don't concern you. This is the last and only warning you will get. The next time you try to make trouble I'll be sure to leave your body on the ground for the Watch to remove, not let you live as I am doing now.'

So saying, he flung Neville away from him to hit the wall of the house behind them and slide down it before he ran off into the dark, leaving his victim to haul himself painfully to his feet.

He had not been wrong: he had been followed and the only explanation for the threats that he had just received was the business of the servant girls and his enlisting of Jackson's support.

But to the devil with threats! In future, not only would he go carefully, but he would pursue this matter to the end. Taking his aching head and his bruised body to his Chelsea hiding place—which seemed to be no hiding place at all—he was not too dazed to realise that his attacker was no ordinary ruffian—which made the whole wretched business more mysterious than ever.

But stop he would not. Neither threats nor pleas nor indifference by the authorities would move him from his path now—in fact, they had made him even more determined to find why both a magistrate and the Runners and now the representative of criminals should be so determined to prevent him from investigating what at first had seemed to be a fairly simple mystery.

Lem, who had been waiting up for him, exclaimed at his master's bruised face and torn cravat. 'Never say that you were attacked by footpads, sir.'

'One footpad,' said Neville ruefully, 'but he was not out to rob me, only to warn me not to pursue this matter of the servant girls further lest worse befall me.'

'And will you, sir? Give up trying to find Belinda?'

'By God, no!' Neville roared, as astonished by his belligerence as Lem obviously was, so foreign was it to his usual calm self, 'but I would not wish you to be prey to these rogues. If you would prefer me to pursue this matter on my own, you are free to do so.'

'What! Leave my Belinda to them while you risk your life for me? What sort of man would that make me, sir?'

'You are sure, Lem? Quite sure?'

'Yes. I will do whatever is necessary to rescue Belinda. Remember what I told you earlier, sir. I would dare anything to save her.' He fell silent and then added, 'We will carry out your plan then?'

'Tomorrow. Each day that we dally makes Belinda's situation worse. Now let us try to get some sleep. Neither of us is used to being awake in the watches of the night.'

Sleep, though was long in coming to both of them. Lem was grieving for Belinda and Neville was thinking about Lem. He'd never really taken much notice of any of the footmen before. They were simply part of the background of his life, like the furniture and the other treasures which filled his home: he had always employed a valet, but had never had anything resembling a conversation with him. His valet was away at the moment, attending his father's funeral, and Neville had not found a temporary replacement for him; he was looking after himself for the first time since he had been a boy. His absence gave him a freedom of action that was making the plan he had devised for finding Belinda easier to carry out.

Lem, indeed, insisted on playing the role of a valet and also looked after him in the little house in Chelsea whenever he used it. A woman came in daily to clean it and prepare Lem's meals—Neville usually only visited in the evening and rarely stayed there overnight.

What suddenly struck him, before he fell into an uneasy sleep, was that, to some extent, he was the prisoner of the servants who surrounded him. Their hard lives made his life easy, but without them he would be lost. When this wretched brouhaha was over he would pay more attention to them.

Lem, for example, was showing a livelier brain and understanding than George Alford or Frank Hollis, yet he was doomed to open and shut doors and carry out menial tasks for the rest of his life. He had also learned to talk like the gentlemen and gentlewomen whom he served, although Neville would never have known that without his involvement in the disappearance of the girls.

Yes, somehow, when this business was over he would find a way for Lem to put his undoubted talents to use.

This decided, he fell asleep, only to wake just before dawn, haunted by Diana Medbourne, another gifted person who was also causing him to question his whole way of life. But whatever changes he made, he would never do anything that might cause him to follow in his father's doom-laden footsteps.

Chapter Five

'Forgive me for saying so, sir, but you don't look a bit like
your usual self.'

Lem had just finished helping Neville into the clothes he
was going to wear on this night's venture: he and his master
were visiting one of the houses on Jackson's list.

'No forgiveness needed,' returned Neville smartly. 'It's exactly the response I was looking for. I don't think anyone
would so much as recognise me in these togs, do you?'

'Flash, very flash,' Lem said, airing his knowledge of
thieves' cant. 'I wonder that you will be able to walk in trousers which are so wide at the foot, sir, and that waistcoat you
are wearing is a model of bad taste.'

'Isn't it just!' Neville grinned, eyeing himself in the mirror.
'I don't think that Beau Brummell would have approved of a
single thing I have on. Even my boots look wrong.'

'Particularly your boots, sir,' said Lem, entering into the
fun of the thing.

'True, but, if I may say so, you look a remarkably good
imitation of a flash cove yourself. And forgive me for asking,
Lem, where did you learn to speak so beautifully?'

Lem blushed. 'Your butler, sir. I asked him to help me

improve my speech because some of the other servants made fun of my country voice.'

'Um—' Neville regarded him quizzically. 'It might be a good idea if you used your country voice tonight—you would then be regarded as a typical bumpkin visiting the sights of London with no notion of how the gentry behave.'

Lem nodded agreement and Neville wondered at himself a little. Where was all this ability to deceive coming from?

'And I,' he added, 'am obviously also not a gentleman, but trying to pass as one by taking dated fashion to its extremes. I shall, though, be sure of a welcome when it becomes apparent that my pockets are full to bursting.'

And all this to go to a house of ill fame off the Haymarket, visited by everyone from minor members of the Royal Family like Prince Adalbert and ambitious thieves seeking prey. With luck he would not meet anyone who might recognise that puritanical fellow, Sir Neville Fortescue.

The Haymarket, when they reached it, was ablaze with light from the new gas lamps. Neville had never been in this part of the capital late at night and was surprised to find the streets so crowded. When they turned into the alleyway that led to Madame Josette's, one of the two brothels of which Jackson had told him, Lem touched his shoulder and whispered, 'Look, sir.'

He was pointing at a man in decent black clothing wearing a top hat. He was seated on a chair and holding up a pole with a board attached to it. Written on it in large letters were the words BEWARE BAD HOUSES.

'A little late to tell us that,' was Neville's dry reply before they reached the door, guarded by two bruisers, which was the entrance to Madame Josette's.

To Lem's astonishment Neville gave a reasonably accurate imitation of Frank Hollis at his silliest. So much so that the bruisers immediately let them in and they found themselves in an entrance hall, and after that a drawing room very similar to those in the best houses of the *ton*.

Good pictures were on the walls. A pretty girl was playing a pianoforte; several men and women sat at ease; at the far end of the room was a long table on which food and drink were laid out. Everything, indeed, was in the best of taste. It was hard to believe that a vicious trade in children and young women was going on elsewhere—everything looked so civilised.

Neville recognised no one present save for one half-cut gentleman who was taking up most of a sofa. He was a well-known MP noted for his upright character. He frequently spoke of the dangers of drink and of immorality. Neville had no time to dwell on the fellow's hypocrisy.

'What now?' whispered Lem.

'Wait,' said Neville. A large woman, handsome and dressed in the latest fashions, but well past her first youth, was walking towards them. She stared at them doubtfully before saying when she reached them, 'I do not know you, sirs.'

'Not surprising that,' Neville drawled, 'seeing that we have not been here before, but your name was given to me by a friend who told me that you were always discreet and that you catered for those whose tastes are a little out of the ordinary.'

'Did he, indeed? And pray, sir, who was this gentleman?'

Neville's response was to lean forward smiling confidentially and murmuring, 'Now that I cannot tell you for he is my physician and matters of medicine are, naturally, confidential. He also said, though, that certain…er…ailments could be overcome if the right cure was available—as I am sure that you know.'

'Perhaps—but I must warn you that these cures are vastly expensive.'

'So he told me before I left the country to visit London and

I have come armed with enough in the way of payment to satisfy you, as well as myself.'

She thought for a moment before saying, 'I can see by your attire that you *are* up from the country—so you are speaking the truth about that. But before you come to my office, sir, you must give me your name and that of your companion.'

'Willingly,' replied Neville, discovering how easy lies were, which, he was beginning to realise, was why criminals used them so often. He was aghast at his own proficiency, but needs must when the devil drives, he told himself, and, indicating Lem, he informed her that he was his young cousin, Leander Parks, also up from the country and that he was John Wilkinson of Barton Elms, Leicestershire, and a magistrate in that district.

'And if,' he added, 'you will be good enough to allow me into your office, I can assure you that I have enough guineas on my person to pay for anything Leander and I wish from you, because...' and he winked at her confidentially '...we engage in these adventures together.'

Lem, listening to him come out with such outrageous untruths, scarcely knew whether to laugh or to cry at his severe master's brilliant impersonation of an unscrupulous lecher. It was all that he could do to keep his face straight. The only flaw in the jest was that he had sworn to Sir Neville that he would never inform anyone of what they were doing, so he would be unable to share the joke with his fellows.

Madame was mollified. A country bumpkin would be an easy mark whom she could heavily overcharge for any services she could offer him.

She led them to her office where a haggling match began, but it was plain to her that this oaf covered his desire for a virgin with the pretence of seeking a cure for his venereal ailment—or perhaps his doctor had convinced him that such a cure was possible.

Finally, grumbling and cursing with seeming reluctance,

Neville paid Madame a sum that left Lem aghast. Madame was so keen to rid him of it that she asked him for no further proofs of his identity, merely saying, 'We have recently acquired what you need—for medical purposes, of course.'

Now what? Her smile never disappearing—it was apparently her stock in trade—she called over a footman who was plainly yet another bruiser and, standing a little apart from them, engaged him in conversation. At his final nod she led him to Neville.

'Giles will take you upstairs and introduce you both to the person whom you require. That is all. I bid you good luck, sir.'

This easy dismissal of them as though they were engaged in some idle piece of merrymaking left Neville wanting to wring her neck, but he refrained and the pair of them followed Giles upstairs.

Lem had asked earlier, 'What do we do if the girl we are offered is not Belinda?'

'We'll cross that bridge when we come to it,' had been Neville's answer. Everything would have to be impromptu, decided on the spur of the moment. As he mounted the stairs he asked himself what the devil he thought he was doing to set out on such a mad enterprise with no notion of whether it would succeed or fail.

And if Belinda were offered to them, how were they to rescue her? Another problem to be solved on the spot.

They were taken to the third floor into a bedroom near a landing, which was also furnished in the best of taste.

'Wait,' said Giles, and left them.

Minutes later he was back, leading a pretty girl with a terrified expression on her face.

Neville raised his quizzing glass and stared hard at her while Giles prepared to leave. He looked at Lem, who shook his head to indicate that she was not Belinda.

It was Neville's turn to say 'Wait.'

'Yes?' replied Giles.

'The child does not please me,' Neville drawled. 'It is most important that she does. Have you no others to offer me? May I not choose one?'

'Did Madame say that you might?'

'Yes,' lied Neville.

'Oh, very well.' Giles took the rejected girl by the hand and dragged her out. Neville made an instant decision—even if Belinda were not here he would choose a girl, any girl, and try to save her from this hell-hole.

When Giles returned he had three young women in tow, all of whom were strangers to Neville—as was Belinda. This time he asked Lem, 'Which one do you favour, cousin?'

Lem pointed at the girl in the middle, who was hanging her head and trying not to look at them. The other two girls were bolder. 'That one, please.'

'A good choice,' approved Neville. 'She is not too forward. You may take the others away.'

Giles and the girls left them, but not before he had said, 'When you have both finished with her, knock on the door and I will take her away. Her name is Phoebe.'

Once they had left, Lem walked over to the girl whom he had identified as Belinda. Her head was still hanging as though the patterned carpet at her feet was the most important thing in the world.

He took her hand which she immediately wrenched away, and turned her head to avoid looking at him. He said softly, 'Bel, my darling Bel, don't you recognise me?'

This time she stared at him as though she had never seen him before. 'Lem! Why are you here? Who is this man with you? Have you come to use me as the other girls have been used?'

It was plain that she now saw every man as an enemy and probably most women, too.

'This, my darling, is Sir Neville Fortescue for whom I

work. We have come to rescue you, to take you away from this vile place.'

'Yes, Miss Jesson, and in order to do that you will have to help us.'

Her dull-eyed gaze was turned on him now: tears were running down her face.

'How can you rescue me since this place is so well guarded that it might as well be called a prison? I have seen other girls brought to this room, and afterwards they are taken downstairs—they have been successfully broken in. Because I am a virgin I have been saved for those who will pay highly for me. Have you paid highly for me, Sir Neville?'

One thing was plain: the people who ran the brothel had spent their time persuading her that she was simply prey, a thing not to be considered and this had made her suspicious even of her possible saviours.

'Yes, I *have* paid highly for you,' Neville said, 'but only in the hope that we might find you here and take you away. Believe me, and believe that Lem has nearly run mad since you disappeared. He asked me for help and I have given it.'

Her lips trembled. She said, tremulously, to Lem, 'Is that true? Are you being honest with me?'

He took her hand and kissed it, even though she would have wrenched it away. 'Always honest, my only love. Remember, I never once tried to take advantage of you when we were alone together before you disappeared.'

She gave a great sigh. 'Giles is outside the door, waiting for you to have done with me. How shall we get past him? He will have locked the door, too.'

'Patience,' Neville told her. 'Lem and I have thought long and hard of how to deal with him. Remember, he has no notion that we are not ordinary clients and will not be expecting anything to go amiss. Are there backstairs here?'

She nodded. 'Yes, I was brought up them after they kidnapped me.'

'Excellent. Try to remember where they are. Now, we must be a little noisy and take our time before we deal with Giles. It would not do to be in too much of a hurry since they will believe that I will want my money's worth.'

He was so gentle and kind that Belinda's lips quivered. 'Aren't you afraid of what they will do to you if your plans fail? They are very cruel.'

'Let us not talk of failure, but be ready for success,' was Neville's reply, and although he was thinking, God help us all if matters go awry, he seemed so calm and sure that for the first time Belinda gave a small, hopeful smile.

At first they talked noisily, making a great commotion and then fell quiet. After about half an hour Giles hammered on the door, calling out, 'Aren't you done in there, yet?'

'Not quite,' shouted Neville. 'God damn me, man, allow me to finish my fun in peace—I've paid enough for it.'

Giles grumbled for a few moments before falling silent himself.

'Now,' said Neville briskly, 'he will not be expecting anything untoward. When he comes in I shall stand behind the door, out of sight. You, Lem, will address him as he enters, Belinda must be pretending to cry on the bed. I have brought my stoutest stick with me, one that befits a country bumpkin. I shall stun him with it—or so I hope—and then we shall all make for the backstairs. And may God defend the right.'

'Amen,' said Lem while Belinda clasped her arms about her and shivered.

Neville was right about Giles. When they called he strode, grinning, into the bedroom and was about to make a lewd remark to Lem when Neville, praying that the blow would not kill him, struck him hard on the back of his head.

He fell like a stone, unconscious.

'Now,' said Neville, hanging on to his stick, and pointing to the door. Lem and Belinda darted through it, and he followed them.

'This way,' whispered Belinda, leading them along a short corridor to a wooden spiral staircase, as functional as the rest of the building was decorative. They ran down it.

Neville had no idea how long it would be before Giles recovered consciousness, or was found in the empty bedroom from which 'Phoebe' and her customers were missing. All he knew was that they must find their way out into the Haymarket where they could mingle with the crowd and disappear.

After that, improvisation would again be the order of the night, and the hope that their luck would not run out.

'You're quiet tonight, Diana. Is anything troubling you?'

Diana looked at her companion before answering her. They were at Leominster House, supposed to be enjoying themselves at a large dinner party. Isabella had been most particular in urging her to attend it because the Leominsters' heir, Jeremy Hamlyn, had come up from the country and was certain to be present. He would, Isabella thought, make a most suitable husband for Diana.

Diana had regretted her acceptance of the formidable lady's invitation to them both. She didn't particularly want to meet Jeremy since she was very worried about Neville and the dangers he might have to face in any attempt to rescue Belinda. She had almost decided to cry off at the last minute on the plea of not feeling well since she didn't care for the idea of enjoying herself while Neville might be putting himself at risk.

She could hardly tell Isabella that, though, and it was only to placate her good friend that she had decided to attend after all, so she simply said, 'I'm feeling a little tired, but I don't think I'm sickening for anything.'

They were drinking tea in the great drawing room while waiting for the men to arrive after their session at the dining table with port, brandy and cigars.

Isabella looked at her curiously. She had grown used to

Diana's zest for life, and to see her so sombre and reserved was quite a new experience.

'Then I suggest that we leave as soon as decently possible,' she said briskly. 'An early night might work wonders.'

It was while she was talking that Diana, who was still worrying about Neville, experienced something quite untoward, something completely alien to her. The room around her disappeared and she was suddenly in the dark, surrounded by unseen enemies and overwhelmed by a feeling of great danger. So great, indeed, that her senses began to swim and she started to fall forward.

Lady Leominster, who had come over to speak to her, saw at once that something was wrong and barked at Isabella in her usual domineering manner, 'Catch her, Mrs Marchmont. Your mistress looks as though she's about to faint.'

Isabella put her arms around Diana and pulled her upright again, then made her lean against the back of the sofa they had been sharing. Diana's face was ashy pale; after a moment she opened her eyes to stare at the distressed Isabella and the totally undistressed Lady Leo-minster.

'I'm so sorry to have made such a cake of myself,' she murmured, 'but for a moment I was overcome by a feeling that I was about to faint.'

She said nothing of the sensation of great danger that she had also experienced, for that would have made her sound ridiculous despite the fact that it was still present, though fading.

'The heat!' proclaimed Lady Leominster. 'It's the heat! I've reprimanded the housekeeper more than once for overheating the salons. Cold is good for you.'

No sooner had she come out with this, however, than she could not fail to see that Diana had begun to shiver again. At this her tune changed completely and she bawled at the assembled company, 'Will someone please fetch the Duchess a shawl, at once.'

A nearby matron slipped off the one she was wearing and came over to drape it 'round Diana who said, numbly, 'I am sorry to have caused such a commotion, I am already beginning to feel a little better.'

A statement that was not strictly true since not only was her right cheek paining her, but troubling her much more than that was the question of what in the world could have brought about such an odd reaction. She had never in her whole life come so near to fainting. Could it possibly be that her worries over Neville had caused it?

Was he in danger? And if so, had she felt it? No, that could not be true. She was not a character in Walpole's *The Castle of Otranto*, or one of Monk Lewis's eerie novels, nor even Mrs Radcliffe's *The Mysteries of Udolpho*. No, she was down-to-earth Diana Medbourne, trained by a husband who despised 'mystical frivolity', as he always termed anything to do with the odd or the supernatural.

And yet, and yet… No she would not think of such things. She allowed herself to drink a little water and be sympathised over by Jeremy Hamlyn, before being driven home in the company of Isabella. Nevertheless, her dreams were troubled and she knew that she would only find relief when she heard that Neville was safe and well.

Neville was far from being either. The three of them had made their way down the backstairs as quickly and quietly as they could. It was essential that they were well away from Madame Josette's before Giles recovered to find that Mr Wilkinson, his cousin and 'Phoebe' had all disappeared.

They had just reached the bottom of the stairs, which had led them to a small room with two doors—one of them obviously opening on to the back of the house. Neville was just congratulating himself that they were about to get away without being caught when two things happened at once.

Firstly, there was the sound of shouting coming down the

stairs and, secondly, one of the doors burst open and an obvious bruiser, wearing some sort of fancy uniform, came in. They were not to know that he had decided to answer the call of nature in the small courtyard at the back of the house.

He took one look at them, roared, 'What the devil are you doing here?' and struck Neville a hard blow in the face, which sent him backwards. Neville thereupon shouted at Lem, 'Run, boy, run, you know where to go.' They had previously decided that, if either of them was trapped, the other would take Belinda by the hand and make off with her.

Fortunately for Lem—and for Neville, too—the new arrival was diverted by the howling that was coming down the stairs. Neville ran after Lem and Belinda, but he had already lost sight of them: they had, he hoped, reached the Haymarket and possible safety.

Behind him, Giles, who had just arrived, was shouting at the bruiser that one of the girls had been taken and she was to be recovered before the boss knew that she had gone— 'If we don't get her back there will be the devil to pay.'

The blow to Neville's face had been a cruel one. His right eye was swelling, his cheekbone hurt him and he was more than a little dazed. They caught him up before he had gone many erratic yards and pinned him against the wall.

'Where's the gal?' roared the bruiser, giving him a slap this time rather than a blow since he wanted him conscious and able to answer questions.

'Gone,' croaked Neville. 'Gone where you'll not find her.'

Giles immediately set off at the double to try to catch Lem and Phoebe, but they were already out of sight. The alley was a short one and by the time he reached the Haymarket they had disappeared into the press of people who were making the night day. He ran a little way further on, but the task was hopeless, particularly when, in his haste, he jostled a group of aristocratic young bloods out on the town who were of-

fended by his trying to push past them and surrounded him,
singing a lewd song and refusing to let him pass.

When finally the game palled he returned to the alley to
find Neville still held by the bruiser and now barely conscious
from his attentions.

'They've gone—and now what?' moaned Giles. 'What's to
do with him?'

'Kill him?' asked the bruiser.

'I'd like to,' grumbled Giles, 'but not wise. The boss
wouldn't want no scandal. T'other chap might go to the authorities and what then? No, let's lug him along to some alley
a fair way from here, pour whisky down his throat and leave
him for the Watch to find and bang up in gaol. The boss said
he was only some bumpkin up from the country, so who's to
worry about him?'

'What about the gal? Why did he take her?'

'How the hell should I know what he thought he was doing? For his own amusement, possibly. You keep him there
while I fetch a bottle of whisky and then we'll be rid of him.
Let him try telling the law that he was nabbing a gal from a
bad house and see what they say to him then.'

And so it was done. Giles poured spirits down the semi-
conscious Neville's throat before dragging him, now reeking
of whisky, to throw him down in a doorway in a nearby alley
where he moaned for a moment or two before subsiding into
drunken slumber.

The unholy pair spent their time on the way back trying to
concoct a story that would satisfy Madame. Yes, they had lost
the girl, but, no, nothing further would be heard from the
villains who had stolen her, and the prime villain had been
left for the Watch to find and take to the magistrate's court.
Best of all there would also be no scandal.

Not that this mollified Madame completely, but, after all,
she had received a goodly sum for the girl from the bumpkin
and, given luck, there would soon be others to take her place.

Unknown to Madame, or to Neville, there had been someone present while the sale of the girl had taken place downstairs, someone who had recognised Neville beneath his disguise and who grasped that the warning which he had sent
him had been ignored. He decided that it would be useful to
inform those who paid him well of his true identity and that
he had rescued Belinda, so that further action might be taken
against him.

He joined in the laughter over the escape of the girl and
the beating of the country bumpkin—and left to go and earn
his money.

Lem arrived back at the house in Chelsea where Belinda
immediately began to question him feverishly.

'Where are we? How did you discover that I was at Madame Josette's? Oh, Lem, I've never been so frightened in all
my life as I was when I was there.'

'Did they hurt you?' he asked her. He could not bear to
think that she had been cruelly treated.

She shook her head. 'No, they examined me and found I
was a virgin and they saved me, with two other girls, for any
rich gentleman who would pay highly for us. Giles…' she
paused for a moment, tears filling her eyes '…was annoyed,
because he had first choice of all the other girls who came in,
but he dared not touch the three of us, so instead he made
our lives miserable… But oh, Lem, where is this place you
have brought me to?'

'We're in Chelsea and the house belongs to my master, Sir
Neville Fortescue. It was he who discovered where you were
and who came with me to rescue you. He should be here by
now—unless they have caught him.'

His worried face distressed Belinda.

'Never say so. Oh, Lem, they will mistreat him if they do.
Giles likes to cause pain.'

* * *

Time wore on, and still Sir Neville did not return. Lem persuaded Belinda to go to bed in the room Neville had set aside for her. He decided that, if his master had not returned by morning, he would take Belinda to the Duchess's house and ask her how they might find him. From what Belinda had said and he had seen, he thought that it was a strong possibility that Madame's bruisers had killed him.

Neville was not dead, but when he awoke the next morning he felt that he might as well have been.

He found himself in a cell behind bars, his head thundering and his whole body aching, in the company of four other wretches, who, like himself, reeked of strong drink, and had been picked up by the Watch in various parts of the city. He bore no resemblance to the sober and severe gentleman he had once been.

His wits were slightly addled too, for he found himself saying, or rather, half-groaning, 'Where the devil are we?'

The only one of his companions who had recovered enough to speak spat at him, 'Where the devil do you think we are, cully? We're penned up here, waiting to be taken to the magistrates and charged.'

Neville, still a little dazed, but with the fuddled and painful head of a man who was a moderate drinker and had ingested a large quantity of whisky, said fuzzily, 'Charged? What with?'

'Being took up dead drunk in the street like the rest of us.'

Neville tried to recall what had happened to him the night before. He remembered escaping from Madame Josette's, being struck a punishing blow, then being kicked…and after that, nothing.

All he could say, feebly, was, 'But I never drink to excess.'

His new-found friend roared with laughter. 'Try tellin' that to the beak, cully, and see where that'll get you.'

Neville shook his head, which seemed to clear it a little.

By now he was sitting up and able to look down at himself. It was true, not only did he reek of whisky, but his clothing was soaked in it and he looked as though he had been rolling in the filth of the alley through which he had been running in order to escape from Giles and his cohorts.

He said, 'I have never been in this situation before. What will they do to us?'

'Send us to the House of Correction, most like to do hard labour with a warning not to be taken up again.' He added with a sideways look at Neville, 'You talk like a gent—come down in the world, have you?'

Neville, appalled by the prospect before him, could only nod at the fellow. Good God, what was he going to do? He was, alas, indistinguishable from the wretches around him. Like them, he had been taken up by the Watch in a bad part of the city and brought here for judgement. Feverishly, while he waited for the policemen to arrive and take them before the magistrate, he tried to think up a reasonable explanation for his sorry condition, but nothing came to mind.

Unfortunately he could not tell the truth; and to report that he had been brutally attacked did not explain his drunken state, nor how he came to be lying in an alley in a district where every vice known to men was for sale.

He had little further time to decide on anything. Two burly policemen entered, one of whom dragged him to his feet and shouted at the rest of the prisoners, 'Let's be having you. We've got the Lord God himself here today to sit in judgement on you, so behave yourselves.'

With difficulty the pair of them managed to get three of the company to walk between them; the fourth, still unconscious, was left behind. They were then led into a room that was a cross between a parlour and a court of law. A crude pen stood at one end of it, facing a large desk behind which sat a man whom Neville immediately recognised.

Of all people it was Sir Stanford Markham, JP, before

whom he had been brought, which explained the first policeman's description of him as the Lord God. Two members of
the Watch were also present to give evidence on the condition
in which they had found the prisoners.

Neville had no time to think since he was the first of the
four to be pushed to the front of the pen to be judged. He had
thought that he might try to throw himself on Sir Stanford's
mercy, but as soon as he tried to speak the first policeman
struck him fiercely and bade him be quiet, 'for the witness to
your arrest has not yet been sworn.'

What to do but obey? One of the watchmen, Jonty Beagle
by name, was sworn and gave evidence that the prisoner had
been found dead drunk and lying in an alley off the Haymarket.

Sir Stanford, who had barely taken the time to look at the
prisoner, and had certainly not recognised Neville, said in a
bored voice, 'Your name, man, and quick about it.'

How to answer? It would be stupid to give a false name
and be sent to the House of Correction since no one, not even
Lem, would know where he was, and his disappearance would
become a nine days' wonder. He would have to speak the
truth and shame the devil, as the saying had it. His hesitation,
however, had annoyed Sir Stanford. 'Speak up, man,' he said
irritably. 'We have more to do than wait for you to make up
your mind which name you are using today.'

'My name is Neville Fortescue and that I am he you may
plainly see if you look carefully at me.'

'What!' Sir Stanford flung down the quill pen that he was
using. 'How dare you make such a claim!'

'No claim, but the truth,' said Neville stubbornly. 'If I may
come nearer to you, I think you will see that I *am* speaking
the truth.'

For a moment Sir Stanford hesitated, then, picking up his
pen, he waved it at Neville. 'Constable, let him come forward.'

Nearer to, he was, indeed, able to recognise that, beneath his dirt and dishevelment, the prisoner was indeed Sir Neville Fortescue. If Neville had thought that this was going to mean that he would be released straight away, he was mistaken.

'Yes, I recognise you, but I must ask you how you came to be found in the condition that Beagle has described. Your current appearance amply demonstrates that, in giving his evidence, he was speaking the truth.'

Nothing for it now but to tell Sir Stanford a little of what had happened to him—but neither the complete story, nor why.

'I was minding my own business, walking quietly along, when I was attacked and robbed. All the valuables on my person have disappeared.'

Sir Stanford stared at him. 'From the Watch's description of the condition in which you were found, I cannot believe that you were walking along quietly—nor, for that matter, even staggering quietly. Is there no one who could come forward to confirm that what you are telling me is true?'

Lem could have borne witness for him, but there were two problems connected with that: he was Neville's servant, and it would therefore be suspected that he had influenced him as to the nature of his evidence; and Neville had no wish to involve Lem in this—to his detriment—or to explain to Sir Stanford, whom he did not trust, what he had been engaged in with Lem.

'Alas, no, I was on my own,' was thus all that he could reply.

'Most unfortunate,' said Sir Stanford severely. 'You leave me in something of a quandary. You have the reputation of being a most upright man and citizen, which reputation now seems to me to be undeserved. Indeed, your presence here makes your previous pretensions smack of hypocrisy.

'Were you, as most who are brought here in your condition are, a beggar or poverty-stricken, I should have no hesitation in sending you to a House of Correction in order to learn to mend your ways, and help you to find a useful trade. That sentence, however, is, given your rank and wealth, obviously most unsuitable, so the question of how to sentence you becomes a difficult one.'

He leaned back and considered for a moment, his hands pressed together in the fashion of a man praying.

'I consider,' he said, assuming an expression of great gravity, 'that the damage to your reputation is, in itself, a most condign punishment. You have been shown to be a drunkard, a liar and, worst of all, a hypocrite. That the whole world will know you for what you are must be your penalty.'

What could he say to that? One thing was plain. He had succeeded in saving Belinda, but at the expense of ruining himself. Put bluntly, his name was now like the mud with which he was covered.

His one hope was that he—and particularly Lem—had saved Belinda: something which he had yet to learn.

Chapter Six

Morning had arrived, but not Sir Neville. Lem had spent a restless night, for while he had helped to save Belinda, he might also have lost his kind master to the wolves who served Madame Josette and her patrons.

What to do? He decided to carry out the rest of Sir Neville's plan by taking Belinda, as soon as they had broken their fast, to the Duchess's home in Piccadilly. It had been arranged beforehand that were she to be rescued she would leave London immediately, being sent to Medbourne Castle in the interests of her safety. This might grieve both her and Lem, but it was essential that her kidnappers should have no idea of where she had gone.

It would also mean that if he were not present there would be no one to admit the housekeeper-cook when she arrived to perform the day's duties, but he dare not delay their visit to the Duchess: the sooner she knew that Sir Neville was missing, the better.

Belinda said, when Lem had told her where they were going, 'But what about Sir Neville? Shouldn't we inform the authorities of what has happened to him?'

'On no account.' Lem was energetic. 'Sir Neville said that it's quite possible some highly placed persons are connected with this trade. The less anyone knows about what we did, the better.'

Belinda fell silent after that. She had not yet recovered from her ordeal and the only person in the whole world whom she felt that she could trust, now that Sir Neville had gone, was Lem.

'I don't want to lose you, too,' she told him, for, being no fool, she had already guessed that to be safe she might have to leave London.

'Not me, you'll not lose me, and, if we're apart I can write to you. You told me you could write.'

'It won't be the same,' she sniffled, but she didn't argue with him.

Diana was eating a late breakfast. She was feeling very much better after her malaise the night before, and had just begun to peel an orange when Lubbock, her butler, entered.

'I am sorry to disturb you, your Grace, but a young man, one Lemuel Banks, has just arrived and has asked to see you. He says that he has a message from Sir Neville Fortescue to be delivered to you personally. He is accompanied by a young woman wearing a veil, whose name he refused to give me. He was most insistent that he sees you and no one else. If you consider his request to be impertinent, I can send him away at once.'

Lemuel Banks! That was the name of the young man with whom Belinda had been walking out. She decided not to appear too hasty in agreeing to receive him. Servants gossiped, as she well knew, so she appeared to think hard for a few moments before saying, 'Oh, send him in, I may as well receive him. If his message is from Sir Neville it may be important, or it may not.'

'Very well, your Grace.'

Diana could hardly contain her impatience until Lubbock

escorted Master Banks and his unnamed companion into the breakfast room.

'Please sit down,' she said, pointing to a sofa opposite to her before Lem could speak.

Lem shook his head. 'Beg pardon, your Grace, but, being a servant, I should prefer to stand. I have news for you, some good and some bad.'

'From Sir Neville?'

'Not exactly,' Lem replied. 'I have to tell you that last night we—that is, Sir Neville and I, rescued your servant, Belinda Jesson, from the bad house where she was kept a prisoner.'

Diana's rapid gaze took in the veiled woman standing beside him.

'And this is Belinda.'

'Yes, your Grace. Take off your veil, Belinda, so that the Duchess may see that it's really you I have brought. She wore the veil,' he explained, 'so that she might not be recognised if anyone from the bad house recognised her on the way here.'

Belinda did as she was bid and bobbed a shy curtsy. She had always been a lively girl and it was plain from her shadowed face that her ordeal had left its mark upon her.

'Oh, I am so happy to see you again, Belinda. You were not mistreated, I hope.'

'No, your Grace. I was lucky.'

She was thinking of all the girls who had not been and the shadow on her face deepened.

'And Sir Neville?' For Diana was wondering why he had not brought them to her home himself.

'That is the bad news, your Grace. We were surprised while we were leaving after freeing Belinda. Madame's guards caught up with us and Sir Neville bade me run off with her since we were ahead of him. He refused to allow me to return to help him. I hoped that he had escaped from them, but I fear the worst because he has not returned to his house in Chelsea where I took Belinda on his orders.'

Neville caught! 'You don't think…?' She was so shocked that she could not finish her sentence.

'That my master is injured, perhaps badly. I don't know.' Anguish was written on his face, too. 'He told me that if aught went amiss I was to bring Belinda to you this morning, as early as possible, which I have done.'

Diana rose and began to pace the room. 'Can you tell me where you last saw him?'

Lem shook his head. 'My master said that I was not to tell you anything for he feared for your safety if I did.'

Diana hardly knew what to say. She could not ask Lem to break his word to his master.

Were she a man she might be able to consult various persons in authority to ask them to help her to find him, but as a woman she was helpless. Nor, for Neville's own sake, since she had no notion of what he might have done before he was attacked, did she want to ask any responsible man whom she knew to try to find out what might have happened to him.

She felt like wringing her hands as though she were an actress in a silly play demonstrating distress, but refrained. She tried to imagine what advice Charles might have given her but even that did not answer. She needed time to think, so she sat down and asked Belinda and Lem to sit also. This time they consented, after which she ordered tea and biscuits to be sent in. Isabella was fortunately absent, visiting a friend; Diana's mind boggled at what she would have made of the pickle in which they found themselves.

Tea having arrived, and all of them having been served, Diana said, 'I think that I ought to accompany Lem when he goes back to Chelsea and wait there with him for a time in case Sir Neville should return.'

The expression on Lem's face immediately told her that he thought this a most unlikely, if not to say improper, thing for the Duchess of Medbourne to do, but he dared not say so.

'How would that benefit us?' was all he could say.

'It might comfort him to have someone whom he trusted and who he could safely speak to about what happened to him last night, since I am the only person who knows about the trade in girls.'

'He also consulted that Runner, Jackson,' Lem offered, 'but I don't think that he told him he intended to kidnap Belinda from Madame Josette's.'

It was a slip of the tongue for him to name the house where Belinda had been kept prisoner and Diana immediately pounced on it. 'Madame Josette's. Is that where Belinda was taken? A most notorious place. Even I have heard of it.'

Lem recognised his error. He said, ruefully, 'Aye, so it is', and said no more.

'That being so, it is even more necessary for me to accompany you to Chelsea. Belinda must remain here. I shall ask the housekeeper to find a room for her: tomorrow, as privately as possible, I shall send her to Medbourne Castle.'

She rose, saying, 'Enjoy your tea, while I arrange matters,' and swept out of the room.

Diana knew that she had left behind her a dazed Lem, unused to ladies troubling themselves with such matters, but she was beginning to feel responsible for Neville's misfortune, seeing that she had not discouraged him from trying to rescue Belinda. He had not wanted her to help him in any way lest she put herself at risk—but pooh to that.

First of all she settled matters with the housekeeper and sent word for the stables to have her phaeton made ready for her to use. After that, she retired to her room to make ready for the journey. She did not send for her lady's maid, but undressed herself before assuming the boys' clothes and boots that her late husband had ordered her to wear whenever she rode out with him. Last of all she put on a small jockey cap, thanking God that the fashion these days was for women to wear their hair short.

Thus accoutred, she returned to the breakfast room where

Lem waited for her—Belinda having already been removed by the housekeeper.

'We are travelling in my phaeton and you must tell me the way to Sir Neville's home.'

'Just the two of us?' replied the dazed Lem, who had imagined that they would be driven off in state in the Medbourne coach.

'Why not? I used to drive my late husband out in it, dressed like this, and now I shall drive you. My staff will not be shocked since they have seen me in boy's clothes before. Everyone will believe that I am some young buck taking the air with a friend. Come, we must waste no time.'

So off they went, with Diana's head groom, Corbin, shaking his head and muttering to his second-in-command, 'Whatever will she do next? I blame the old Duke for encouraging her to behave like a headstrong boy, but I must confess she handles that phaeton better than most young fellows do.'

Neville reached home by mid-morning. One of the court's officials had called a cab for him when his business at the court was over and told him that, seeing that Sir Neville's pockets were to let through theft, Sir Stanford had handed him a sum of money to pass on to him, enough to take him anywhere he might care to go.

He let himself in by breaking a side window—his keys had been stolen, too, and he made a resolution to have the locks changed and the window reinforced. The house was empty, something that worried him. Had Lem not managed to escape with Belinda after all? Only the fact that he needed to rid himself of his filthy clothing and have a bath as soon as possible stopped him from worrying too much at first.

Once he looked more like the man he had been until the night before, he visited the kitchen to find some water to cure his raging thirst. His head had almost ceased to ache, but the idea of food was still repulsive to him and, now that his thoughts were coherent, he was plagued by the notion of what the night's events might do to his hitherto spotless reputation. He could not believe that they would remain unknown.

A hypocrite! Sir Stanford had called him a hypocrite, but be damned to that. He had been trying to right a wrong, and whether or not he had succeeded in rescuing Belinda he would not cease in his efforts to stop, or at least reduce, this filthy trade. He would visit Jackson again and this time he would not allow himself to be fobbed off. He would demand to know why those in power were turning a blind eye to this wickedness.

He had just made this decision when he heard a commotion outside in the drive. He rushed to the window to see that a phaeton, driven by a lad, had drawn up and that Lem was scrambling down to hold the horses, preparatory to leading the carriage into the stables at the back. There was no sign of Belinda.

Neville was so desperate to learn what had happened to Lem and Belinda that he ran to the front door, opened it and arrived in the drive in time to lend Lem a helping hand. Lem nearly let go of the horse he was leading when he saw his master, dirty clothing, bruised face and all, as he later told Belinda just before she left for Nottinghamshire.

'Oh, sir, you're safe! We thought you dead or left for dead.'

'Not dead—left for, but still alive,' said Neville briskly. 'No time to talk now. Let's dispose of the phaeton and its driver,' and he put out a hand to help the lad dismount.

Lem's first thought was that his master had changed. There was something hard about him, about his unusual brusqueness, but there was no time for him to worry about that. Rather he said, in as neutral a way as he could, 'You won't be disposing of the driver, sir, no indeed.'

Before Neville could take this in, the driver had saved him the trouble of asking Lem what he meant by taking off his cap and saying as briskly as Neville had done to Lem, 'No, Neville, I really must insist that I am not sent to the kitchens.'

Diana! It was Diana, dressed like a boy, cap, jacket, breeches and boots all perfect, a most inappropriate turn-out for a woman to be tooling around town in.

Not that this distressed him, no, indeed, for on looking at her mischievous face he had the most dreadful desire to take her into his arms and—no, better not think of that… Instead he croaked, for at the sight of her, his voice, as well as his other senses, seemed to be fatally disturbed, 'Why in the world are you dressed like a boy?'

Diana, not in the least discommoded, replied, 'In order to drive Lem to Chelsea, of course. What else?'

Neville tried to assemble his scattered wits. After his awful night, even worse morning, and now this, he was beginning to think that the devil himself was persecuting him for his noble attempt to lead a good life.

'I know *that*—I mean, why have you driven him here dressed like a jockey?'

'Neville, if you will allow the three of us to come indoors once the phaeton has been disposed of, I shall be delighted to explain everything in return for you doing the same for us.'

Belatedly Neville remembered that the most astonishing thing about Diana was that alongside her extraordinary behaviour went an equally extraordinary amount of common sense.

'Yes, indeed. I am afraid that my manners have disappeared overnight. Let us take your horses and carriage to the stables and then we may all adjourn to the drawing-room.'

And so they did. Lem would have disappeared into the kitchen as a good servant should, leaving his betters to get on with the business, but he was drawn up short before he reached the kitchen door by Sir Neville's bellow.

'Where the devil are you going, man? Come back at once. We need your assistance in this.'

Yes, his master had changed and he was shortly to find out why.

Once he was seated Diana took the lead by saying, 'Let me explain why I have arrived in this fashion with Lem. Since secrecy is of the essence in this matter, as you have so often said, rather than come here with him in the Medbourne coach with all its various attendants, outriders and so on, which might have caused comment, I drove him here as inconspicuously as possible. When you first saw me you did not even recognise me, so I am sure that no one on our journey thought that the lad driving the phaeton was the Duchess of Medbourne.

'Now, as to why we came. Lem was worried when you did not return home either last night or this morning so, acting on your orders, he brought Belinda to me, and asked me for advice and help. I am sure you will be relieved to learn that she is safe. I insisted that I drive him to Chelsea in case you were still missing and what we should decide to do next if you were.

'Happily we have found you here and we may make our plans together when you tell us how you spent your night.'

This concise report, delivered in Diana's most charming manner, was as businesslike as those of any of the young men whom he had employed as secretaries. Nay, more so.

'Yes, you acted most properly.' He did not comment further on her clothes. From the way they fitted her they had obviously been made for her—but that was not to the point at the moment. 'And now I must tell you my story, which is not a very pretty one, to say the least,' he continued, and in the same fashion, no words wasted, he told them of everything that had passed since he had lost sight of Lem the night before.

They were silent when he had finished. Even Diana's ready tongue was not up to commenting on his untoward adventure immediately, once she had grasped the implications of his being taken up from the gutter as a drunkard and brought before Sir Stanford Markham JP.

Neville knew what she must be thinking. 'Yes,' he said. 'I am thoroughly discredited, am I not? A proven hypocrite. That alone should stop me from pursuing this matter further. Well, damn them all, I will not be stopped! There is more to this than meets the eye. How did Sir Stanford, who knows me, come to be on duty this morning in a petty court for minor criminals? The usual man would not have recognised me. He did not appear to know me at first, but he might have been acting. Or am I seeing a conspiracy where none exists?'

Diana said, slowly, choosing her words with care, 'First of all you were fortunate that they did not kill you. Did the two blackguards who beat you know who you really were?'

'That is the weak point in my belief in a conspiracy. I am sure that they did not,' Neville admitted.

Diana, not at all in her usual cheerful and robust manner, but speaking as she would have done to her late husband when they were considering a difficult proposition in logic, suggested, 'Is it possible that there was someone at Madame's who recognised you despite your disguise, but did not care to reveal your true identity until her bruisers returned and told her that you, and your friend, had made off with Belinda? After that either he or Madame must have sent word to Sir Stanford who then attended the court in the district where you were found and arrested.'

'That means that there must have been someone there who knew me, but I didn't recognise anyone present.'

Lem said shrewdly, 'We were so busy playing our parts that I don't, begging your pardon, sir, think that either of us took a real hard look at Madame's clients.'

Neville nodded. 'True, very true. If you are right, Diana, it also means that the man who identified me is most likely involved in the kidnapping and sale of girls—and that Sir Stanford Markham is, too. If so, it explains why he refused to help me when I went to him about Belinda. In any case, I shall immediately visit the Runner, Jackson, again. He also, I believe, knows more than he cared to tell me. He might cooperate with me when he hears my story.'

On hearing this Lem exclaimed agitatedly, 'Would it not be better to abandon this whole dangerous business, master? After all, we have saved Belinda, which is what we set out to do.'

If Diana had ever thought that Neville's patent goodness also meant that he lacked backbone—as her late husband would have said—his instant and fiery response to Lem's proposal told her otherwise.

'Indeed not! If there is such a trade, then it ought to be stopped and those who run it punished.'

Both Diana and Lem were beginning to understand that his dreadful and humiliating experiences had had an effect on Neville, which those who had brought it about could not have anticipated. Instead of destroying him, it had changed him by creating in him a hard determination and a certain ruthlessness that had previously been foreign to his nature.

He had also, Diana noted, several times called her Diana in front of Lem—something that, before the previous evening, he would never have done. Indeed, he had found difficulty in speaking to her with such familiarity when they were alone.

'I can drive you to Jackson's office,' she offered. After all it was the least she could do.

Neville shook his head. 'No, you must not risk being recognised. Think of the damage that would do to your reputation. Remember what happened to Caroline Lamb.'

Diana was about to say, 'Pooh to that! Lady Caroline was a little light in the attic, you know,' but she was sensitive enough to see that, if she did, she would distress Neville and this was no time to upset him after all he had been through. What she really wanted to do was comfort and reassure him, and this feeling was so strong that it surprised her.

Instead she rose, and said briskly, 'That being so, I must leave at once. Be sure to tell me if Jackson informs you of anything useful. I, too, am sorry that we can do nothing for the other poor girl who disappeared in like fashion to Belinda.'

Neville waved a hand at Lem. 'Come, we must help the Duchess on her way.'

And if he held her hand a little longer than he should have done when he assisted her into the phaeton, it was not long enough for Diana. Afterwards she thought that it was perhaps significant that she had agreed to his command that she go home immediately, rather than insisting on having her own way. Why it was significant she preferred not to think.

She tried to keep her mind on the task of driving through streets crowded with the business of the day. At one point she had to struggle through a flock of sheep, which were trying to behave as though they were still in the fields from which they had been brought to help to feed London. Thoughts of Neville and his problems kept breaking in, however, and she was unusually brusque when, on reaching the stables, she handed the phaeton over to the head groom.

It didn't help matters when she met Isabella on the landing outside the door that opened on to her suite of rooms.

Isabella took one look at her boy's clothing which she had never seen before, and exclaimed, 'Goodness, Diana, why in the world are you parading around dressed so indecently? Your reputation will be as bad as Caroline Lamb's—and remember what happened to her!'

If that wasn't the outside of enough—to be compared to Caroline Lamb twice in one morning! Diana's reply was a stony one. 'My dear Isabella, if my late husband encouraged me to wear breeches when they were more suitable than skirts for the task in which I was engaged, who was I to quarrel with him?'

'Nevertheless...' Isabella began.

'Nevertheless, nothing. I have ordered nuncheon to be served immediately and you are delaying me in my new task—that of changing my clothes yet again in order to be *comme il faut* when I eat it.'

Diana walked off, regretting her small outburst of temper. She had not meant to be unkind to her companion, but there were times when Isabella's pious rectitude grated on her. Coming as it did after hearing of Neville's dreadful news and his refusal to allow her to assist him, the drawbacks of being a woman in a world arranged for the convenience of men had never seemed more plain.

Not that she wanted to emulate the late Mary Wollstonecraft and campaign for the rights of women to behave exactly like men, since by doing so Mary had ended up trying to commit suicide when she was unmarried and pregnant after her lover had abandoned her. It brought home to her the truth of what Charles had once said when they were discussing the rights of men and women: 'I agree that women, particularly married women, do not deserve to be treated as they are—having no legal existence, and left being prey to the unscrupulous whom they have the misfortune of marrying—but, alas, the time for reform is not yet.'

It was then that he had told her of Mary Wollstonecraft's subsequent marriage to the philosopher Godwin, and, alas again, she could not help but agree with him.

Nevertheless—and she had the grace to laugh at herself, remembering the way in which she had twitted Isabella—she was not going to allow Neville Fortescue to fob her off again. Help him she would—and he would have to like it, or lump it.

Besides, to be fair to him, Neville was by no means as arrogant as most men were—which was perhaps why she could not stop thinking about him.

* * *

'So, you took matters into your own hands—with predictable results,' was Jackson's first comment on Neville's news, now that Neville had come to see him.

He also made no mention of his changed appearance for, although he was dressed in his usual careful manner, Neville could not disguise his black eye and his bruised face.

'But we did rescue Belinda,' Neville retorted.

'True, but we both know that the news of your apparent downfall will be around town in no time, do we not?'

'And I know that you know much more about this business than you have cared to tell me. Don't you think that it's time that you did me the honour of telling me exactly what is going on?'

Jackson played the idiot boy to perfection. 'I am sure that I don't know of what you are speaking, Sir Neville.'

The old Neville would have retreated at this point, but the new one said, roughly, 'Don't serve me gammon, Jackson. I know when I am being deceived. Moreover, I'll pay you highly for the truth.'

'If you want my advice, Sir Neville, which you plainly don't, you'll forget this whole business. You are an amateur in my line of work.'

'Which is why I came to you, after being fobbed off by everyone else. Honest whoring is one thing. Kidnapping and ruining innocent young girls is quite another. I am astonished to discover that while we can, rightly, make a great noise about the wickedness of the slave trade, we are apparently prepared to do nothing to protect the innocent women who are being kidnapped and turned into slaves in our own country.'

Jackson gave a great sigh. 'What you say is true and, because it is, I am, for once, prepared to break my word and not only give you some more information but also, discreetly, help you in your campaign to try to stop it. Although I warn you that, because it is underground and exploiting only the lowly, it will be difficult to end it permanently.'

Neville gave a long sigh of relief. 'That is better than nothing and I thank you for it.'

'I hope that I don't regret this but, briefly, there is a rumour that some exalted names are involved and I have been asked to try to discover who they might be. They are said to use a go-between, another member of good society, but his identity is also unknown. As a result of last night's work we are now aware that Sir Stanford Markham may be part of this vile coterie.'

Neville could not help noticing that when he was speaking privately to him Jackson dropped the uncouth manner of speech which he usually employed in public. There was more to him, too, than met the eye.

'That is not all,' Jackson continued. 'Some of them, it is feared, may also be engaged in plotting revolution and subversion, and meet privately in houses of ill fame—and gambling dens, too. You begin to see why it is difficult for me to confide in you fully.'

'Yes—and I suppose you are doing this on behalf of the Home Office.'

'You may suppose what you please,' was Jackson's cheerful reply.

'And you will not reveal to me any of the exalted names you may know?'

'No, because I have, as yet, no evidence that would stand up in a court of law.'

Neville couldn't fault Jackson over that, particularly when, at the end of their meeting he said, with no bravado or exaggeration, 'I must warn you that you might be in real danger if you continue your campaign. You may be putting your life at risk and the next time you might not survive.'

'Too late. Like Caesar I have crossed my Rubicon. But if you do find something that would help me, you will inform me, I trust. As I shall inform you.'

Jackson nodded, 'Of course—but remember, be careful.'

Chapter Seven

The *on dits* ran round the *ton* like wild fire. That respectable bore, Sir Neville Fortescue, had been picked up, dead drunk and dirty, in one of the alleys in the worst part of the city, had been dragged before the magistrate, Sir Stanford Markham, and been heavily reprimanded to mend his ways before being sent home, disgraced. What a hypocrite!

Naturally the tale grew in the telling. The men spoke openly of his downfall in their clubs and less reputable haunts: the married women whispered it behind their hands, their daughters tried to overhear what was being said because it was causing so much amusement.

One odd consequence, however, was that the less respectable, while laughing at the joke, tended to end their comments with phrases such as, 'Never thought he had so much red blood in him. All goes to show that you can't tell a book by the cover, ha, ha!'

Neville did not go into society again until the bruises on his face had faded. He had hoped that some new scandal might have made the memory of his misadventure fade a little, but no such thing. He had only to enter a room for heads to turn, winks to be exchanged and meaningful remarks made just loud enough for him to overhear them.

Isabella Marchmont was one of the most shocked at the apparent contrast between the public man and the private one. 'Well, I never,' she exclaimed to Diana when she first heard the titillating news. 'Whoever would have thought it of him? It only goes to show how mistaken one can be,' she added, unconsciously echoing some of the more notorious rakes whom she also despised—Neville now having been added to her list of those to be avoided.

She added as a further gloss on Neville's new-found non-acceptability, 'I do hope that you are not going to receive him in future.'

'On the contrary,' Diana told her. 'I am sure that there is a rational explanation of his misfortune. Indeed, I overheard Lord Burnside, when we were at Emily Cowper's last reception, saying that he thought that there must be another side to this story.'

'Well, I can't think what that could possibly be,' Isabella declaimed dramatically, 'but if you do receive him I shall be sure not to speak to him.'

Diana had not seen Neville since that fateful morning, although she had received a letter from him—delivered by Lem—thanking her for her kindness and encouragement.

Did she want to encourage him? One thing had become quite plain and that was that those engaged in this trade would stop at nothing. She would tell him so when she next met him.

This proved to be at a soirée given by Lady Leominster, who never let anyone's bad reputation deter her from inviting them to any event that she was hosting at the time. His presence would certainly add to the liveliness of the occasion, rather as Lord Byron's had done when he and his many lovers were behaving at their naughtiest.

That Neville chose to attend was not to demonstrate his defiance of the polite world's opinion of him, but because he hoped to hear, or overhear, something that might help him and Jackson in their quest. Also there was the possibility that he might meet Diana, whom he needed to see as a dying man needs water in the desert.

He was not to be disappointed. One of the first persons he saw in the entrance hall when he arrived was Diana. She was accompanied by a much older man and his wife. Someone had told him when she had first arrived in London that she was related to the Marchmonts. He was a little behind them in the line of people who were mounting the stairs where Lady Leominster, her mild husband in attendance, waited like a baleful goddess to greet her guests.

Several people had already cut him dead and he wondered what her reception of him might be. He need not have worried. She gave a great scream when a footman bellowed his name. 'So! You have come. I did so hope that you would. I trust that you have recovered from your recent ordeal. Boys will be boys, you know, and men will be men,' and she gave him a great wink before turning to her husband and roaring at him, 'Isn't that so, Henry?'

'If you say so, my dear,' was his mild response.

'Oh, I do say so. Do not let yourself be overcome by this business—all will be forgotten in a few weeks' time, unless, like Byron, you perpetrate even worse *bêtises,* but I am sure that you are too clever for that.'

After which she waved him on with her fan and he found himself alone, with many curious eyes on him. He scarcely knew whether to laugh or to cry at the antics of her lunatic ladyship of Leominster, as she was commonly known. One thing, however: if he had thought that everyone would cut him, he was wrong. The trouble was that those who didn't were already on the edge of being consigned to the demimonde if their own behaviour didn't improve.

The first person to accost him was a grinning George Alford. 'Well, well, coz, what the devil have you been up to?

Thought you didn't go in for that kind of thing.' This was accompanied by a great clap on Neville's back as though he had been admitted to some new form of knighthood.

After that it didn't surprise him that Frank Hollis came up and virtually congratulated him on having joined the ranks of drunken sinners—he being such a conspicuous example of one of them himself.

All of this unwanted attention prevented him from finding Diana. Perhaps he ought not to find her. What would it do to her reputation if he was daring enough to greet her?

He needn't have worried about that, either.

She was talking to the Marchmonts when she saw him walk away from Frank Hollis. She turned and said something to them, they appeared to remonstrate with her, but she shook her head and walked towards him.

'Sir Neville,' she said, aware of curious eyes on them and trying to appear as though she were not aware of the gossip that would follow her conversation with him.

'Duchess,' returned Neville, bowing to her before saying, 'Are you sure that you ought to be speaking to me in public?'

'If I weren't I shouldn't be doing so,' she retorted. 'In any case, I am not being any braver than you are in coming here, knowing what is being said of you.'

'Since what is being said of me is in essence, untrue, then I take no notice of their mistaken opinions.' Neville was aware that he sounded stiff, but how else could he respond to the riotous emotions that filled him at the very sight of her?

'My feelings exactly.' Diana smiled. 'Tell me, have you seen Jackson and did you learn anything from him? When you answer me, be sure to raise your eyebrows and smile a little as evidence that we are talking polite nonsense.'

'Would a smirk be better than a smile, perhaps?' Neville was astonished at the sudden ease that he felt in talking frivolously—something that he had always avoided doing before. 'I can only say that he told me that he had received confirmation that several persons well-known in good society are involved in this, but he gave me no names. He did, however, agree, to help me, in return for my telling him if I came across anything that might help him.'

Diana flirted her fan at him. She was looking gloriously flamboyant in a low-cut green and gold gown, her hair dressed high and, for once, was wearing the famous Medbourne emeralds around her neck and on her wrist.

'Not very helpful,' she remarked, 'but perhaps better than nothing. There is, though, one thing that I must say to you. Do you think it either wise or safe for you to continue searching for those who run this dreadful trade?'

'Exactly the same warning which Jackson gave me and I will answer you as I have already answered Lem, and him. No, I don't but that will not stop me.'

'Even if your career and Parliamentary prospects are ruined if you do continue?'

'I would not stop because of that any more than you would cease to live your daring life because a few old gossips spoke ill of you and blew on your reputation.'

'True, and I respect that. I see that you no longer wish to compare me with Caroline Lamb. We shall have to part shortly because we are fast becoming the rival of a Punch and Judy show in attracting attention. Daring though I may be, there are also limits beyond which it might be unwise for me to go. Is there nowhere that we can speak freely?'

Neville laughed. 'I thought that we were speaking freely now.' He had never before found it so easy to talk to a woman. It was like talking to his other self. Diana used no artifices such as fan and eyelash fluttering, simpering and tossing her head, which other women employed as a matter of course whatever the nature of the conversation.

'Up to a point,' she told him. 'Do you know what I miss most since the death of my late husband? It is the free and frank conversations that we had on every subject under the sun. There is so much of which we women cannot speak and that includes many of those issues that affect us the most. You are the first person who reminds me of him in his willingness to converse with me as an equal.'

'You flatter me,' he said, and that was the truth.

'No, I don't, I never flatter anyone. And now, Sir Neville, bend that acute mind of yours to think of where we may meet without prying eyes. You could visit me any time you please, but I do not put it past Isabella Marchmont to tattle about us because she disapproves of you so profoundly since your downfall—as she usually speaks of it.'

'You break my heart. I had thought that she doted on me.'

He had thought nothing of the sort, but banter came so freely to him this evening that he was to wonder afterwards whether this was another of the changes that his recent encounter with brute reality had brought about.

Diana's laugh was a genuine one. 'If she dotes on anyone it is, of all unsuitable people, George Alford—and now we must part.'

Neville bowed and she retreated, to be cornered, after going a few yards, by Lady Leominster.

'My dear Duchess,' she began. 'I am so pleased that you have seen fit to recognise Sir Neville. *Entre nous* I believe that there is something awry about this business of him having... But I need not repeat the gossip to you since you must know it already. Of course, should he offend again, why, that would be another matter.'

She leaned forward and said confidentially, 'Do you know, my dear, you remind me of myself at your age.' And with that she was gone to descend upon another victim.

God forbid, was Diana's reaction to that, and yet, and yet... Crass though she often was, Lady Leominster was unlike most women in that she spoke her mind freely even if a lot of what she said was silly. More than that, for some reason, despite being so downright, she had survived to lead society—probably because everything was forgiven of eccentricity provided it was eccentric enough. It was a thought that she would share with Neville when next they met—and pray God that would be soon.

Neville, after speaking to those few of the guests who condescended to recognise him, decided that it was time to leave, particularly since he had learned nothing that might help Jackson, which did not surprise him. He was on the way out when he was stopped by Lord Burnside.

'Ah, happy to see you, Fortescue. I had hoped that I might. Brave of you to come, all things considered. What I really wanted to say to you was that I feel that there was more to your recent escapade than meets the eye. I have never thought of you as being a voluptuary—if you will excuse the use of the word. I can only hope that your career as an MP will not be impaired. If it was a moment's madness, then you still have my sympathy.'

Neville hardly knew what to say. The man's kindness moved him after the way in which many had received, or rather not received him.

'Thank you, m'lord. I can only hope that one day the whole truth about what happened to me may become known. If so, your kindness to me would be more than vindicated.'

It was enough, perhaps it had almost been too much, to say, but Burnside's sympathy had affected Neville more than he might have expected. They spoke for a few more minutes of other matters, before Burnside moved on.

Neville set off to leave again, but was immediately accosted by Henry Latimer, with George Alford in tow, as usual. Latimer said, 'Hello, Fortescue. Shan't speak to you of what is occupying everyone else tonight. Nine days' wonder, I shouldn't be surprised.'

This was said with such leering offensiveness that it raised Neville's hackles. He was about to reply when Latimer continued with, 'Burnside a relative of yours? You have a great look of him.'

'No relative,' returned Neville stiffly, 'and I think you must be mistaken as to the looks.'

'Not I. Besides, you have his manner, too—odd, that.'

What to reply to that? Other than to say, 'Not odd at all, everyone in society today sounds like everyone else,' which was not a strictly truthful answer but should serve to silence Latimer. It did, and he babbled away about other matters—something to do with Frank Hollis paying court to one of the season's heiresses.

'Not Duchess Diana, of course. Who, without as much tin as she possesses, can aspire to her? Perhaps it's as well, seeing what a hoyden she is, difficult to be married to her! Ah, well, old chap, must go and pay my respects to her. Who knows, she might favour me as much as she appears to favour you— though I doubt that.'

He left, leaving Neville fuming. If anyone was odd, it was Latimer, for there had been a sneering note in his conversation that Neville particularly disliked. Latimer had attacked not only him, but also his friends, for so he thought of Burnside and Diana. Although they had been friends as boys, he had never liked Henry Latimer when he met him again as a man, and had always considered him to be a posturing lightweight.

He had already decided to take his life one day at a time; by tomorrow, he would be almost at the end of the nine days with which Latimer had twitted him.

Unfortunately, however, both Diana and Neville were to find that they were not to be allowed to escape being reproached before the nine days were over. The next afternoon Diana had just sat down to read a treatise by Immanuel Kant entitled *The Critique of Pure Reason* when Isabella, whom she had thought had been safely away on a day's outing with some friends, came bursting in.

'Really, Diana, it is the outside of enough that I should have had to be twitted by half London society today on your latest escapade.'

Diana, who found reading Kant in the original German hard enough when she was on her own, grasped that it was going to be impossible if she were to be constantly interrupted by Isabella whenever she sat down to master what her late husband had described as one of the most remarkable books of the last century.

'I really cannot imagine of what you speak,' was her frosty reply.

'No? It is all over town that you and Sir Neville Fortescue had a lengthy tête-à-tête in full view of all those attending Lady Leominster's soirée last night. I am only too happy that I did not receive an invitation—I would have felt compelled to remonstrate with you publicly had I been there.'

'Oh, and what was my offence, Isabella? That our tête-à-tête wasn't held in private?'

'Do not mock me. You know perfectly well what I mean. You appointed me to help you.'

'I didn't appoint you to be tiresome. I happen to believe that Sir Neville has an explanation for what happened to him that he does not yet wish to make public. Until then I shall reserve judgement. Remember your Bible and what it said: ''He that is without sin among you, let him first cast a stone at her.'''

'Are you implying that I am a sinner?'

'If the truth be known, Isabella, we are all sinners: some of us commit small sins, others great. Now, if you please, do go away, drink a soothing draught and leave me to read Kant in peace. I don't expect to see you again until supper.'

She had never spoken harshly to Isabella before, but she would not have her conduct criticised by someone who had no notion of the truth and saw only what she wanted to see.

From favouring Neville and pushing him at Diana as a possible husband, she had now taken him in violent dislike!

She flounced out and Diana resumed her reading with a weary sigh. She could not dismiss Isabella from her service because the poor creature had nowhere to go, but keeping her was becoming more and more of a penance.

Neville had spent his morning with his secretary, who gave no indication that he was at all aware of the scandal surrounding his master although he must have heard of it long ago. By the afternoon he retired to the front drawing room to try to forget his recent unhappy experiences by reading a report from the Board of Agriculture, but he could not keep his mind on the text because it wandered between dreaming about Diana and of how he could continue his campaign, which he was now almost wishing that he had never begun.

No, that would never do, he must soldier on. He was not a coward to want to withdraw from the war simply because he had lost the first battle. He had just come to this conclusion when he heard a great commotion outside. Looking through the window, he saw that a coach had been drawn up on the gravel sweep before the front door. It was his mother's and she was being helped to alight from it by a footman who was now escorting her into the house.

He gave a great sigh. She was the last person he wanted to see and he could only imagine what she might have to say to him.

He was soon to find out.

The door was flung open and she entered the room like a thunderstorm without waiting for the butler to announce her.

'How could you do this to me,' she began. 'Think what I went through when I received a letter from Lady Leominster yesterday, informing me of your dreadful behaviour. All society knows that you were found dead drunk in a squalid alley in the worst part of London where all the bad houses are to be found. To make matters worse, if that were possible, you were then hauled before a magistrate to be sentenced. On top of that she had the gall to order me to forgive you because she thought that there was something awry about this story.

'Something awry! Of course there is something awry. The something awry is your appalling conduct. I suppose that every fool in London will be laughing behind my back. It was bad enough when Sir Carlton was alive, but that you should follow in his footsteps…words fail me.'

'Oh, I wouldn't say that, Mother,' Neville gritted at her.

She took no heed of him but ranted on. 'I had thought that you would be different from him, but you have proved me wrong.'

'After all,' replied Neville recklessly, knowing that it would provoke her, 'like father, like son, they always say.'

'You are not in the least like your father. Oh, my God, what am I saying? Of course you are. I shall run mad after this. To think of all the trouble I took to bring you up as a Christian. I might have known that something was amiss when you failed to convince Harriet to marry you. And the next thing I hear is that you are running around with that mad Duchess.'

She began to sob before throwing herself on to the sofa in the most abandoned fashion.

Well, this really was a fit of the vapours and no mistake, was Neville's dazed conclusion. He scarcely knew what to say or do, for the sight of her with all her usual icy calm shattered was too much for him. After all, she was not only his mother but she had cared for him devotedly since birth. More than that, she had been proud of him because he was so unlike Sir Carlton in every way and now that pride had been brutally shattered.

He walked over to the sofa to sit beside her and take her hand in his. 'Mother,' he said, as gently as he could, 'do not distress yourself overmuch. I was attacked and left for dead.

I am fortunate to be alive. I am sorry that silly people have seen fit to taunt you, although to give Lady Leominster her due she was publicly kind to me, and did not mean to hurt you, but to support you.'

His soothing voice had its effect on her. She sat up after giving a few more sobs. 'Were you attacked because you were drunk? I suppose that you were robbed, too.'

'Yes, although I had not much in the way of valuables on me. I can only assure you that I have done nothing to be ashamed of, but alas, I cannot tell you, or the world, the whole story. One day I might be able to offer you an explanation. That is all I can say for the moment.'

'And the Duchess? Is it true that you are *épris* with her?'

'I am her friend, that is all. It is true that I admire her greatly, but to say that I am *épris* is to use too strong a word.'

Lady Fortescue sniffled into her handkerchief, which was already sodden. 'Am I to believe that you are speaking the truth?'

The truth was that he was, indeed, more than Diana's friend and was beginning to hope that he might be even more yet, but in her present state he dare not tell his mother so. Life with Sir Carlton had destroyed her ability to believe in any man's word, and he did not wish to distress her further.

'So far as anyone ever speaks the truth, I am speaking it now,' he said at last.

The smile she gave him was a watery one. 'That is to say nothing and everything.'

Neville had to concede that, as she had often proved, his mother was no fool. He kissed the hand he was holding. 'May I give you a piece of advice, Mother? Go back to Aunt Susan and try to forget the squalid gossip with which many in the *ton* fill their days. Even if I were as badly behaved as you believe me to be, it is not the end of the world. You know how much you enjoy the country, so why not spend the rest of the summer there? I might even visit you and Aunt Susan when the Parliamentary session ends.'

She gripped his hand tightly. 'You must understand how shocked I am. Until now you have always been so good— you have never given me a moment's worry.'

Neville could not say: There is another side to that. Perhaps I ought to have done. Not that I should have behaved like my late unlamented father, but a young man ought to sow some wild oats and I never did. I have been too soft, unnaturally so, and I must begin to acquire steel.

Not that he was sowing any wild oats now, far from it, but he couldn't tell her so.

She offered him another watery smile and kissed him on the cheek, murmuring, 'You are right to recommend me to return to the sweet green fields of Kent. London smells vilely at this time of year.'

Neville thought that it was time to bring this to an end. He rose, saying, 'Let me send for some tea, Mother. It might soothe both of us.'

She nodded agreement. 'And I will stay overnight. Your Aunt Susan is giving a small dance at the weekend and I must not miss that. You will be careful, now, won't you? No more drinking.'

'Rest easy,' he told her, and nothing more. He silently cursed the vile pair who had poured the liquor into and over him. Wickedness affected not only those who were immediately harmed by it but also those who weren't, like his mother. If he had ever doubted that he wanted to cry vengeance on his enemies, that doubt had now disappeared.

'You must understand, Fortescue, that any question of you gaining promotion in this Parliament is now quite out of the question.' Thus Lord Liverpool said when Neville encountered him outside Parliament one bright afternoon.

The great men of his world were letting him know that his

indiscretion, as they put it, had harmed his prospects, possibly permanently. Never mind that none of them was whiter than white, their indiscretions had been discreetly committed in private and the general opinion was that Fortescue had let the side down.

It was a bad time for those who ruled Britain to be discovered misbehaving. Radicalism was on the march. Working men were demonstrating in every major town and in the countryside, too, roused by the depression that had followed the end of the war in Europe. The ghost of the French Revolution was walking again and this was no time for those in power to demonstrate that they had feet of clay, as one pro-government newspaper put it. The radical press was even more insulting.

'There is another matter, too. Sir Stanford Markham told me that you had been troubling him about a missing servant girl—hardly the most tactful thing to be doing when you were following a course of conduct that resulted in your arrest. My advice to you is to go carefully, and you might yet recover some of your previous good reputation.'

Lord Liverpool's well-meaning counsel, far from encouraging Neville to follow it, had quite the opposite effect. So, Sir Stanford, whom both he and Jackson thought might be mixed up in the affair of missing girls, had been bringing pressure to bear on the prime minister to try to stop him from continuing his investigation. Far from abandoning it, he would redouble his efforts and would begin by telling Jackson immediately of this latest development.

He just bowed and said, 'Thank you for your consideration, Prime Minister. I am sorry that, inadvertently, I have brought shame on the government and my fellow MPs.'

If Liverpool thought that the word 'inadvertently' was simply an attempt by Neville to try to wriggle out of admitting his culpability he did not pursue the matter, merely walked away, hoping that his wise words would ensure the young man's future good behaviour.

Chapter Eight

Neville reached home to discover that George Alford was ensconced in the drawing room, a decanter of sherry, a half-full glass and some ratafia biscuits before him.

'Hope you didn't mind me waiting for you, old fellow. That secretary of yours said that it wouldn't be long before you returned home. He saw to it that I was properly entertained,' and he waved a hand at the sherry. 'I thought you ought to know all the latest gossip seeing that, apart from the Leominsters' dinner party, you haven't been seen much in public lately.'

Neville had not the slightest desire to hear any gossip, either the latest or the oldest, but said wearily, 'Do tell me, George, seeing that I've no way of stopping you other than asking a couple of footmen to escort you out of the room and the house.'

George took this to be meant as a joke. He laughed loudly and started immediately to retail the most prime piece of all. It was about Diana and he could scarcely wait to see old Nev's reaction to it.

'Well, you'll not credit this, but it happened at the Cowpers' ball and I had the good fortune to see it. We were dancing the cotillion. Duchess Diana had Henry Latimer for a part-

ner, and when they got to the bit where they stand waiting
their turn he started talking to her. Suddenly he let out a tre-
mendous howl and hopped away from her. Of course, the
dance was ruined since every one stopped to look at him, and
then at the Duchess when she walked off the dance floor.

'Seems that he must have said something to her that she
didn't like and in return she stamped on his instep, not once
but twice, hence the howl. They've been taking bets at Watier's as to what he said—which is silly really, because no
one can win since no one dare ask either of them.'

'Is that all?' Neville said coldly, showing no emotion of
any kind. 'I've felt like stamping on his foot once or twice,
but haven't had the courage. I shall tell her bravo when next
I meet her.'

This was not in the least the reaction that George would
have expected from the once prim and proper Neville. He
murmured weakly, 'I would have thought it quite enough.'

'Did you, indeed. Well, if you haven't anything better than
that to tell me, let us discuss something else. This trouble
down in Norfolk, for instance.'

'Couldn't do that, because I don't know what the trouble
is.'

Which was, of course, to be expected, since George knew
nothing outside the idle life that he lived in society. Neville
was astonished at himself for putting down George—twice!—
so brusquely. Always before he had reacted with great patience when condemned to listen to his sillinesses. He wondered where this sudden ability not only to think these dreadful things but to say them aloud had come from. It seemed
that having a nasty knock on the head had had more consequences than he could have imagined.

Well, he had wished for more steel and could not now
complain when he was displaying it. He endured George's
nonsense for some little time before he sent him away after

inventing some lying nonsense of his own about having urgent correspondence to deal with.

'Oh, you men of affairs,' was George's cheerful answer to that. 'You're all the same, you should take a holiday from work from time to time, do you good. Go to the races, play cards at Watier's.'

God forbid was Neville's silent response before he went to his study to discover that he was not a liar after all. There were two letters waiting for him, both marked urgent.

One was from Jackson and the other from Diana. Both were asking him to visit them as soon as possible. Jackson had decided that since their association was now known to their enemies, secrecy was no longer necessary. Neville pulled out his hunter. He would visit Diana immediately and then travel on to Jackson, but not before he had seen his secretary. He thought sardonically that, if matters didn't improve, he would no longer be having any Parliamentary business for which he would need one.

Diana was at home. Since she had stunned society by physically attacking Henry Latimer in public, even if it were only his foot that she had damaged, she had supposed that she might find herself cut, not received or visited, by anyone. On the contrary, she had had a stream of visitors—she could only conclude that being an enormously wealthy Duchess pardoned most sins that she might commit. She entertained herself by trying to think of what she could do that would damn her forever.

One private source of amusement was that Isabella had not dared to say a word about her most recent piece of outrageous behaviour, but had instead contented herself with sighing and moping. She sighed and moped even more when the butler came to inform Diana that Sir Neville Fortescue had arrived and had asked if she would receive him.

'Certainly,' she said, 'and when you have brought him in

I am not at home again until after he has left.' Which statement brought more sighs from Isabella as she flounced out of the room.

Diana had wondered how Neville was standing up to the furore that he had created, but when he came in she thought that he looked better than ever. The new cynical curve of his lips served to add character to his face.

He was also dressed with a little more panache. There was even a hint of the dandy about him, instead of the air of the sober rising politician that he had possessed before. He was even wearing a decorated waistcoat—she guessed that it might be some relic of his early youth at Oxford.

She rose and put out her hands to him after he had bowed to her. 'You look extremely well for a man living in the centre of society's version of a tornado.'

He laughed, and said, 'So I should. After all, I have not killed anyone. One would think that no one had ever been caught drunk before. And I was not even disorderly since I was just lying quietly in the gutter—instead of lying noisily in Parliament like my supposed betters.'

Her laughter joined his. 'Now it is your turn to reproach me for my disorderly behaviour. I am sure that you have heard the gossip already.'

'Indeed, I have. And I can only congratulate you on making your victim Henry Latimer. I have taken a dislike to him and I am sure that you would not have punished him so severely without good reason.'

'Do sit down before I tell you why I attacked him, because it concerns you. He has been chasing me for some time. Last night he was whispering endearments to me throughout the dance and then, because I have never given him any real encouragement, he made a truly unpleasant innuendo about me—involving you.'

Neville started up. 'By God, I'll call him out, that I will.'

'No, no, that is not why I told you. Besides, think of the

scandal. A duel in which two of the people involved are already in deep disgrace—it would dish us both forever. Besides, you must not endanger yourself for me.'

Neville controlled himself with some difficulty and sat down again. He didn't know what had come over him. When Diana had told him of the insult to which she had been subjected he had felt a red rage the like of which he had never known before. He wanted to take her in his arms and comfort her, except that she most manifestly did not appear to need any comforting at all.

She was the strongest woman he had ever known, and the more he saw of her the more his admiration of her increased. He recalled what she had been saying when he had been overcome by his desire to defend her good name. 'Just now, before I so rudely interrupted you, you made a remark about the reason for telling me of his misbehaviour—that it involved me.'

'It is this. Because I have so often fended him off before, and always politely so as not to make a scene—which is amusing enough in the light of what happened next—he said something to the effect that while I rejected him I was favouring a priggish fool who had no more sense than to stick his nose in other people's business.'

She stopped. Neville's expression was a picture. 'Latimer said that!' he exclaimed. 'How could he know of my involvement with the missing girls—to which he must have been referring, because I am not, at the moment, involved in anything else—unless he is privy to the whole wretched business? He must have been very angry with you to commit such a mistake.'

'So I thought. But I had, in his eyes, humiliated him by refusing to take him seriously and so he lost his temper. Then I lost mine and I don't regret it.'

'Did you answer him in any way?'

'Not verbally. I just brought my right shoe-heel down hard

on his left instep, to be precise. I thought it best to say nothing.'

'I'd like to do more to him than jump on his instep, but I must not make his mistake and give myself away. You were right to reproach me for wanting to kill him.'

They both laughed together at the picture of Henry Latimer hopping across the floor.

Neville thought for a moment before he said soberly, 'Someone told me recently that they could not understand how Latimer could live so high, seeing that his father died a bankrupt. Like a fool I said perhaps an inheritance from a rich relative might explain matters. But this alters the picture. I must say I've never heard of him being connected with Sir Stanford Markham. He's not at all the sort of person I could imagine being a boon companion of Sir Stanford's. In fact, I doubt whether Sir Stanford is anyone's boon companion, whereas I rarely see Henry Latimer without a glass of wine in his hand, although I have never seen him drunk.'

'Hail fellow well met,' suggested Diana.

'Very much so, although not my sort of fellow. But, if he is connected with the trade in women, I can imagine that he would make a splendid go-between. Now, I must inform you that your letter arrived at the same time as one from Jackson, asking me to visit him as soon as possible. I intend to do so once I leave you.'

This piece of news brought a sparkle to Diana's eyes. 'Is it possible that I could go with you? I should like to meet him; if the message is so urgent, he might have some good news for us.'

Neville liked the *us,* but not the thought of her accompanying him to Jackson's.

He told her so. She demurred. He insisted.

Exasperated, Diana said mutinously, 'Why not? I would very much like to meet him and I could tell him myself of Henry Latimer's slip of the tongue.'

'It would not be fitting for me to escort you to such a place.'

'Pooh to that—we could go there separately.'

Neville said, 'If you will not think of your reputation, then I must.'

At which Diana charged back with, 'Now who's to know?'

'Those who wish to silence me are almost certainly keeping a watch on me now. No, my dear, believe me, it would not be wise.'

Diana could see that there was no moving him. Well, she would do as she pleased and he could like it or lump it. 'So be it,' she apparently conceded at last.

Neville had reverted to his old pompous self a little because his reaction to her apparent concession was to remark with a kind smile, 'Very wise of you.'

Diana offered him a deceitfully winsome one in return. 'You will inform me of any news that Jackson might have for us.'

There was that *us* again. Neville had never been part of anyone's us before and it gave him a warm feeling. Until he had met Diana he had never grasped how lonely he had always been.

'Of course, I promise not to keep you in the dark. It is only my feeling for your good name that prevents me from putting you into any danger of your losing it.'

Her good name! What did that matter if, in order to help him right a great wrong, she lost it? But she said nothing more and when he rose she held out her hand like a frank boy, saying, 'I like being a conspirator and I believe that my late husband would approve of me helping you.'

'Well, I approve of it,' were Neville's final words for her when he took her hand and kissed it—only to release it as though it had stung him. He looked at her to find that Diana had a dazed expression on her face as though she, too, had been stung.

Danger! The danger was here with him, for it was plain that she was as much affected as he was.

Good God, was he falling in love at last? If he were honest, no woman had ever affected him as much as Duchess Diana did and he took that thought with him all the way to Jackson's lodgings.

Jackson was at home and was pleased at the speed with which Neville had responded to his letter.

'I had not expected you so soon, Sir Neville.'

Neville smiled wryly. 'I am not very busy these days and I would like to see this business over and done with. I take it that you have further information for me.'

'Indeed, I have, but it is vague in the extreme except that my informant, who must remain nameless, has told me that Sir Stanford Markham is certainly involved at some level in this wretched trade.'

Jackson had just reached this point in his report when there was a timid knock on the door. He paused and shouted, 'Come in.' It was his landlady.

'I thought that I told you not to interrupt me.'

'I would not have done, Mr. Jackson, but a lady has arrived who has said that it is most urgent that she sees you at once.'

'A lady? Did she give you her name?'

'Yes, she says that she is Mrs Diana Rothwell.'

Neville gasped and Jackson swung round to question him. 'Do you know the lady?'

'Indeed, I do, and that is not her whole name. If we may speak privately, I will enlighten you.'

'Pray leave us for a moment, Mrs Barton. Now, Sir Neville, please enlighten me at once.'

'Diana Rothwell is a part only of the lady's name, but it is not the whole. She is the Duchess of Medbourne and, at the moment, the bane of my life.' Neville said this ruefully, so ruefully that Jackson gave a bark of laughter.

'I have heard of the Duchess, but why is she is your bane?'

'Because it was her servant who was kidnapped and consequently she is so eager to be of help to me that I am afraid that she might lose her reputation should she do so. She is, however, now in possession of some further information that will probably reveal who the go-between is.'

'Is she, indeed? Then I think that we ought to invite her in, don't you?' and he called to the landlady to send Mrs Rothwell upstairs.

'That would please her greatly. She has expressed a wish to meet you, but I advised against it lest she put herself in danger. She must have followed me here.'

Neville's feelings about Diana's impudence were a mixture of exasperation and admiration. His exasperation grew when she entered. She was dressed plainly, although to his besotted eyes that seemed to enhance her beauty rather than conceal it. She offered first Jackson, and then him, her sweetest smile.

'Sir Neville!' she exclaimed. 'How fortunate that you are here. We can both give Mr Jackson an account of the recent information we have acquired and save him some valuable time.'

'Not fortunate at all,' Neville growled. 'You have followed me here quite against my express wish that you should not be further involved in this dangerous business.'

Diana was all innocence. 'But I am only trying to be helpful…'

Neville was about to challenge her again when Jackson tactfully forestalled him. 'May I suggest that, now Mrs Rothwell—I mean the Duchess—is here, we might as well take advantage of her presence.'

'Splendid,' exclaimed Diana. 'It will save a great deal of time.' And she gave him a brief and lucid account of what Henry Latimer had said and the circumstances in which he had said it.

Jackson could not refrain from giving a snort of laughter

on hearing about the episode of the stamped foot, but looked suitably grave when Diana told him that Latimer had, perhaps inadvertently, spoken of Neville as sticking his nose in other people's business. She tactfully left out the description of him as a priggish fool.

'The only thing that I don't understand is why he should suddenly give himself away—if he did, that is.'

'Hmm,' Jackson said after thinking for a moment. 'It is my experience that when people are angry or distressed, as Henry Latimer undoubtedly was when you rejected his advances, they often give themselves away without meaning to in the heat of the moment. I've come across his name before, but I can't recall when or why.' He paused. 'It'll come to me if I leave it for a moment, but something tells me that I wouldn't be surprised if he were engaged in something not quite legal.'

Diana leaned forward eagerly. 'Sir Neville and I believe that he might be a go-between. Someone who runs errands and carries out dubious offices for his superiors. We think he could be arranging the provision of girls and young women for those in power who might need their services in secret.'

If Jackson thought that Duchess Diana was the most unusual young woman he had ever met, he did not say so. Instead he said, 'That is possible and I think it would be useful for me to investigate Mr Latimer. But for the moment, I have to tell you both that I have arranged to meet an informant of mine this evening; I would be pleased if Sir Neville would consent to accompany me—disguised of course. He has hinted that he has some useful information to give me.'

To this, Diana said passionately, 'But would not that be rather dangerous, Mr Jackson?'

'Perhaps,' he said, smiling a little, 'but if we are to discover something helpful, this is the kind of thing we have to do.'

Diana privately thought that it was the kind of thing that Jackson did, but if his 'we' included Neville then that was quite another story. Neville had no right to tell her not to put herself in the way of danger or loss of reputation if he was going to endanger himself by accompanying Jackson. She opened her mouth to say so and was then transfixed by Jackson's steely gaze.

'You wish to say something, Mrs Rothwell?'

Neville had to prevent himself from laughing out loud. His darling and dauntless Duchess had met her match in an ex-Bow Street Runner—and she knew it.

When she did speak it was to say, 'If I had ever doubted how shrewd you are, Mr Jackson, I no longer harbour any such false belief. I think that you would have liked my late husband—he being so similar to you in so many ways. He could read minds, too.'

'So, it is settled, then,' Jackson said. 'Tomorrow morning Sir Neville and I will meet at the coffee house we visited before and you, Sir Neville, must contrive to look a little more of a ruffian than you did then.'

'With pleasure,' returned Neville with a conspiratorial grin. 'I have looked extremely respectable for far too long.'

He's enjoying himself, thought Diana incredulously. *I can't beg him not to, for he is finding in himself depths that he never knew existed.* And thinking this, she felt the most extraordinary rush of love for him. There was passion in it but there was something more: an admiration for the true man he was beneath the impassive mask that he had worn for far too long. A man of honour and of strength, a strength which he had only just discovered.

'And you will be careful,' she begged him.

His reply was an unexpected one. 'Until recently careful has been my middle name and, begging your pardon, Mrs Rothwell, my life has been damned dull and I have achieved very little of real note or value. Now I have been given an opportunity to right a real wrong, and if it leads me into danger, so be it.'

'It has already led you into danger,' she reminded him tactlessly.

Exasperated, Neville turned to Jackson who had kept, with difficulty, a blandly neutral expression on his hard face. 'Now you see what I meant when I called her my bane.'

'Your bane? What about *my* bane—having to deal with a man who thinks that he has the right to tell me what, and what not, to do—and he's not even my husband?'

Diana put her hand over her mouth the moment that she had finished speaking. She had managed to give herself away and no mistake.

'Do I take it then, Mrs Rothwell, that if I were your husband you would instantly obey me?'

'Yes—no,' exclaimed the flustered and blushing Diana. 'Neville, I think that we ought to stop entertaining Mr Jackson, he will think that we are light in the attic.'

'More like light in several attics, Mrs Rothwell.'

'And please stop calling me Mrs Rothwell.'

'May I remind you that you called yourself Mrs Rothwell before I did?'

'And you—what are *you* going to call yourself when you join Mr Jackson at the coffee house? I'm sure that you won't be there as Sir Neville Fortescue and you certainly won't be dressed *à la mode* any more than I am now.'

Neville opened his mouth to answer her back as cavalierly as she had spoken to him, and then he saw her sparkling, mocking eyes and realised that she was flirting with him and teasing him into the bargain, and that he, careful, respectable Sir Neville Fortescue, had no more common sense than to take her seriously. So much for him trying to change himself.

It was all that he could do not to take her into his arms and kiss her senseless on the spot. Instead he threw up his hands and said, in mock surrender, 'I cry you quits, in any name you choose to call yourself, and you may offer me mate, checkmate, or whatever you please and put Mr Jackson out of his misery.'

'Not at all,' said Jackson. 'I was enjoying myself, but it is time that we started to work. I hereby adjourn this meeting to another day.'

For some reason his reply, which had no overt humour in it, set them all laughing hysterically. In this happy mood Diana and Neville left together and the temptation she presented to him had never been greater.

If he was unrecognisable when he entered the coffee house that night, Neville thought, then so too was Jackson. He was entirely different from the smooth man whom he and Diana had met that morning. He was dressed like every rogue who was trying to earn a dishonest penny.

Neville had asked Lem to borrow some clothes for him from one of the grooms who was about the same size as he was, on whatever pretext he could contrive. They were clean, but had been heavily patched, and were obviously those of a working man. Above them his face betrayed his origin and status.

He had groaned a little at his image in the long mirror in his bedroom—until inspiration struck. The small fire in the grate had long gone out and would not be remade until he was dressed for the day. He bent down, ran his hands into the cold ashes and smeared his face with a handful of them. To clean them he then ran them over his jacket and breeches, reminding himself to have them washed before they were handed back to their owner.

He thrust a small French breech-loading pistol into one of the capacious pockets of his workman's trousers. It could only fire one shot, but he would have something to defend himself with if matters went awry.

At this point Lem knocked, calling 'Master,' to identify himself, since he was the only member of staff who knew of

Neville's intentions. Anyone else would have been turned away. On entering he stared at Neville and said in his countryman's voice, 'Eeh, you look a reet rascal, Sir Neville, and no mistake.'

'Exactly the impression I am trying to give.'

Lem said anxiously, 'Forgive me, sir, but your voice will betray you immediately. It is that of an educated gentleman.'

Neville groaned. 'I'll try to say as little as possible, but if I have to I shall grunt a little and stammer as though I'm hard of hearing.'

'That might do,' said Lem doubtfully.

'It will have to,' said Neville robustly, and, after Lem had wished him good luck, he had walked through the streets where London's night life congregated until he reached the Turk's Head.

Whatever happened now, he was committed to this venture. He walked briskly in to where Jackson sat in one of the booths furthest from the door where they could not be overlooked.

'Well done,' was all he said on seeing Neville in his version of *mufti*—a foreign word Jackson had picked up, meaning something different from a man's normal clothing. 'I might have known that you'd be up to snuff.'

Neville laughed wryly. 'Is that what I am? I feel a right gaby in this.' He looked about him. 'Has your informant arrived yet?'

Jackson gave vent to a sardonic laugh. 'Not he. He's what's known as a queer rooster—that is, a fellow given to overhearing other thieves and using his knowledge to his own advantage. Tonight it's to sell it to us. Even in this place he'd stick out like a sore thumb; besides, he wouldn't want to be seen with me in public. No, we're meeting him in a back street not far from here where it's unlikely that anyone will be about at this time of night. Drink up your coffee and we'll be off.'

He had already dropped into the coarse speech he used on

these occasions. Neville obediently did as he was bid and followed him out of the coffee house into the dimly lighted street—the night was moonless—and then through a series of alleys and dark, narrow passages until he stopped before an open pair of iron gates in front of a decayed and rotting town house, which long ago had been someone's pride.

Jackson pulled a battered hunter out of his pocket in order to check the time. 'He said he'd be here by now, but he believes in keeping me waiting for a few minutes. After all, it's he who's doing me a favour.'

They stood in silence for several minutes. Somewhere a public clock chimed the half-hour. Neville thought it best to say nothing; since he was the novice in this game, even though he had the strangest sensation of being watched.

Finally he said tentatively, 'It may be my fear speaking but I have the distinct feeling that something is wrong.'

Jackson nodded agreement. 'You may be right. Perhaps our queer rooster is waiting for us in the house's forecourt. It's more private there than here. You go first, I'll keep watch to check whether we're being followed.'

Neville walked through the gates until he arrived at a small arcade before a once-imposing front door. It was pitch dark in the arcade and he immediately stumbled over something.

He looked down—to see that the something was the body of a man, lying in his own blood. His neck was at an odd angle and Neville could only suppose that the body was that of the queer rooster whom they had arranged to meet. He turned to run back to Jackson to ask him to come and try to identify the dead man, but before he could do so the house door was flung open and two men burst out, one brandishing a cudgel and the other a pistol.

Afterwards Neville realised that he had not even paused to think what to do next; acting on blind instinct, he quickly wrenched the pistol from his pocket, cocked it, and shot the attacker in the chest before he had time to fire his own pistol.

Instead he fell to the ground across the body already lying there.

Meantime Jackson was wrestling with the man with the cudgel, a battle that he was having difficulty winning. Neville hit the second would-be assassin hard on the head with his pistol, so that Jackson could wrench the cudgel from him and hold him helpless in an iron grip.

'Kill the bastard!' Neville shouted—later to be astonished, and a little ashamed, by his own ferocity, but after all survival had been everything.

'Not now, only after he's talked to us.' Jackson smiled. 'Who knows what he has to tell us?'

'Naught, I know naught,' babbled number two, as Neville was beginning to think of him.

'Really? If that's so I'll hand you over to my companion so that he can make his second kill of the night. He can use your late pal's pistol.'

Words poured from the wretch in an attempt to placate the pair of them. 'We was told to follow Leary and then do for him before the Runner arrived. Then we was told to do for you and anyone with you.'

'We know that,' said Jackson, all weary patience. 'Tell us something we don't know—such as who sent you?'

'A gent, it wor' a gent. Leary had been boasting about how much he was going to get from a Runner when he told him who ran the trade in gals.'

'His name?'

''Ow should I know his name? Jus' that he wor' a gent and gev us each a golden guinea. Didn't say why he wanted you done for. Jus' told us to do it. He gev Jem his pistol.'

'Where's the guinea?' asked Jackson.

'In my pocket a'course.'

'Then you may give it to me,' was Jackson's answer to that, and on receiving it, after a lot of grumbling from his prisoner, he tossed the coin to Neville, saying, as he casually broke the would-be murderer's neck, 'Have that, chum, you've earned it tonight.'

Neville stared at Jackson and then at the dead man, and said, 'What do we do now?'

Jackson replied immediately, 'We go home, of course.'

'And just leave them here? Three men who have all died a violent death?'

'Why not? A falling out of thieves is what the authorities will think and good riddance to bad rubbish without having to trouble the hangman. Besides, you surely don't want anyone to know what we've been up to tonight. Think what that would do to your reputation.'

He seized the thunderstruck Neville by the arm and hurried him along. 'No need to worry. Even if our queer rooster was unable to name any names, we found out one useful thing tonight—that someone knows that we are after them and tried to silence us.'

Neville started to say something, then changed his mind. How was he to explain this night's work to Diana? Need he tell her all the gruesome details? If he did, she would worry even more about his running into danger and begin to nag him about it all over again.

'The Duchess will want to know what happened, how can I tell her about this?' And he pointed back to where the three dead men lay.

'You mean Mrs Rothwell? I like that name better, she's too down to earth to be a Duchess—pity she's a woman, she'd have made a grand duke. Why not simply say that the informant never turned up—and that's not a total lie?'

It was all that Neville could do not to choke back a grim laugh. 'Indeed it isn't. We have arranged to visit Hyde Park tomorrow afternoon where I am to inform her of what we discovered tonight. I am sure that no one will suspect that we might be openly discussing such secret matters before the whole of society.'

'Aye.' Jackson grinned. 'I can see that you're fast learning the ways of criminal trickery.'

'I think, if I don't tell her the whole truth, that she'll be disappointed that we didn't learn anything substantial.'

'Tell her anything to keep her happy—I've found that's the best way with women.'

Neville grimaced, 'Not with Duchess Diana, I do assure you.'

'Oh, you'll think of something,' Jackson told him jovially. 'You're learning fast and no mistake. I've never thanked you for ridding us of the cove with the pistol. What made you bring one along? And such a little fellow it was.'

'I don't know. Perhaps Diana's prattling about danger spurred me on. I was given this by my father because it was small, and I found it easy to hide in my pocket, these breeches being so capacious.'

By now they had reached the Haymarket again. Even though it was now one in the morning the street was still crowded with people going about their dubious business.

'I never thought that I was going to kill a man with it,' said Neville abruptly, 'but needs must, I suppose.'

Jackson nodded. He had wondered how Sir Neville Fortescue would behave when he was in a tight corner and now he knew. He could depend upon him.

'Tomorrow,' he said, 'I shall start a new line of enquiry—mostly around Mr. Henry Latimer and that fraud, Sir Stanford Markham. I'll let you know how I fare and whether I shall need you again. You might try to start a few hares, too. Some of your fancy pals probably know more than they ought. You're a dab hand at playing the innocent, if I may say so, and you never know what might turn up.'

But I *was* innocent, Neville thought while walking back home. I've been blooded tonight and the whole world looks different to me, as though I have been reborn. When I become my orderly, soberly dressed self again, will everything I see still be changed?

And would he be able to conjure up some half-truths tomorrow good enough to satisfy Diana?

Chapter Nine

'Now,' commanded Diana, 'you may tell me what you and Jackson found out last night.'

They were walking together in Hyde Park, the subject of many curious eyes. Diana had been driven there, Isabella by her side. Neville had arrived shortly afterwards driving his two-horse curricle. Seeing Diana, he had leapt out to greet her, leaving his carriage with his tiger, a cynical midget who had once thought it odd that his master was so indifferent to pretty women.

Neville had ignored Isabella's fierce stare and her refusal to greet him properly, saying cheerfully to Diana, 'Ah, my dear Duchess. Dare I propose that we walk together on this sunny afternoon?'

Diana refrained from answering him with *You may dare to propose anything to me that you please, Sir Neville*. Instead she came out with, 'Of all things that would be most delightful. You will excuse us, Isabella, I trust.'

'Willingly,' Isabella snorted, taking care not to look at Neville when he handed Diana down. Her reckless patron was looking charming in a cream, high-waisted gown devoid of fuss and frills. Her glossy raven-black hair had been cut even shorter than the current fashion and she carried with her a tiny parasol, which not only shaded her from the sun but made it difficult for curious onlookers to guess what she and Neville were saying.

She thought that there was something different about him, but what the difference was she could not tell. He had a twinkle in his eye and an expression which she had never seen before—something to do with the set of his lips and the way in which his eyes roved over her.

Now that he was answering her question, his expression became rather rueful. 'I'm afraid there isn't much to tell you, Jackson's informant never turned up. He's always been reliable before and Jackson fears that he may have come to some harm. If so, it might mean that someone important is determined that we shall not find anything out. Jackson is going to investigate Henry Latimer and Sir Stanford Markham—he agrees with us that they are most likely go-betweens.'

'So really, we are no further on.' To give the impression that they were having a light-hearted, flirtatious conversation, Diana then took his arm, and excitedly pointed to where the Duke of Wellington had just driven into the Park in his beautiful new curricle, painted a bright yellow and with silver harness.

'I should so like to meet him,' she exclaimed deliberately loud enough for those around to hear her.

Neville shook his head. 'Before I lost my reputation I would have taken you over to introduce you to him, but for your sake I dare not risk being given the cut direct before everyone in the Park.'

'What a pity,' Diana said, still deliberately loud, but she didn't have long to repine. The Duke, on seeing Neville, drove over to them, with half of the Park breathlessly waiting to see what would happen next, Wellington being notorious for his forthrightness.

His first words, delivered from on high, were, 'Happy to see you out in public, Fortescue. Damned bad business of yours recently, didn't believe a word of it. Don't try to explain what it was all about, but I know a good man when I see one. Pray introduce your companion to me, I have not had the privilege of meeting her before.'

Diana blushed and Neville, astonished at the Duke's dismissal of the scandal that haunted him, did the honours. The Duke's response was to hand the reins to his tiger and dismount to walk along with them.

'So you're the Duchess of Medbourne everyone is talking about. I knew your late husband when I was a lad and he was visiting his property in Ireland. I believe he sold it some time ago.'

'Yes,' said Diana, 'he wished to give all his attention to his lands in England and he didn't like being an absentee landlord—he thought that a great deal of the troubles in Ireland were caused by that.'

'Ah, so he discussed politics with you, did he?'

'Yes, Duke, and philosophy, chemistry and mathematics—in fact, everything in which he was interested, and his interests were many and various.'

'As I have heard.'

Neville listened, fascinated by being privileged to hear two such free-spoken people talking together. To his astonishment he found himself a little jealous of the speed with which the Duke and Diana had become friends. Wellington's success with the ladies was notorious, although lately his friendship with Mrs Arbuthnot, who was also present in the Park, held most of his attention.

Finally the Duke said, 'We must not leave Sir Neville out of our jolly *causerie,* particularly since I wished to hand him a piece of advice. It is this: in life, as in war, it is always best to go carefully whether you wish to attack or defend. Prepare your ground before you act. Even that will not give you certain victory, but it at least gives you the chance of it. I am sure that your late husband would have agreed with me, Duchess.'

'Indeed, and it is the advice that I have been giving Sir Neville—doubtless as the result of my late husband's tuition.'

The Duke beamed at her and then bowed to the pair of them. 'Splendid. Now I must wish you well and leave you. I have arranged to meet several friends in the Park today and I must not be remiss. I bid you both adieu and good luck.'

They watched him walk away. Neville said in a hollow voice, 'He knows what we are up to. How much is not plain, but he must, or why else the warning?'

'If he does know—' and Diana was a trifle indignant '—why did he not give us some information—name a few names, for instance?'

'Because he's not only a soldier but a politician. He has to go carefully, and what he said and how he said it must mean that our enemy—or enemies—are most powerful.'

'Perhaps so,' said Diana doubtfully, 'but surely if he really does know something it is his duty to inform the authorities.'

'Ah, but do we know where he believes his duty to lie in this matter?'

Diana's retort was a rather sour. 'I should have thought it plain—but then I am only a woman.'

'My dear Duchess,' was Neville's riposte, 'you are not an only anything, but we live in a cruel world where difficult choices have to be made.'

He could tell that he had not mollified her, but for once she let the matter go and they continued their walk around the park, talking about the many small matters that filled their world. In this, as in all things, Diana spoke with the common sense that Neville had come to expect from her, even if it was expressed in a vividly interesting and downright fashion.

It was a pleasure just to be with her, although it was something of a mixed blessing, for his passion for her was growing, not diminishing, while she was being her usual teasing self so that it was difficult for him to gauge whether or not she was beginning to feel for him what he felt for her.

Perhaps, after all, it was simply the case of the missing girls that interested her and nothing else. From what she had said to him, and to the Duke, her feelings for her late husband were strong ones.

They parted at last, and Diana was as reluctant to leave Neville as he was to leave her, although from her manner no one would have guessed it, least of all Neville.

'I shall tell Jackson of the Duke's advice tomorrow,' were his last words to her on the way back to her carriage. While he helped her in, he was well aware of Isabella's disapproving eyes on him, but he was as pleasantly courteous to her as he was to everyone. He knew, though, that she would badger Diana about the length of time she had spent with him.

Isabella's first words to her, after he had moved away, were, 'Was it really necessary to be with him for so long? You must know that you have both been the main topic of spiteful conversation this afternoon.'

'Really,' returned Diana, all innocence. 'Was that because the Duke of Wellington chose to spend so much time in our company?'

'You know exactly what I mean,' snorted Isabella.

'No, I don't—and even if I do, I have never let idle chit-chat and *on dits* govern my life. It was one of the lessons which my late husband taught me.'

Since Diana's late husband had been a Duke of spotless reputation whom Isabella could not bring herself to criticise, she being so far below him, this served to silence her. She spent the whole of the rest of the journey home with a grim expression on her face that told the world of the suffering which she had to undergo with her thankless mistress.

Isabella was not to know that the only reason that Diana chose to retain her services was because she knew that if she were to turn her away, Isabella would be left without a home, all her other relatives having long ago tired of her lengthy and unwanted advice.

Neville was not sure that he had convinced Diana that the edited version of his previous night's experiences was the whole truth. She had already shown him that she was well aware of when she was being lied to, but nevertheless his duty remained quite plain to him. At all costs he was bound to try to protect her from the wolves with whom they had become involved.

He had been invited to a reception at the Templestowes' grand house in Piccadilly; since Harriet Templestowe, always known as Harry, was one of the few women whose intellect he respected, he had accepted the invitation. In her quiet way he thought that she and Diana shared many good qualities. Since the Templestowes had already shown that whoever else chose to cut him, they would not. He was looking forward to his evening even though he was a little worried that Diana might, on second thoughts, have decided that he had prevaricated with her and would punish him accordingly.

There was rather an unusual crowd present when he arrived. The Templestowes always invited a very mixed bag and besides several grandees, Wellington, Lord Burnside and Sir Stanford Markham among them, there were a large number of poets, would-be poets, littérateurs and natural philosophers, all friends of Alex Templestowe who belonged to the Royal Society. Fortunately for Neville this meant that many of those who had been most harsh towards him since his downfall—as everyone called it—were not present.

'So pleased that you felt able to come,' were the words with which both Templestowes greeted him when he reached the top of the stairs. Later Alex was more blunt. 'Take no notice of the silly upstarts who think that they run society. I know you, Fortescue, and I would trust you with my honour and my life.'

Neville smiled and said, 'There are many who have been waiting for me to follow in the disastrous path of my father and are only too happy to cry, ''I told you so!'' I assure you that I have done nothing dishonourable or to be ashamed of, even though circumstances made it appear so.'

Was he imagining it or did Templestowe give him an odd look when he had finished speaking? It must have been imagination, because Alex went on to discuss with him the present disastrous state of farming after the terrible weather of the last two years. Neville remembered that he was reputed to help with bringing in the harvest in person when assistance with it was needed.

From then on his evening was, for a time, an unqualified success except that Diana was always surrounded by a crowd of people. He decided to wait until the fuss about her had died down before he spoke to her.

Wineglass in hand, he retired to the privacy of an alcove devoted to a display of miniatures of members of the Templestowe family and was busy inspecting them when he heard someone coming up behind him. He turned, to find that it was Sir Stanford Markham, who offered him a frosty smile.

'So here you are, Fortescue. I thought that I might find you present tonight. I hope that you have recovered from your previous…er…trouble. Most unfortunate for both of us that you should find yourself before me that morning.'

This came out in such a would-be tactful, two-edged fashion, particularly since Neville had come to believe that Sir Stanford was only present on the bench that day because he had been arrested, that he scarcely knew how to reply to him.

Finally he came out with a murmured, 'More unfortunate for me, if I may say so, than for you. I am quite well at the present, but then, I was never ill.'

Sir Stanford's bushy eyebrows rose. 'Hardly well, though, that morning,' he offered, 'but if you will blunder into dangerous situations you must take the inevitable consequences.

A word to the wise might help. Next time, I fear that you may not be the principal sufferer. I am sure that you would not wish your mother—let alone yourself—to be the subject of open scandal, to say nothing of Lord Burnside, also, whose own spotless reputation for virtue might suffer if the truth about him and your mother were known. Live a quiet life and all will be well.'

White to the lips, Neville said, 'Is that meant to be a threat? Even though I cannot believe what you are telling me to be the truth.'

Sir Stanford smiled. 'Continue to associate with that ex-Runner of yours and persist in your present course of action and you will soon discover how much truth there is in it. I have no more to say than that, other than be careful,' and he walked negligently away.

To follow him, to take him by the throat and force his lying and blackmailing words down it was Neville's first fierce re-action, but that would merely be to create an instant scandal—and at the home of his best friend! His mother's honour and that of Lord Burnside had been impugned. It must be a lie. Burnside could not be his father—and yet, if he were, it ex-plained so many things.

For example, how unlike he was to his supposed father both in appearance and in behaviour. Was that why Alex Tem-plestowe had looked at him oddly when he had told him that he did not resemble his father? If Burnside were his true fa-ther, then it would also explain why he was taking such an interest in his career and had recently been so supportive.

What he found difficult to believe was that his mother would ever have had an affair outside marriage; she had al-ways been such a strict moralist, complaining about the loose conduct of those in the best society.

And yet, and yet, what people, even his mother, said and what they did, were often two quite different things... He remembered suddenly her rather peculiar remarks about his taking after his father when she had visited him to reprimand him for having been found dead drunk in the street—and how hysterical she had been then.

The only good thing about Sir Stanford's threats was that he had given himself away as one of those involved in the trade in girls—which must mean that he and his associates were fearful of what he and Jackson might have discovered, or might yet discover in the future, which would incriminate them. Hence the direct threat that he had made to Neville in an attempt to persuade him to give up his campaign to unmask the organisers of the trade.

A threat that Neville ruefully admitted might succeed. He had no wish to create a scandal that would ruin his mother and Lord Burnside. Since both of them were believed to live good and Christian lives, they would immediately be branded as hypocrites and worse.

His mind in turmoil, for what Sir Stanford had just hinted was something that he could never have anticipated, Neville considered leaving at once—except that Diana, who had been cornered by Henry Latimer once the crowd around her had thinned, turned her back on him and, seeing Neville, made straight for where he stood, still half-hidden in the alcove, debating with himself whether he ought to continue his campaign.

And, if he did not, what would Diana think of him? Because for his mother's sake, he dare not tell her of Sir Stanford's threats.

'Save me,' said Diana melodramatically, in best Drury Lane style, 'from Henry Latimer who, believe it or not, claims that he wishes to mend fences with me.

'I told him that I had never mended a fence before and did not wish to mend one now with him, especially at the Templestowes' reception—a most unsuitable place. And than the idiot began to explain to me what mending fences really meant, as though I didn't already know.'

'So you don't wish me to explain, either,' said Neville in an attempt to get rid of his Friday face lest he worry Diana with it.

Diana, however, had already seen that he was greatly troubled. 'Forgive me,' she said, 'for being frivolous. I can see that something is worrying you.'

'Yes,' said Neville, wondering how he could convey the desperate mental state he was in without lying to her. 'I have been confronted by a moral dilemma—yet another unsuitable thing to happen at the Templestowes' Reception—and as a consequence I am exercised as to whether I ought to continue our campaign.'

Diana was so surprised that she nearly dropped her fan. 'Never say so, just when we seemed to be making a little progress. But what can this dilemma be that might make you change your mind so dramatically?'

Neville was uncomfortable. 'Since it involves persons other than myself, I cannot tell you, only assure you that I shall have to sleep upon the matter.'

He thought dismally that he had never before told so many lies and half-truths as he had done in the last few weeks. He was not going to sleep on the matter at all. Instead, he had decided to travel to Surrey on the morrow and speak to his mother to try to discover whether Sir Carlton was truly his father.

It would not affect his place in the world if he weren't, because a child born to a married woman who was living with her husband was, in law, the husband's son, even though another man was his father. But for his own peace of mind he needed to know the truth.

Only after that would he come to any decision.

Diana's gaze on him was steady. 'Was it something that Sir Stanford Markham said?' she asked him.

'Now, how do you know that?' exclaimed Neville, startled into indiscretion.

'While Henry Latimer was fawning on me—why, I do not know—I could see that Sir Stanford was talking to you. Bearing in mind our suspicions about him, I wondered what you could be saying to him. Immediately afterwards you tell me that you might have to withdraw from our venture, so the logic of the situation is that he told you something that has disturbed you greatly.'

She was far too shrewd for her own good and if he were to lie to her now she would never forgive him.

'I will not prevaricate with you. You have guessed correctly, he did say something to me, but on my honour I cannot speak of it to you now.'

Regardless of where they were, or of who might be watching, Neville leaned forward, took the hand that was not holding the fan in his and looked deep into her glorious eyes. 'Believe me, if I were free to speak I would tell you everything. Wait but a little and I may be able to. As for our joint venture—any decision will have to be deferred.

'Are you prepared to trust me, Diana, as I trust you?'

The intensity of his gaze, the expression of sorrow on his face, almost undid Diana. She, too, had forgotten that they were standing in a public place and that for both their sakes she must not publicly be too particular with him.

Neville released her hand, but not before he had turned it and kissed her open palm, and they both experienced a *frisson* of delight so strong that they were surprised by it.

'And now I think that we must part,' he murmured. 'We have entertained the company long enough and I have a journey to make tomorrow. After that we will talk again.'

'*Bon voyage,*' Diana said and watched him walk across to the door, nodding to an acquaintance on the way before she lost sight of him. He managed to avoid speaking to Lord Burnside since, after Sir Stanford's revelations, he would have had difficulty in carrying on a conversation with him. The sooner he spoke to his mother, the better. Until then his whole life would have to go into abeyance.

He had to admit that what he most disliked about the whole wretched business was having to be so evasive with Diana.

Chapter Ten

'My son has arrived and is waiting for me in the blue drawing room. Are you sure of that? It is most unlike him not to inform me of his proposed visit beforehand.'

'Quite sure, m'lady. He has asked that you see him as soon as you returned from your engagement since he has urgent business in London, which he needs to attend to immediately.'

Lady Fortescue and her widowed sister had just returned from an afternoon party spent at a neighbour's house nearby. Neville's aunt Susan was quite unlike her sister. She was a jolly woman, plump and rosy, with a great sense of humour. Neville's mother was beautiful, but cold and severe; her sense of humour appeared to be non-existent.

Susan Harrow thought that the difference between them had been the consequence of Emily's dreadful life with Sir Carlton Fortescue because when they had been children together there was not a pin to choose between them in their enjoyment of innocent mischief. She said, briskly and kindly, 'You must join him at once, Em.'

'I do wish that you would not call me Em,' was Lady Fortescue's frosty reply. 'You make me sound like a junior parlour maid, but I suppose that I must go to him as soon as possible.'

'Of course, Emily, it is your duty to oblige him since he has never given you a moment's trouble—unlike most young men these days.'

'Except that he consistently refuses to marry.'

'Well, that is his choice, not yours. Now off with you and, while you are gone, I will arrange for some refreshments for us all when his business with you is over.'

Neville knew the moment that his mother came in that his sudden unheralded arrival had displeased her. His heart sank. How the devil was she going to behave when, however delicately and tactfully he phrased it, he asked her if she had had an affair with Lord Burnside and whether he was the unfortunate result: a bastard in fact, if not in law.

His internal language was getting worse and worse these days!

His mother, as he had expected, remarked repressively, 'What on earth can be so urgent, Neville, that you dispense with all the normal courtesies and arrive here unexpectedly?'

To his surprise Neville, who had always before given way to her bullying by going on the defensive, replied coldly, 'Well, since you ask me so politely, Mother, my errand concerns you and your possible lack of manners in the past.'

The moment that the words were out, and spoken in such a cavalier fashion, too, he regretted them, but there it was. He had changed, profoundly, since he had become involved in matters of life and death.

His mother, shaken by his manner, a manner that he had never used to her before, sank on to a nearby sofa and said faintly, 'Whatever do you mean by that, Neville? Have you taken leave of your senses?'

'On the contrary, I think I have only just come to them. Let me get to the gist of the matter. Yesterday I was informed by someone, whom I believe to have been speaking the truth, that my father was not the late, unlamented Sir Carlton Fortescue, but was, instead, none other than Lord Burnside.'

He had not meant to be so brusque and sound so unfeeling, but his mother's unkind and critical reception of him had, for the first time, provoked him to retaliate—and he had meant to be so tactful. But there it was, he had been brutal and as a result the truth was written on her face.

'Who told you that?'

'The name of my informant is of no moment. I only know that I must ask you to tell me the truth, or I shall go to my grave not knowing whether or not I have lived a lie all my life.'

His mother shook her head. 'What a thing to ask me.' She sounded brave, but her quivering lips gave her away. 'You are, rightfully, Sir Neville Fortescue and that is all you need to know.'

Now this was prevarication and Neville knew it. He also knew that he was desperately sorry for the manner in which he had confronted her. He went down on to his knees before her and took her hands in his.

'Mother, I apologise for speaking to you so harshly, but the truth, whatever it is, cannot hurt me. Know that if Sir Carlton was not my father and that Lord Burnside is, I shall feel no regrets, only relief. Do me the honour of being honest with me. Believe me when I say that I have no wish to reproach you, but I must know the truth.'

She began to cry, great shuddering sobs. 'I thought that no one but myself, Sir Carlton and Lord Burnside knew the truth. My life with Sir Carlton was a living hell. He frequently beat me and on one occasion knocked me downstairs—and all because I couldn't give him a child. It was my fault he said, but I believe that it was his. He had no children by his many *amours*—many of them with servant girls. Oh, people knew that he was unkind to me—but not the full horror of his behaviour.

'And then, one day, we were at a house party and he was taken ill. It was many months since he had tried to give me

a child. Lord Burnside was there and I think that, from something he said, he knew the truth of my marriage. He was so
kind and I was so lonely, and so was he, for he had recently
lost his young wife in childbirth. How it happened, I shall
never know—and believe me, I was only an unfaithful wife
on one occasion—but on that one occasion I conceived you.
The reason that I was barren must have been Sir Carlton's
fault and not mine.

'I thought that Sir Carlton would throw me out, disgrace
me, because he knew that the child could not be his. But no
such thing. He desperately wanted an heir to spite the man
who would have inherited after him, and now I had given him
one. He was only too happy to agree to be your father and
I…I was desperate not to be disgraced.

'He did not live overlong after that, and I was sure that no
one would ever know the truth. I don't understand how your
informant came by his knowledge.'

She stopped and her weeping stopped, too. Neville leaned
forward and kissed her on the cheek. 'Mother, why did you
never tell me how cruelly Sir Carlton treated you?'

'No one knew the whole truth of his cruelty—only Lord
Burnside—and since you were brought up to think that Sir
Carlton was your father the less said, the better. I am still
surprised that the matter is common knowledge.'

Neville kissed her again. 'Two things. Firstly, I can believe
that the man who informed me knew that Sir Carlton suffered
from an illness which made him barren and impotent, so that
he knew that Sir Carlton could not have been my father. Secondly, do you remember the names of anyone else in the
house party? By the by, someone remarked recently on my
likeness to Lord Burnside both in face, manner and behaviour.'

'I was so relieved,' his mother whispered, returning the
kiss, the first direct sign of affection she had given him for
many long years, 'when you were not like Sir Carlton, but

like *him*. I did my best to bring you up as a good man. As to your question, I remember nearly everything about that house party. Lord Marchmont was there, and Prince Adalbert, and Stanford Markham—he had not yet been knighted.' She gave a few more names, concluding, 'Oh, and Henry Latimer's father and George Alford's. You must understand that we were all very young.'

So, Sir Stanford had been present—which was probably how he knew the truth of something that he did not care to use against either of the two principals until Neville had begun to try to find out who was behind the trade of the kidnapped girls.

'Suppose I told you that someone has tried to blackmail me into giving up a campaign, which I feel in honour bound to pursue, by threatening to expose my true parentage and ruin the reputations of both you and Lord Burnside. Would you say that I ought to agree to surrender my honour to save yours?'

His mother gave a great shudder. 'My impulse is to say yes. I have tried so hard to live a pure life ever since. How could I face the world if the truth of your birth was known? But you are my son and I suppose that I ought to consider you as well as myself. I know that I have always been hard on you, but I wanted you to be a credit to me and your true father and, if I am honest, you always have been. I don't know what decision I ought to make…except that I suppose that you could ask Lord Burnside what we, I mean he and I, ought, in honour, to do.'

Then she repeated the fear she had expressed a moment ago. 'How shall I ever be able to hold up my head again if the truth comes out? It was wrong of me to keep you from your real father—but think, had I left Sir Carlton before you were born, you would have become a nameless bastard. It was partly to protect you, as well as myself, that I continued to live with him. The law made you his son.'

'Mother,' said Neville, who had risen to sit beside her, 'you must know, as well as I do, that many of the women leaders of fashion today have committed graver sins than yours and have defied the world to censure them.

'Think of Lady Melbourne, for example. All the world knows that of her five children, only one, the first, was her husband's. The present Melbourne heir, William, is Lord Egremont's son, and she still manages to hold her head so high that it is a wonder that she doesn't fall forwards, having fallen backwards so often.'

This dreadful joke even provoked a faint smile from his mother. 'You mean that if I agree to allow you to carry on and a public scandal erupts, I should refuse to be put down and, like her, behave as though nothing has happened.'

'Exactly. But if you wish me to speak to Lord Burnside before I make a decision, then I will do so.'

For almost the first time in his whole life his mother looked at him with love on her face before saying, 'You may tell him that I have agreed to allow you to continue your campaign even if it provokes a scandal involving the pair of us.'

'One last question, Mother. Does he know that I am his son?'

'Yes. I thought it only right to inform him of that shortly before Sir Carlton died. It was the last time I ever spoke to him.'

He wanted to ask her if she had loved Lord Burnside, but he had caused her enough pain.

'Do you wish to come to London with me and speak to him yourself?'

She shook her head. 'No, but you may return to him something that he gave me when we parted all those years ago.'

It was over, and neither of them knew what to say. Except that when Neville rose to leave her alone with her memories, she called his name before he reached the door.

'Neville, it was very wrong of me not to tell you the name

of your true father when you reached twenty-one, but I have always been a coward and now it seems that I may have to pay for my cowardice.'

He presented her with an expression on his face that she had never seen before, so hard it was. 'Mother, you may rest assured of this: if ever anyone says a bad word about you and I come to hear of it, I shall punish them after a fashion that they will never forget.'

If ever Emily Fortescue had feared that her son had been influenced by that craven brute Sir Carlton Fortescue, she now had the satisfaction of knowing that she had brought up a man who was his opposite in all things.

She said to him, shyly, 'Neville, it would please me, and your aunt Susan, if you would stay here overnight. We see so little of you these days.'

Were it not that he wished to return to his duty—and to Diana—he would have agreed to stay longer than one night, but they both called to him, so he did not ask for an extension, although he would dearly have liked to have done so.

'Of course,' he said, and wondered whether they might have had a more loving relationship if his mother had told him the truth long ago, because once she had enlightened him her whole manner towards him had changed.

Better late than never, though, and he must be pleased that having told him it was as though she had shed a burden that she had carried all her life.

'Yes, you are my son, and my one regret is that I was never able to be your father, but there was your mother to think of.'

Neville did not ask his father the one question that had been troubling him all the way home from his aunt Susan's place in Surrey: *Why did you not marry her after Sir Carlton died?*

As though he had read his mind, Lord Burnside, who had risen and walked to look out of the window of the study in which he had received Neville, turned to face him.

'You were twelve years old when Sir Carlton died, and you were the living image of myself as a boy—and you have grown up to resemble me even more in every way. I could not face the scandal and whispers of what would surely follow if I had married her—and of how it would affect your mother. We have both prided ourselves on living a virtuous life, which made matters worse, for our fall would have been the greater.'

Neville wanted to say, *But what of me, living all my life in the shadow of a cur like Sir Carlton, fearful that I might be like him if I were not careful, and all the time I was the son of a man of whom I could be proud?*

Instead Neville asked him what advice he would offer him: to defy his blackmailer and continue his campaign, or keep quiet and abandon it?

'What was your mother's verdict?' was Lord Burnside's reply to that.

'Roughly what the Duke of Wellington is supposed to have replied when the courtesan Harriette Wilson tried to blackmail him. "Publish and be damned!"'

'Then she must have changed greatly since I knew her.'

'Yes, I think that for the first time she asked herself whether she was right to stay with Sir Carlton after she knew she was carrying your child, and by doing so make me legitimate.'

'Indeed, and knowing how badly he treated her, that took courage.'

'So, what is your answer?

'Briefly, that if your mother is prepared to face the scandal, then so am I. But is it possible that you can tell me of your campaign? I should dearly like to know why it is so important.'

'Alas, I am sworn to silence, to protect not so much myself as those who are helping me. You may be sure that it is one of which you would most heartily approve.'

'And your mother, does she know?'

Neville shook his head. 'No, but she trusts me. And now I

must give you this.' And he handed his father the book that his mother had given him that morning shortly before he had left her—for the first time in love.

Lord Burnside opened it, and read something that was written on the first page. 'Have you looked at this, Neville?'

'No, the book is between the two of you and has nothing to do with me.'

'She has asked me to visit her. What do you say to that, my son?'

'It is your decision, Father, but were I to offer you an opinion, I would say that you might think it both wise and kind to oblige her.'

Lord Burnside's sad face softened. 'I see that you are truly my son. It is what I would have said in a similar situation.'

Amusement rode on Neville's face. 'Begging your pardon, Father, but I find it difficult to believe that there are many situations similar to this one.'

'True, but I will take your advice. Might I ask who is blackmailing you over this?'

'Again, no, but suffice it that it is someone who knew you both and had reason to believe that his attempt at blackmail would succeed.'

'In which he was wrong—because we have created a strong-minded son who will always try to do what is right, not what is expedient.'

Neville shook his head in denial, but his father smiled and said, 'You must know that to be true. I also know that the blackmailer has done one good thing: he has brought us together. At long last I know that I shall be leaving behind me when I die a worthy heir, even though I may not acknowledge him. It is more than I deserve for abandoning you to Sir Carlton. Emily and I did better than we knew.'

After leaving him, Neville felt that he had suddenly been set free, that the black cloud which had hovered over him since birth had been lifted. He had spent his life denying himself even minor pleasures in the belief that by doing so he was showing how unlike he was to his wastrel father. More than that, he had a fond hope that Lord Burnside and his mother might come together and enjoy in their declining years what they had lost in their youth.

His father's last words to him were, 'I trust that you will be careful in pursuing your campaign. It seems to me that anyone who would seek to influence you by blackmailing you would not hesitate to stoop to other more dangerous means of silencing you.'

Well, that was true enough; now he would visit Diana and try to persuade her to stop playing an active part in helping him. He could put his own life in danger, but he dare not risk hers.

'I am happy to note that you have stopped seeing so much of that young man,' Isabella Marchmont said to Diana that afternoon. 'Very wise of you.'

They were seated in the main withdrawing room. Diana was engaged in canvas work, thus pleasing Isabella, who thought that Diana ought to spend more time on ladylike pursuits rather than in pretending that she was a man. Diana, however, was finding it soothing after a morning spent with her agent, who had come from Nottinghamshire to go over the estate's books with her.

The words had hardly left her mouth when the butler entered. 'Sir Neville Fortescue has arrived, your Grace, and has asked if you would do him the honour of receiving him.'

Diana put down her canvas work, trying not to appear too excited by the news. 'You may show him in at once, Lubbock,' she said, and added to the frowning Isabella when he had gone, 'I think that you would prefer to leave before he arrives, since you disapprove of him so strongly.'

Isabella, embroidery frame and bag in hand, rewarded her with a forbidding stare and departed, fortunately not passing

Neville on his way in. Diana picked up her work again and pretended to be engrossed in it when the butler escorted Neville into the room.

She wondered wryly what the other servants would say when he told them that she was entertaining Sir Neville on her own—again! They would probably think the worst and there were times when she wished that they were right, for often, after he had left her, she asked herself whether she wished him to be so tiresomely honourable all the time.

'Sir Neville Fortescue, your Grace,' intoned the butler and left.

Neville thought, yet again, that Diana was looking at her best in a simple dark blue gown, devoid of frills and furbelows so that her essential beauty was not diminished by the interfering fuss of high fashion.

For her part Diana thought that Neville had changed yet again. The only phrase that she could think of to describe this new Neville was that he looked like a man who had found something—but she had no notion of what that something might be.

Even the manner in which he bowed to her as she rose to meet him was subtly different, and when he spoke he sounded frank and eager, not as though he was carefully considering each word before he uttered it.

'As always,' he said, sitting opposite to her at her behest, 'you are in looks, but I need not tell you that. Your mirror should have told you so already.'

Oh, he was indeed in her toils: he only had to see her to desire her. It was as though the short time he had spent away from her had made her more precious to him than ever. It was not only simple lust that was inflaming him, although that was present, too, but it was becoming impossible for him to imagine a world in which he was away from her for long.

'You are looking well, too,' Diana said.

'I am feeling well.' But the pity of it was that for the sake of his mother and new-found father he could not tell her why the world seemed so new-minted to him and share that joy with her.

At the last, when he had been walking with her towards his carriage, his mother had said hesitantly, 'You are a grown man, Neville, and if you wish to befriend Diana Medbourne that must be your choice and not mine. When next you see her, remember me to her.'

What he did say was, 'I have been visiting my mother in Surrey. She sends you her regards and hopes to meet you again when she returns to London—which may not be for some time. She is happiest in the country.'

Perhaps that might change if his father visited her—another thought that he could not voice. He did not like having secrets that he could not share with Diana.

He said impulsively—and when was he last impulsive?—'Did you miss me, Diana? I missed you. I was constantly on the verge of turning towards you to make some remark, only you were not there.' He had leaned forward when he came out with this so that they were eye to eye.

Diana made no effort to retreat. She stared gravely back at him, and her gaze was so intense and her eyes so blue that Neville thought that they were part of another sea in which he might drown.

And thinking thus, he left his armchair to sit beside her on the sofa, and again she made no effort to stop him, saying nothing, but still keeping her eyes on his. She had no notion of what he might do next, but the passion that she was beginning to feel for him was consuming her—the passion between men and women of which her husband had spoken but had never been able to enjoy.

When he leaned forward again and raised his right hand to cup her chin and gently brought his lips down on to hers, so rosy red, so perfect, her answer was to return the kiss, so that

Neville gave a little groan and, putting his arms around her neck, bore her gently backwards, still kissing her.

Oh, the bliss of having his arms around her and of being able to show the depth of her feelings for him by kissing him back. His right hand strayed down to caress her left breast and the pleasure which that gave her caused her to give a little cry, so sweet it was.

One thing soon led to another and, since neither of them had been prepared for the power that they had unleashed between them, it was not surprising that they rapidly reached the point when the next step was final consummation.

Afterwards neither could clearly remember what stopped them. At the time Diana, on the verge of a delight that she had never before experienced, suddenly remembered that, although she had been a married woman, she was still virgin with all that that might entail if events took their inevitable course.

'No!' she cried, pulling away, at the very moment when Neville, unbuttoning his breeches flap, recalled what reckless passion had done to his father and his mother. God forgive him, he was behaving after a fashion that he had always despised, carelessly ready to risk Diana's reputation and his own in a rush of feeling that had been partly provoked by the sense of release which he had felt on hearing his parents' news.

Like Diana, he pulled away and they stared at one another again—this time in dismay.

'Forgive me,' Neville began, trying to rearrange his dishevelled person. 'I never meant to go so far.'

'Nothing to forgive,' Diana retorted a trifle tartly, while pulling the neck of her dress back over her shoulders, since bliss denied was having a bad effect on her temper—even if she had pulled away from it at the same time as Neville. 'I was your willing partner until common sense told me that we risked discovery or worse.'

'But I am the man, and I led you on.'

'And I followed you most willingly.'

'It still remains my responsibility—'

'Are women supposed to be so weak that they can do nothing without a man's taking the lead?'

They had become so cross with each other, when a moment before had been engaged in the most time-honoured activity between a man and a woman, that it seemed that, somehow, the very strength of the rapport which they had mutually enjoyed had served only to increase their anger.

'And are men supposed to stand by and see a woman come to harm?' he shot at her.

'If the woman wishes to make her own choice, then that is the risk she must take!'

'Of all the cross-grained arguments—' Neville began, to be furiously interrupted by Diana.

'Oh, one is always certain that one's adversary knows that he is losing an argument when he feels it necessary to resort to vulgar abuse.'

'So we are adversaries now?' Neville retorted hotly, surprised at his own anger that, to his astonishment, was mixed with an insane desire to bear her down on to the carpet and teach her who was master.

'If that is what you wish—but I don't. I wish to be at peace with you.'

'Then you choose some strange ways to achieve it!'

'So now I am strange, am I?'

Diana was about to add, 'My late husband never thought that I was,' but fortunately for them both, since God knows how Neville would have riposted to *that,* there came a sharp rap on the door.

Diana shouted weakly, 'Come in,' and Isabella entered to stare at the pair of them, standing face to face, their faces scarlet, glaring into each other's eyes.

'Is there anything wrong?' she asked, aware that there was something awry.

While Neville was wondering desperately what he ought to offer as an explanation, the ready-tongued Diana, taught by a master, gave a light laugh before saying cheerfully, 'Sir Neville has been telling me a most amusing story which he heard in Surrey last night about an encounter between a bull and a townie in which the bull came off worse.'

It was one that her late husband had told her and which was hardly appropriate to be told in mixed company, as Neville knew, and he was unable to stifle a grin at his daring Duchess's impudence, which, fortunately, served to silence Isabella who was not sure that Diana had been telling the truth.

The looks that she offered them both were suspicious, but since they were now both smiling cheerfully at her, she tossed her head, and said, 'Lady Devereux and her companion have arrived and wished to know whether you are at home today. I told the butler I would come and ask you to save him the journey.'

The real reason, both Diana and Neville suspected, was that she had hoped to catch them *in flagrante delicto,* but, alas for her, she had arrived five minutes too late.

'You may ask the butler to show them in, they might like to enjoy Sir Neville's story, too.'

Neville, his anger at Diana's refusal to listen to his well-meant advice still hot within him, could not prevent himself from admiring her ready wit, even if he continued to deplore her refusal to consider her own safety.

Isabella rewarded them both with a glare of her own and added a toss of the head before leaving to carry out Diana's bidding.

Neville, thinking this a useful opportunity to take his leave himself, now that Isabella's arrival had ended the impasse between them, bowed to Diana, saying, 'I have just remem-

bered that I have another important engagement. Pray present
my excuses to Lady Devereux that I could not remain to see
her.'

If Neville, because of Cass Devereux's arrival, had not been
able to continue to try to persuade Diana not to take unnecessary risks lest she put herself in real danger, he found when
he arrived at Jackson's home-cum-office that she was not the
only one at risk as a result of their campaign.

He was so shocked when he saw Jackson that he could not
prevent himself from exclaiming, 'Good God, man, what the
devil has been happening to you?'

Jackson, who was sporting a black eye and a heavily
bruised and swollen face, replied in his usual dry manner,
'You have no need to ask. It was your business that provoked
this attack. It happened last night when I was on my way
home. Two queer roosters attacked me and gave me a hearty
larruping, before warning me to have nothing further to do
with you lest worse befall.'

'And will you obey them?'

'Not I—I shall just have to go more warily. I think that we
have frightened our enemies—I believe them to be more than
one.'

'I do not like the thought of you risking your life for me,'
said Neville slowly.

'I am not risking it for you, but for the poor bitches whom
they have ruined and sometimes killed. I am not much further
on, but patience is everything, and if we *have* frightened them
they are likely to do something stupid.'

'They have already done something stupid and in the doing
have confirmed our belief that Sir Stanford Markham is a
prime mover in this.' He proceeded to tell Jackson of the
attempt to blackmail him, not omitting its nature.

Jackson offered Neville a wry and painful smile. 'Aye, I
thought that might turn up as a threat.'

'You knew? About my mother and Lord Burnside?'

'Oh, aye, I always make a point of investigating anyone who employs me to investigate for them. You might be surprised to learn how useful that often is.'

Neville's laugh was a rueful one. 'So, it must have been common knowledge after all, despite my mother's belief that no one knew.'

'No, what *was* common knowledge was that your supposed father died of syphilis and had been impotent for many years before that—or so I discovered through underworld gossip. I wonder how Sir Stanford came upon the truth.'

'My mother told me that he was present at the house party where she and Lord Burnside met all those years ago—as were Henry Latimer's father and George Alford's.'

'Hmm, Henry Latimer again. I like the look of him as being part of Markham's conspiracy—but from what I hear, the present Lord Alford is a foolish nonentity. I take it that Markham's threat was that if you continued to work against him and the others the truth about you, Burnside and your mother would be revealed. Do you intend to continue?'

'With my mother's and Burnside's permission, yes—although I have told them nothing about our venture.'

'I suppose that the truth is that they are shielding not only themselves but someone powerful. From what you have told me, I would lay odds that Henry Latimer is a go-between— he has an unsavoury reputation among the queer roosters even if he is one of society's pets.'

'But not Diana Medbourne's,' remarked Neville with a grin.

'No, and I think that you ought, as soon as possible, to advise her that she ought to draw in her horns and allow us to continue on our own. They are ruthless enough to try to use her as a weapon against us.'

'I meant to do that today when I saw her. To that end I have told her nothing about Sir Stanford's threats or of the truth of my birth which I learned from my mother yesterday.'

'Very wise of you. The lady is a headstrong lass and I can only hope that she will listen to you for all our sakes. We don't want to waste our time running around trying to rescue her from abduction—or worse.'

Privately Neville wondered whether she would take any notice of either him or Jackson, but said nothing other than, 'I'll try to persuade her to use her common sense.'

'Good. Now are you ready to accompany me on another fishing expedition? I have paid a colleague to watch Henry Latimer—no use watching Markham, he won't do any of the dirty work—and he says that he has some useful information to pass on. We are to meet him in secret tomorrow night, when I hope that we might be more successful than we were the last time. And wear your ruffian's garb for the meeting place is a greasy tavern in one of the back alleys leading off the Haymarket.'

'Very well, I'll do as you ask and I'll speak to Diana tomorrow in the forenoon before going on to Chelsea.'

So it was decided and, driving home, Neville decided that persuading Diana not to risk herself was likely to be nearly as difficult as going with Jackson to try to discover what Henry Latimer was up to—if anything.

Chapter Eleven

'So, you are giving me an order, Sir Neville Fortescue, that I am to withdraw from our joint enterprise and sit at home with my needlework and the latest Minerva Press novel.'

'I didn't put it quite as bluntly as that,' exclaimed the harassed Neville. He was finding that trying to persuade Diana not to put herself in danger was proving as unhappy an experience as he had feared it might be—something that would not have surprised Jackson.

'There is no other way of putting it,' Diana told him, 'and since you are not my husband and I have never promised, either in a church or anywhere else, to obey you, you may take it for granted that I shall behave exactly as I please.'

'I am only thinking of your safety—and Jackson agrees with me in this.'

'Oh, does he? And who is he to decide how I should regulate my conduct? Even if he were old enough to be my father, that would not give him the right to tell me what to do.'

She had never sounded so wilful, nor ever looked so lovely.

'It is your safety that we are thinking of, Diana.'

'That is for me to decide, Sir Neville, not you.'

The glare she gave him after she had come out with this was not play-acting, it was real.

How had they reached *point non plus*—and quite so quickly? Their meeting had begun so well. Diana had plainly been happy to see him, and had asked him eagerly about his meeting with Jackson, of which he had given her an abridged version.

But then he had tried to persuade her that it was in her own best interest to withdraw; now both he and Jackson had been attacked and threatened twice, it was intolerable that she should hazard her virtue and her safety. The more he tried to explain that he was trying to protect her, the crosser she grew with him.

'I suppose,' she said, 'that you will still be carrying on— despite the danger you are in, and Jackson as well. Are you not to protect yourselves, too?'

'We are men, that is the difference.' Neville dismally saw that, far from making matters better, this unwise statement had made them worse.

'Tell that to Joan of Arc,' was Diana's riposte.

'She is not a good example to quote—after all, she was burned at the stake.'

'But not before she had saved France by her example,' Diana threw back at him.

It was useless, the woman would not listen to reason and, what was worst of all, the more her eyes shot fire at him, the more his wretched body reacted in the most improper and, given the circumstances, the most inappropriate fashion.

He wanted to take her in his arms, bear her down to the floor and silence her with his mouth on hers. Was it not Aristotle who had said that when a man and a woman fight, either verbally or with blows, they inevitably ended in one another's arms, playing the eternal mating game, even if their intentions had been quite otherwise?

Instead he glared back. 'I see that it is useless to talk sense to you today.'

'Or I to you, for that matter.'

Damn her, must she always insist on having the last word! And that inflamed him, too. He could only imagine the passion that she would bring with her if he ever got her into bed—and for that he would have to marry her. Dare he marry her, so wilful was she? And yet the very thought of it excited him so much that he had to turn away from her, lest she see the effect she had on him.

He was becoming a veritable satyr, was he not? Except that no other woman, before or since he had met her, had ever affected him so profoundly. The fashion for tight breeches was becoming a curse!

'Come,' he said, turning towards her again and speaking in as coolly controlled a voice as he could muster—which gave no indication of the turmoil within him. 'Let us try to discuss this wretched business rationally.'

'But that is what I was doing—it is you who is being unreasonable.'

Neville was about to retort, 'Unreasonable to try to protect you from harm?' but realised that were he to do so would simply result in a repeat of what they had already hurled at one another—hurled being the only word he could think of that did justice to their verbal struggle.

How had she managed to live in peace with the old man she had married? How had he been able to control her?

Which provoked a further question: did *he* want to control her? To suppress the dauntless spirit with which she faced the world? If he truly loved her, then surely the question of control ought not to arise. He must remember that, for all her strong-minded wilfulness, she had never behaved in the outrageous fashion that had brought about other women's decline into disgrace and exile.

Despite the passion that informed nearly everything she

said, Diana always displayed a cool logic in using it that was difficult to refute. So what was different this time?

It was precisely because he had come to love her that he wished to protect her, to shield her from harm. And when she had twitted him with running into danger, was it not because she was beginning to feel something for him?

The difference lay in their sex, that he could defend himself physically and she could not, and—however unfair it was—scandal rarely destroyed a man while women were vulnerable to its nastinesses. Because of that he wished her to withdraw—but he could not compel her to obey him, and he was beginning to recognise that the more he tried to control her, the more resentful she became.

Best, perhaps, to cease to argue with her. He said instead, 'I would ask you to reflect on what I have said and consider that there must be justice in it. Of course, I have no power to organise your conduct for you, but think that my respect for you—' he dared not yet say love '—lies behind my urgent wishes.'

And that was a piece of Machiavellian cunning, was it not, of the kind that he had never practised before. He came out with it as gently as possible, but she rewarded him with a knowing smile and he knew at once that he could not fool her because her mind was as sharp as his, or any man's.

'You reminded me,' she said, 'when you said that, of a man who gives a baby a rattle to keep it quiet.'

His response to her shrewdness was a shout of laughter and before he could stop himself Neville took her in his arms and kissed her passionately, before releasing her, lest his desire for her became so strong that he could not control it.

'No rattle, my heart, but only the wish that you will take care of yourself and behave with the common sense that I know you to possess.'

'You may be sure of that, Neville, and now let us cease to quarrel, for you have much to do today, and, by the by, if you do not leave soon, Isabella will burst in on us on some pretext or other to check whether or not you are engaged in trying to ravish me.'

Which told him that she was fully aware of the power that she was beginning to exercise over him. All the same, it was a real quarrel and he had to hope that it would not destroy the rapport between them which was growing so strongly.

The greasy tavern Jackson had spoken of not far from the Haymarket was the Moor's Head and on the following evening Neville found him inside, a pot of ale in front of him, and puffing at a long pipe. He was seated in a booth from which he could see the door. He looked like every dirty rogue who prowled round this seedy part of London.

Neville was equally disreputable in appearance. Instead of his usually spotless cravat he wore a Belcher around his neck: a grubby-coloured handkerchief decorated with blue and white spots, named after the pugilist Jem Belcher and worn by those who aspired to be part of the Fancy, as the boxing world was generally called.

When he looked at himself in the mirror before he left for his rendezvous with Jackson, Neville decided that if he met the man pictured there he would run a mile before he had anything to do with him. As a last convincing touch he had awarded himself an unlikely black eyepatch.

Nevertheless Jackson still recognised him, beckoning him over to his table as soon as he walked through the door.

'How did you know me in this disgraceful getup?' Neville asked.

Jackson offered him a shark's grin. 'Your walk, the way you hold your head. You should cultivate a bent-shouldered slouch whenever you are out with me on an errand like this— not a ducal strut.'

Neville laughed. How many more times would he be out on an errand like this? To his surprise he was enjoying himself. What a dull life he had led before chance had put him in the way of the world in which Jackson lived.

'Our man has not yet arrived?'

'Not yet, but he is a stouter fellow than our previous informer—in every way. Now sit down and drink the pot of ale I have ordered for you.'

Neville did as he was bid. No one had ever told him what to do so smartly since he had been in baby clothes—usually he was the one who gave the orders and was deferred to. For a moment he understood how Diana felt when he was laying the law down to her.

The grin Jackson offered him when he put the tankard of vile ale to his lips and managed to swallow it without gagging was even more feral than usual. The arrival of a barrel of a man who was more decently dressed and who addressed Jackson as mate enabled him to put the tankard down and pay attention to what was going on.

'Who's he?' asked the barrel.

'No one, just a come-by pal. A bit useful.'

'He don't look it,' said the barrel, sitting down. 'You might order me a pot of ale while we talk and introduce us.'

'Looks often deceive. Ned Springer, this is Thad Newman,' Jackson said. 'Thad fought the Gentleman once.'

'And lost,' said the barrel cheerfully. 'How'd ye get the eyepatch?'

'An argument with a railing—t'other chap was using it as a rapier—he had sharpened its end, and all I had was a tree branch. I lost, too.'

Jackson's expression when Neville came out with this piece of piff-paff was a sight to behold. Neville was astonished by his own inventiveness, particularly as his explanation was taken at face value.

'Bit of a gent, was you, once?'

'Once—got a bit too fond of gambling.'

Where in God's name was all this coming from? What in

the world had happened to decent, prudent, priggish Sir Neville Fortescue that he should tell such flaming lies with such panache?

Thad abandoned Neville as a subject for conversation, took a great swig of his disgusting ale, which had just arrived, and expressed his appreciation of it to Jackson.

'Now, where do you want me to start?'

Jackson was terse. 'At the beginning.'

'The cove I was watching for you, Latimer, is a tricky feller, and no mistake. Goes to the Coal Hole off the Strand all bright and lively and then leaves by the back way. Lost me once or twice at first, but I soon twigged his little game. Cully Watson works there and keeps an eye on him for me.

'Goes after that to a fancy address off the Strand. Stays there for a short time and then off to Madame Josette's, which he enters by the back way and rarely visits the public rooms. Friend of mine there tells me that quite a few gents meet once a week on Tuesday in a private room on the first floor—they never visit t'other part. Food and drink's taken in to 'em and later on they disappear one by one, never together. Don't know who they are or why they are there. No women and nothing rowdy. Latimer might be one of that party.'

He stopped. Jackson said, 'Does Madame Josette ever visit them?'

'Sometimes, not always.'

'Did you manage to see any of them?' Neville asked.

'With my friend's help, one or two, but I didn't know any of 'em—all nobs, you see.'

'And that's all?' Jackson said.

'Not quite. My friend let me in once when they needed someone at the door at Madame's to keep the riff-raff out and I managed to enter the room they used. If I'd been caught I would have said I'd lost my way, but I wasn't. There was nothing there but a long table, chairs and two locked cupboards that I hadn't time to break into.'

'No more than that?'

'A little… My friend watched for them one night and recognised one of 'em. Captain Knighton he calls himself,
though whether he ever captained anything is doubtful.'

'Captain Knighton? The man who helped to organise the
Spa Fields Riots?'

'Aye, and fled to France after that to avoid arrest, Toby
said. Toby being my pal, you understand.'

'But you learned nothing about the girls?'

'No, except that when I asked about them—cunning like—
I could get nary a word from anyone. More'n my life's worth
to say owt, one cully said.'

So they were no further on, thought Neville dismally, except that Jackson seemed to be exercised on hearing of Captain Knighton and handed over to his informant a small purse
in return for his information. Thad pocketed it, saying,
'Thanks, guv, allus ready to oblige you,' before drinking up
his ale and preparing to leave with them.

'What now?' Neville asked.

'We go to Madame Josette's and, since it's not Tuesday,
we break in and try to find the room and the cupboards.'

We—so he means me to accompany him. Aloud Neville
said, 'I gather that you are interested in this Captain Knighton—I've never heard of him, but plainly you have.'

Jackson laughed. 'Was I so obvious? I don't think that he's
part of the conspiracy involving the girls, but I'd lay odds
he's involved in another and I'd dearly like to know who he's
meeting there—and if any of them are the ones we're after.'

'And Knighton is…?' queried Neville.

'You might as well know. He's an ex-soldier and a radical
who wants to start a revolution here—with a guillotine in
Trafalgar Square, no doubt. He fled England some years ago
because he was suspected of plotting to overthrow the then
government while they were fighting against Boney and the

French. Someone peached on him so he crossed the channel to what was supposed to be permanent exile.

'What are the odds he's started his tricks again now that unrest has become general what with the bad harvests we've had, the soldiers who've been laid off with nothing now we don't want them and the framework knitters rioting in the Midland counties and the north? On top of that, Sidmouth has suspended habeas corpus and given magistrates new powers.

'Knighton wants to be a successful Guy Fawkes and there's always a few prominent men about who have a grievance against the government because they lack money or advancement and think that it might be a good idea to help him.'

'It seems a long way away from what we're investigating,' Neville remarked doubtfully.

Jackson put his finger by his nose. 'Who's to say? One way of bringing down the ruling class is to debauch them...'

He left the sentence hanging in the air, grinned at Neville and said, 'Ready to start work, Ned Springer?'

What the devil! He might as well be hanged for a sheep as well as a lamb and if, on the way to finding out about the girls, they also caught a few traitors, then that was a bonus, was it not?

It was all that Neville could do not to shout, 'Tally ho!'

As it was, he exchanged grins with Jackson before saying, 'England expects...pray lead the way.'

If Neville was having an exciting night, Diana was enduring a boring one. She was at a dinner party given by Lady Leominster and had been seated between Henry Latimer and Prince Adalbert. This was doubly unfortunate for both of them were men whom she most wished to avoid. Never mind that the Prince was a distant cousin of the Prince Regent's through his notorious wife, Princess Caroline.

Diana didn't know which of the two men she liked the least, and whenever she met the Prince always felt an overwhelming desire to ask him why he was neglecting his subjects back in Eckstein Halsbach by staying so long in London.

She knew why he pursued her—for the fortune that Charles had left her and she had to assume that Henry Latimer's motive was the same. Gossip had it that he was ruined—stony broke being the usual phrase employed—yet he still managed to remain in society impeccably turned out and welcomed everywhere and he certainly didn't appear to lack money. She had hoped that by stamping on his instep she would prevent him from pursuing her, but no such thing. It seemed, in fact, to have encouraged him!

For some reason the talk at table turned to matters political—a subject usually avoided by society when eating—probably because there was a lack of other more interesting gossip and *on dits*. Word had come that day of a merchant having been shot dead by Luddites in Leicestershire.

Behind all society's gaiety lay the fear of revolution: it was a spectre at every feast—something often thought about but rarely mentioned.

'If I were ruling Britain, I'd hang the lot of them,' was the Prince's charming solution to the problem of the Luddites who were busy breaking the new knitting frames that were depriving them of their living. 'I wouldn't countenance such behaviour back at home. What say you, Latimer?' he asked across Diana.

Henry was at his most suave. 'Oh, I fully agree with you. We are too soft here.'

'After a proper trial, of course,' was Diana's contribution.

The Prince gave her a pitying look. 'What a waste of time when guilt is plain, eh, Latimer?'

'Quite so.'

After that Diana said nothing, and was only too pleased when it was time for the ladies to leave the dinner table to the gentlemen and their port and retreat to the Chinese drawing room, where at least the dragons on the many screens were silent.

Alas, however, the conversation among the women was no better and Lady Leominster was at her worst, bellowing at everyone in turn. Fortunately, when she reached Diana, she lowered her voice a little, saying, 'I hear that you and Sir Neville Fortescue have become very friendly. You know, I never believed all that recent nonsense about him. Such a good young man—take care that you treat him properly. On the other hand, best not to marry him. Someone like Prince Adalbert would be far better. He could do with a strong wife.'

So that was why she had ended up with him sitting beside her at dinner! Which left the problem of why Henry Latimer had been gifted to her. She had scarcely had time to wonder about this before her hostess smiled confidentially at her before raising her voice again. 'I do so hope that you made peace with Henry Latimer after your recent contretemps—he's such a charming young man, too, even though he's a little wild. I like to see all my friends happy, you know, and you must know that you are one of me truest friends.'

Well, you don't make me happy by sandwiching me between the debauched Prince and the ruined roué, was Diana's somewhat savage response. She didn't tell Lady Leominster so, although later she wished that she had when, soon after the men finally emerged from the dining room, the indefatigable lady rushed Henry over to where Diana sat quietly awaiting a convenient moment to take her leave.

'Now you two must entertain one another while I look after those who don't know how to entertain themselves,' she bawled so loudly that the entire room heard her.

Diana and Henry looked at one another. He seemed to be rather more happy than she was. He broke the ice by smiling at her and then saying, 'Before we begin to please our hostess by conversing civilly with one another, I must ask you to forgive my recent misbehaviour at the Cowpers' ball. I fear that I was a little foxed and stupidly expressed my annoyance to you over seeing you favour Sir Neville Fortescue. It was very wrong of me and you were right to be annoyed. I hope that you will accept my most sincere and profound apology—I have forsworn heavy drinking ever since.'

What could Diana say after that but, 'I will accept your apology, and hope that your new-found temperance will prevent you from distressing other young women in the future.'

He bowed his head. 'I see that Sir Neville is not present this evening. Her Ladyship informed me that he had cried off owing to a sudden malaise. I trust that he is not overworking himself these days. Would you think me forward if I suggested that a lengthy holiday at Brighton or in the country would benefit him?'

'Yes. I would. You ought to make the suggestion to him personally, and not to me. I am not his—or any man's—keeper.'

There, that should silence him, thought Diana savagely, but no such luck.

'It was merely that, since you are so friendly with him, I thought the suggestion coming from you would be better than if I should intrude. I wouldn't care to see him damage his health by overworking.'

Madder and madder. Was she to interpret the last sentence as a kind of hidden threat to Neville to be delivered to him by her? Was he aware that Neville was almost certain that he was involved in the dreadful business of the kidnapped girls? Best, perhaps, to make some inconsequential reply, which she did in as cool a voice as possible.

'It is remarkably good of you to trouble yourself over the health of a man who is little more than an acquaintance. Dare I suggest that we drop the subject and talk of something quite impersonal such as our opinion on the latest drama at Drury Lane—otherwise I shall have to disappoint Lady Leominster by cutting short our conversation.'

'And that would never do.' Henry smiled. 'I am giving a picnic by the river at Richmond next Wednesday and I would be honoured if you would accept this as an invitation. I shall be asking Sir Neville to attend, too. We must hope that this fine weather continues. We shall be assembling at Chiswick steps and will float down river to our rendezvous. Do say that you will come.'

'If I can. I must consult my diary when I reach home.' With that they bowed and parted.

Her head whirling, Diana made her way to her hostess to register her thanks before leaving. Had Henry Latimer been trying to tell her something? Where was Neville and what was he doing? Something dangerous, no doubt.

One thing was certain: when next she saw him she would pass on to him this curious conversation with Henry Latimer. Her last thought before leaving was that by his presence at Lady Leominster's dinner Henry Latimer could not be engaged on anything untoward on this particular evening if Neville and Jackson were prowling around London's seedier haunts looking for him.

At that very moment Neville was in the throes of breaking and entering a brothel with the help of a criminal and a onetime officer of the law. Thad, after they had smashed their way into Madame Josette's through a back window, led them upstairs to the meeting room on the first floor, forcing that door, too.

He then moved on to unlock the cupboards of which he had earlier spoken while Neville, who supposed that employing a criminal to make a forced entry made him as guilty as his accomplice, nevertheless helped Jackson to take from the cupboards the few pieces of paper that they contained.

Alas, there was nothing of the remotest interest in them. They were stained and dirty and the few dates on them were ten years old. As far as they could tell, they were a part of an inventory probably made when Madame Josette took over the premises.

Neville, a wry expression on his face, murmured, 'I seem to have made a criminal of myself for nothing.'

'Not quite,' Jackson told him, 'because, had you not done so we would never have known what the cupboards might have contained. Now we do.'

This piece of twisted logic might have set Neville laughing if the occasion had not been so serious, if not to say dangerous. As it was, he merely replied, 'Maybe so,' and looked carefully around the room as though it might have something to tell him.

Thad, meanwhile, had taken up a post at the head of the stairs, ready to warn the other two if he heard anyone about to mount them. Neville had hardly finished speaking before he ran into the room, whispering, 'We must hide, quite a large party is on its way up.'

Their leaving the room was much more rapid than their entering it, was Neville's sardonic thought—but where to go?

Thad, more used to this sort of game than he was, took him by the arm and led them rapidly down the corridor that ran away from the landing and the door. Thad had told them that they usually arrived one by one, but tonight the whole party appeared to be on the way.

Their leader was carrying a lantern whose light could be dimly seen in the alcove where Neville's party was hiding, although it was not possible for them to see the newcomers clearly enough to identify them. On the other hand, their progress up the stairs and along the landing to the door was so noisy that there was no chance that they could have heard Neville and his cohorts retreating.

An even noisier discussion took place when the door was found to be open before they all trooped in and shut it.

All three criminals heaved a sigh of relief. 'Except,' whispered Jackson, still being careful, 'that we have no notion of who they are and what they are doing.'

'Difficult to believe that they are engaged in wrongdoing,' Neville replied, 'when they were being so noisy.'

'True, but they may feel safe here—while we are not.'

Thad said, 'Let's leave, before we're caught. If you two gents don't mind hiding somewhere in the back alley, I'll go in and have a word with my mate Toby who's on duty tonight and try to winkle some information out of him about these fellows. Either of you got a couple of guineas on you?'

'I have,' offered Neville before Jackson could speak.

'Right, let's go.'

As gingerly as possible they made their way back to the stairs and from thence to the window through which they had entered. The alley was smelly and muddy, but by now Neville had stopped noticing such minor nuisances—he was far too busy hoping desperately that he was not going to end up in court again—or be forced to shoot another rogue. He had his small pistol concealed in his grimy clothing.

They found a deserted yard behind an empty building where Thad left them sitting on a barrel. 'Shan't be long, I hope,' was his somewhat glum farewell.

'And I'm hoping,' Neville muttered morosely, 'that my two guineas won't be such a temptation to Master Thad that he will disappear with them.'

'That's a risk we have to take,' was Jackson's dry reply.

Neville had never expected that villainy of this sort would be so varied. He was either being frightened to death—or putting someone to death. Time seemed to pass agonisingly slowly. Both men remained silent, not wishing to draw attention to themselves, until suddenly they heard the noise of the Watch approaching, whereupon Jackson muttered in Neville's ear, 'We must hide, and quickly.' He swung Neville towards the ruined building and its broken doorway, and pushed him inside. Since the night had become windy its shelter was welcome.

Another period of waiting followed while the Watch coughed, hawked and spat outside, wandering into the yard and out of it, swinging his lantern around, until finally he made off. Almost immediately after he had disappeared into the night and they were back on their barrels again, Thad arrived.

'Mum's the word,' he mouthed at them. 'They're on their way out by the back door, one by one this time. Toby had some news for me, but that'll do later.'

No sooner said than the first man appeared, walking slowly by the yard, but his top hat and muffler concealed his face, preventing the watchers from being able to recognise him.

One by one and at some distance apart, as Thad had said, they wandered by until the last man appeared, just as the breeze grew even stronger, so strong that it knocked the top hat from his head and it bounded along the ground. Shouting an oath so loud that the watchers could hear it, its owner bounded after it, his muffler falling away as he ran so that his face was plainly visible.

Neville did not know him, but Jackson obviously did. When the man had recovered his hat and was safely on his way, he turned to Thad. 'Your informant was right. That *was* Knighton and I'll be bound he's at his treasonable tricks again. Follow him home and then tomorrow morning give me the news of where's he's hiding now. There's been a warrant for his arrest waiting for him ever since he skipped to France. And while you're at it, keep a watch on Latimer, too.'

Neville was relieved to learn that they had gained something from the night's work, and although Thad had had no time to tell them of what he had learned from Toby, presumably about the girls, he would surely tell Jackson of it on the morrow.

'We cut line, then,' he suggested.

'Um…' Jackson was thoughtful. 'We might…' And then, 'No, we mustn't push our luck too hard. I know that we've smoked out a traitor at his dirty work, but we shall need to do much more in the way of surveillance if we are to find out who's running the trade in girls. Perhaps Thad did discover something. If so, we may need to risk ourselves all over again—so we'd better make for home and try to catch up on a little much-needed sleep.

'Come to my rooms tomorrow morning in the hope that Thad does have something useful to report on both our enquiries. I am sure that I need not tell you that it would be wise not to inform anyone of the nest of vipers that, by pure chance, we appear to have uncovered.'

So it was agreed.

But Neville could not sleep. In trying to solve the problem of the missing girls, they had come across something just as important that involved the fate of the country he loved and the Parliament in which he served. More than that, he was duty bound to say nothing of this to Diana, which would involve him in deceiving her once again.

He had to hope that Thad had something substantive to tell them about the girls.

Diana had hoped that Neville would visit her in the morning again, that period which stretched from rising from one's bed until some indefinite period after noon. No such thing, however. Time passed and no Neville arrived.

By one of the clock Diana's patience had run out. She decided that if Neville was not going to come to her, she would go one better and visit Jackson and demand—very politely—to be told what was going on. Accordingly she dressed herself as plainly as possible, ordered the landau for once, and had herself driven around to Jackson's rooms. By so doing she hoped to circumvent Neville and teach him that if he would not oblige her, Jackson might.

She had no real notion of why she was so cross with him, and would have been even more annoyed if she had known that Isabella, who had been watching her, had hit the nail on the head and had ruefully judged that she was pining for Neville.

Any hope of having a quiet, confidential meeting with Jackson disappeared after she had followed his landlady upstairs and had entered his rooms to discover that he and Neville were seated together, obviously in the middle of yet another meeting.

Neville had arrived at Jackson's rooms a little earlier in the hope that he might have some news for him. He was back in his normal clothing again and, to his surprise, far from being tired after the previous night's exertions, he felt more than ready to welcome the day.

'I thought that you'd be here at the crack of dawn to learn what Thad had discovered,' Jackson announced cheerfully. 'First of all, he has found out that Knighton is lodging in George Street off the Edgware Road under the name of Captain Johnson. A bribe to his landlady early this morning resulted in her telling him that he seemed to have a great number of visitors. He's been there about three weeks.'

'What do we do next?' Neville asked.

'We notify the Home Secretary, Lord Sidmouth, but it's unlikely that he'll have him arrested immediately since the Home Office will want to find out who the rest of the conspirators are. To do that they will probably keep an eye on him by using one or more of their informers, who will join him by pretending that they, too, want a revolution in Britain. All the conspirators will be rounded up and arrested at the last minute—just when they think that they're safe.'

'Exactly like the Gunpowder Plot.'

'Yes, and the fate of the leaders will be the same. The rest will be transported to Australia—which will be less than they deserve.'

'I'm not surprised, though,' said Neville quietly. 'We've had two terrible winters, the harvests have been dreadful, and many are starving. On top of that that large numbers of the soldiers who won the war for us have been turned off with a pittance. I don't condone what the conspirators are doing, but I can understand why they are doing it.'

'On the other hand...' Jackson shrugged.

'On the other hand, when I remember the misery that the revolution of 1789 brought to France and Europe, I can understand why Sidmouth is being so harsh on any radicals who try to start one here.'

They both nodded. Jackson said, 'Thad had some other news for us. It seems that his friend Toby was so shocked by the tale of the kidnapped young virgins that he passed on to us some valuable information. It's highly likely that Madame Josette's house and some of her regular gentlemen are involved. He named Henry Latimer and someone else called Frank Hollis, who I have never come across before, as possible go-betweens from several conversations he overheard.'

Frank Hollis! Frank Hollis, who had jeered at him for being too respectable! Neville gave a savage smile. It would be pleasant to give him something to think about—he might in the long run find that it would have been more profitable to have been respectable himself.

Something else struck him. 'I can believe that Madame Josette is involved in the trade in girls, but I find it difficult to believe that she would be engaged in helping Knighton to foment revolution.'

'Thad had some news for us about that, too. Toby told him that the upstairs party is rented by a gentlemen's club who meet there to drink privately because they can't afford anywhere more expensive. Some of them stay behind after the meetings to sample Madame's regular girls. It seems that no one knows what they're really up to.

'By the by, Thad says that you still owe him two guineas since he gave both yours to Toby as a reward for his information.'

Neville laughed at Thad's impudence, saying appreciatively, 'I don't object to that; on the contrary, it will be four guineas well spent. I'll leave two with you to give to him when next you see him. There is one thing that I still don't understand, however. Although Sir Stanford attempted to blackmail me about revealing the truth about my birth if I didn't stop my campaign, he must know that I took no notice of his threat, but nothing has happened, which is all to the good, of course, as it spares my poor mother.'

'I agree, that *is* odd, but it's possible that they may be delaying to fulfil the threat in the hope that you may yet change your mind since it must be plain that so far we have run up against a series of dead ends.'

'I suppose that may be the answer,' said Neville doubtfully. 'I can only hope so.'

It was at this point that Diana arrived.

Jackson bowed to her, saying, 'Ah, Mrs Rothwell, so pleased to see you,' for that was the name which Diana had again given his landlady.

'And I you, Mr Jackson,' she replied, before sitting down in the only comfortable chair in the room. 'I see that Sir Neville has been here before me.'

'Oh, no,' Neville retorted, 'if you are Mrs Rothwell, then I must be Ned Springer, a name Mr Jackson gifted me with last night. No Sir Nevilles wanted on our unofficial outing.'

That brought the colour to her cheeks and no mistake. 'Well, Mr Ned Springer,' she retorted. 'Did you learn anything useful from your last night's adventure? Since you are both sitting here obviously in fine fettle, I take it that nothing went wrong.'

'Only that we endured an exceedingly dull and uneventful night learning very little directly,' Neville told her. 'Mr Jackson's informant, a large gentleman known as Thad, paid his pal Toby at Madame Josette's two guineas of my money for information about the girls, from which it appears that Henry Latimer and his great friend, Frank Hollis, are almost certainly involved as go-betweens. Which is not, of course, proof of anything, other than that we were right to suspect Latimer.'

'I suppose that's something,' Diana said dubiously, 'but I have to tell you that Henry Latimer was present at Lady Leominster's dinner last night, and he said something that can only be construed as an indirect threat to you, Neville.'

'Another?' said Neville, raising his eyebrows. 'This is becoming tedious. What was it this time?'

'That it would be a good idea for me to recommend you to take a rest from your labours and retreat into the country for a long holiday in order to recuperate from them. The longer the better.'

'How very considerate of him, Mrs Rothwell. I take it that you heartily agreed with him.'

'Yes, but I did tell him that I would not be his messenger girl, and that he should make this excellent suggestion to you in person.'

'Splendid!'

'It isn't funny,' Diana said suddenly. 'You may be in great danger. Are you sure that you still wish to go on with your campaign?'

'Now, Mrs Rothwell, since you refused my suggestion to you that you ought to withdraw, why should you expect me to? Think, rather, that every time someone threatens me it merely serves to reinforce the notion that we may be getting nearer to the truth than the conspirators think is desirable. Isn't that so, Mr Jackson?'

Jackson, who had been watching and listening to this spirited interchange with some amusement, remarked gravely, 'Exactly so.'

'But we are not much further on, are we? We have no hard evidence against any particular person, only suspicions.'

This plain statement of fact was so true that there was nothing Neville or Jackson could say to refute it. Nor could they tell Diana that, quite by accident, they had uncovered a conspiracy designed to bring down the British crown and government, so that their evening's work had not been entirely wasted.

Something about their manner, she did not know what, made Diana suspicious of the pair of them.

'You *are* telling me everything that happened last night?' she demanded. 'Why do I have the feeling that you are not being entirely honest with me?'

Jackson's smile was that of a man who is doing his best to rebuff an unreasonable remark. 'Come, come, Mrs Rothwell, you cannot think that we would hide anything from you.'

'On the contrary, knowing you both, I am sure that if you thought it politic that you most certainly would. I will not play games with you over this, though, the matter is far too serious. I have to assume that you will find someone to watch Henry Latimer and Frank Hollis. I'm a little surprised that Frank was named—he's always seemed a rather empty fribble to me.'

'Empty fribbles tend to run out of money rather quickly,' Jackson said, 'and when offered what seems to be an easy, if unlawful, way of gaining some, they surrender to their first temptation very rapidly.'

Neville nodded. From what he had seen of Frank Hollis, this seemed a fair judgement of the man. Diana, although recognising this to be true, was still hooked on the notion that she was being deceived by the pair of them, but she decided that for the moment she would not pursue the matter further. What she would do was begin some private investigations of her own. Exactly how she would accomplish this she was not sure.

She would, though, pass on to them something that she thought significant. 'It might interest you to know that Henry Latimer seems to be on excellent terms with Prince Adalbert of Eckstein Halsbach, a man whose reputation where women are concerned is distinctly dubious.'

'Interesting,' said Jackson. 'I have heard rumours about him, but nothing definite. Yes, he might bear watching, too. It would help to explain why anyone who begins to question what is happening to the girls is being so ruthlessly pursued. Certain people in power would do anything to prevent a scandal that involved even a minor member of the royal family from becoming public knowledge. Think what the radical newspapers would make of it.'

They all considered this undoubted truth for several minutes. 'Even so,' Neville said. 'We must not let the consequences of that stop us from pursuing the matter, but I agree with Mr Jackson that it might explain why they are so desperate to silence us.'

Since Diana made no further attempt to try to provoke Neville and Jackson into telling her what it was that she was sure they were keeping from her, the meeting broke up and Neville and Diana made their farewells together. If Diana was angry at their duplicity, Neville was unhappy because of it. He could only console himself with the thought that it was for her own good, but the slight coolness between them that had grown up as a consequence of it served to distress him more than he would have thought possible.

Before they finally parted to go to their separate carriages he tried to make a rendezvous with her on the morrow, but although she gave him a sweet smile she also assured him that, for the moment, other engagements were taking up her time.

'But some time soon,' urged Neville desperately. The

havoc that the mere sight of her wrought in him was being hideously reinforced by the fact that it might be some time before they met again.

How was it that she had become so central to his life and thoughts that the idea of losing her was hateful to him?

Diana, for her part, was equally unhappy about banishing him from her life for the time being, but he would have to learn that she was not to be controlled by him or any other man. Since her husband's death, she had become a free spirit and her freedom was precious to her.

Chapter Twelve

'There seems to be no way of stopping him,' moaned Henry Latimer to Sir Stanford Markham. 'So far we've only dealt in vague threats—except the one about his mother, which was direct, but he simply ignored it. I thought that when he refused to oblige us we ought to have started running as many *on dits* as possible round society about the scandal of his birth and silenced him for good.'

'So did I,' said Sir Stanford grimly, 'but my superior told me that I should not have made the threat. It seems that he and Fortescue's mother were friends in youth and that he had something of a *tendre* for her before she was married off to Sir Carlton Fortescue and he would not like to see her distressed.'

'He'd be even more distressed if this business about the girls was made public,' said Henry savagely.

'True, but there it is. Better to try other ways of bringing Fortescue into line. How about threatening him through Duchess Diana?'

'Now, there's a thought,' exclaimed Henry, who dearly wanted to revenge himself upon Diana because she had so steadfastly held him off whenever he had tried to woo her. 'I doubt whether he'd ignore that. I could set Eckie on her.'

'No, no, Prince Adalbert's a loose cannon. No telling what he might say or do. No, a threat might be enough. Best, though, that you don't make it. You haven't mentioned our biggest worry, and that's the ex-Runner, Jackson. God knows why he can't content himself with doing his duty for the Home Office by keeping watch on all the dam'd radicals who infest this country, without him chasing round London helping that Don Quixote, Fortescue, as well.'

'Couldn't he be persuaded, if that's the right word, to drop the business?'

'Oh, persuasion's been tried, but even a regular beating doesn't seem to have stopped the fellow. I daren't do more, since Sidmouth prizes him so highly.'

'What a mess,' was Henry's contribution to that.

'Indeed. We must remember that Fortescue's the man to deter and soon. If all else fails, more drastic methods might have to be employed, but only as a last resort.'

'That's that, then, we try to reach him through Duchess Diana,' said Henry glumly.

'Unless you can think of a more tricky way of stopping him, yes.'

So it was decided.

Diana, meantime, was visiting her solicitors. They had in their employ a man named Dobbins, who had been one of their clerks and who carried out what they called rather difficult business for them. It was he who had investigated Diana's suitors for her in order to discover their true financial worth—she had no mind to marry a fortune hunter; indeed, her late husband had warned her against them more than once before his death.

'Henry Latimer, hmm,' said Mr Courtney Jenkinson, the chief partner. 'Yes, I've heard that his pockets are almost certainly to let despite, or because of, his extravagant way of life: On the other hand, there are no rumours running around that suggest that he is being dunned.'

As usual, Diana was surprised to learn how much the legal bigwigs in their offices in the Temple knew about those who circulated in London's highest society.

'I have heard,' she said cautiously, 'that he is engaged in a very shady enterprise, which is almost certainly illegal, and I would like to know whether there is any truth in the rumour. He has been pursuing me most diligently, and I would wish to avoid being a friend of anyone whose character is dubious.'

'Exactly. For that we shall have to engage Dobbins. You have no objection to him, I take it.'

'None at all.'

'Good, I shall put the matter in hand and notify you as soon as he has something useful to report. Is there anything else that we can do for you?'

Diana hesitated before adding, as though it were an afterthought, 'I did hear that a Mr Frank Hollis might be a partner of his. Perhaps Mr Dobbins could investigate him, too.'

'I will put it in hand immediately. Is that all?'

'I think so.'

'Should you learn anything more, pray let us know. Allow me to show you to the door.'

With much bowing and scraping he escorted Diana out. As soon as she had gone, he visited the office of his junior partner.

'Fred, you're on the edge of society through your cousins. Have you come across any odd gossip about one Henry Latimer?'

Fred looked up from his work. 'Only that he's too clever for his own good and runs with some queer fish.'

'Frank Hollis, perhaps?'

'Yes, and Prince Adalbert, that worthless cousin of the Princess of Wales. Why?'

'They say that you know a man by the company he keeps.

It seems that Henry Latimer has some deuced odd friends. It's just that his name cropped up recently and you seem to have confirmed my informant's judgement of him, that's all.'

It was never 'that's all' with Courtney Jenkinson; anything that he spoke of was very much to the point in some way or other, was Fred's wry conclusion. His superior's clientele was made up mostly of nobs and Fred wondered which of them was seeking advice about Mr Latimer. He had seen Duchess Diana leave Jenkinson's office, but he did not associate her with his master's sudden desire to know about Henry Latimer.

After all, she was only a woman and what did she know of the world in which men were everything and women were powerless nothings who were merely wives, daughters, sisters and widows, obedient creatures who found it wise to do as they were told. Which was all to the good, since they were so flighty that they would always be making the wrong decisions.

Jackson had once informed Neville that in his business patience was everything. Much time might pass when he learned very little about his current investigation, and then, suddenly, after weeks of nothing, everything happened at once. It seemed to Neville that they were very much in the doldrums and Jackson's optimism was growing wearisome.

He had to acknowledge that there hadn't been weeks of nothing yet, but his impatience was being heightened by the very little he was seeing of Diana. On top of that, the matter of Knighton seemed to have disappeared over the horizon. When he questioned Jackson about it, the only answer he got was that the matter was being taken care of.

Henry Latimer and Frank Hollis were being watched, but were apparently living blameless lives. Jackson's explanation for this was that they were both lying low. It was impossible to know whether girls were still being abducted or whether the trade had been temporarily halted in an effort to deter those who were trying to uncover it.

'You have been avoiding me,' Neville accused Diana when he finally encountered her at the Templestowes' ball. She was at her most radiant, wearing a gown of a colour as blue as her eyes, or the Medbourne sapphires that adorned her tiara and her necklace—to say nothing of her ear drops and the ring on her finger.

She opened her fan and looked at him over its top, her eyes shining defiance at him. 'Yes,' she finally said.

'You admit it, then?'

'Yes.'

'And you haven't missed me?'

'Of course I've missed you.'

'Then dance with me, you naughty minx.'

The latter flew out of him over a choke of laughter that was caused by the mischievous eyes staring at him over her fan.

'Ah, yet another order barked at me by his High Mightiness, Sir Neville Fortescue. Pray tell me why I should obey it.'

His answer stunned them both. 'Because I love you, dammit.'

What in the world was happening to him? Ever since that fateful night when he had overheard Frank Hollis dismissing him as a prig, his careful language and his equally careful conduct had been disappearing as fast as the French fleet at Trafalgar. Again, the mere sight of Diana had him behaving in the wildest manner—all at the behest of his wretched body which seemed to have acquired a life of its own so far as she was concerned.

Down, Rover, down, were the only words he could think of to end his uncomfortable condition—and they seemed to have no effect at all.

It might have been some consolation to him to know that

Diana was also flummoxed, if that was the right word to describe the effect he had on her whenever she saw him.

So long as he was out of sight she could tell herself that she would not flirt with him, would give him no reason to believe that, so far as she was concerned, meeting him was any different from meeting any other man. Instead, here she was, behaving like a hysterical schoolgirl at the first sight of a handsome suitor.

To make matters worse, while Neville was not the plainest of men, neither was he the most good-looking but, for her, he was everything she had ever wanted in the shape of a member of the male sex.

And now he had said that he loved her. In the middle of the Templestowes' ballroom, too.

Worse was to come. He seized her hand and said fiercely, 'Dance with me, Diana, or I shall disgrace myself by falling upon you here and now. Have you no notion of the power you have over me?' and he spun her on to the floor where a waltz was just beginning.

To everyone watching them as they dipped and swayed around, the strength of the passion that they felt for one another was immediately plain. She had stars in her eyes, his were fixed on hers with such intensity that no one could be deceived—even if they were trying to deceive each other.

Henry Latimer, watching them, ground his teeth. By God, he must tell Sir Stanford yet again that one way to bring Neville Fortescue to heel was to attack Diana, Duchess of Medbourne—or have Fortescue killed—which would certainly bring the fool's crusade to an untimely end. Not only that, he would benefit from Fortescue's death, for he had no chance of winning her for himself so long as his hated rival walked the earth.

Why wait for Sir Stanford, though? The sooner Fortescue was threatened with harm coming to Diana the sooner he might give way—and even if he did, it might be possible to persuade Sir Stanford that as a punishment for holding them off for so long he deserved nothing less than the most condign sentence of all: death.

No sooner had he decided on this than the waltz ended—but Diana and Neville were so engrossed with one another that they failed to hear the music end and had completed another circuit of the floor before they realised that they were alone on it.

They looked at one another and began to laugh. 'Dear Mrs Rothwell,' Neville said, 'we are making a public spectacle of ourselves—we ought to find a quiet corner away from everyone.'

'Oh, as to your first statement,' she told him while they walked back to where a disapproving Isabella was ready to reproach her, 'nothing to that, since I have been making a public spectacle of myself ever since the season began. As to the second, I agree with it heartily—so long as you behave yourself.'

'I'll try,' Neville told her, 'but if we are to retire I shall avoid handing you over to your resident dragon first. Let us make a detour by way of the most distant door from where she is sitting and I shall escort you to a corridor where I know Templestowe has a fine collection of paintings acquired by one of his ancestors on the Grand Tour. We can pretend to be looking at them if anyone finds us there.'

'How fortunate for you that I am a widow and thus am allowed a little latitude in the matter of being alone with an eligible gentleman.'

'Is that what I am? An eligible gentleman. I thought that I had forfeited that when I ended up in a magistrate's court.'

Diana's laugh was a genuine one. 'Oh, dear, no. Anyone as rich as your good self—as the lawyers say—is soon forgiven once the *on dits* have run down and have ceased to entertain society. Every mama with an unmarried daughter cannot fail to pursue you once she thinks of the size of your estate and that you bring a title with you—even if you are not a peer of the realm. Money gilds everything, you know—provided there is enough of it.'

There was almost a hint of bitterness in her voice, but Neville thought it best not to remark on it. Besides, he was too busy escorting her through the door and beginning to walk her down the corridor in anticipation of being, at last, alone with her, if only for a short time.

Halfway down the corridor was an oak bench, a legacy of the Tudor earl who had founded the Templestowes' fortunes at the time of the Dissolution of the Monasteries in the reign of King Henry VIII. He led her to it and found that they were opposite to the greatest masterpiece of the Templestowe collection. It was a huge painting by Tintoretto showing Venus tempting Vulcan, while her son, the infant Cupid, hovered overhead, a bow in his hand with which he was about to shoot the arrow that, on piercing Vulcan's heart, would make him mad with love for her.

'Is that why you brought me here?' Diana asked, once they were seated. 'So that I might see a picture portraying a seduction, thereby making me ready to be seduced?'

Neville shook his head. 'It's the wrong way 'round,' he said. 'Vulcan needs Cupid's arrow to persuade him to love Venus, whereas I love you, but I think that you might need Cupid's arrow in your heart in order to persuade you that you love me.'

Well, at least he was being frank about it—and it was the second time that evening that he had told her that he loved her. She loved him, but she dare not tell him so. She was not sure what was holding her back when only a short time ago she had almost thrown herself at him, he had not resisted her, and only at the last moment, panic-stricken, had she held him off.

Was it the sterile years that she had spent with Charles? Had they made her afraid of true passion since she had been content to share a white marriage with him and had thereby become convinced that that might be the safest relationship she could have with a man?

Was she, who was frightened of very little, fearful of the prospect of lying in a man's arms and giving herself utterly to him?

Surely not, but here she was, silent, while a good man spoke to her of love and she was making no answer to him, either of Yea or of Nay. She must say something, but what?

Finally she came out with, 'We are looking at a painting of the gods of Olympus, not of ordinary men and women.'

'True, but if you study the gods' behaviour carefully you will find that they were only ordinary men and women writ large. They were ruled by passion, as we are.'

Oh, he was a cunning devil who could chop logic as well as any lawyer!

Still she could not give him the answer he so dearly wanted. His look for her partook of the fierce when he asked, 'Are you playing with me, Diana? Teasing me? One might almost think you virgin with your sudden fits of reticence.'

This piece of insight resulted in all the colour disappearing from Diana's face and she began to tremble so violently that Neville stared at her aghast. He had touched something deep inside her. He began to tremble a little himself as he came to a conclusion that explained so many things about her.

He took her lax hand in his and kissed it. 'Look at me, Diana... Tell me the truth. You are a widow who had been married for many years—but can it be that you are truly virgin despite that?'

She left her hand in his, but turned her head away from him so that he might not see her quivering lips. 'Oh, Neville, how did you come to guess the truth of me when no one else has ever done?'

'Because I love you. Was it truly a white marriage that you shared with that old man?'

'Yes, and do not blame him. He was always kind to me. He taught me so much…' The sentence ended on a sigh.

'But not how men and women behave as husband and wife. And since you were so young when you married him you never had the opportunity to learn to live in a world where young men and women mixed freely. You were an only child, were you not? And then you became his child.'

Yes, it explained her many contradictions. The mixture of boldness and shyness with which she faced the world. Her shock that time when they had been alone together in her home when he had taken her in his arms and had begun to make love to her and she had been so overwhelmed by him that she had almost given herself to him there and then—only to start back at the last fence.

'Are you afraid of men—and of me—Diana?' he asked her gently.

'A little, I think.' And speaking so she turned at last to look at him, to add, 'Yes, I was his daughter—and at the time it seemed to be enough. Now, I am beginning to learn that it was not. Oh, Neville, you must be patient with me.'

'Always,' he said, 'for that is what love is about, and because I am a man and you are a woman I wish to protect you. You must understand that too.'

'I think,' she said carefully, 'that I resent that because Charles protected me all the time and, if I am honest, I began to feel stifled. I also began to wish to be able to control my own life—which I suppose is why I am a little reckless at times.'

'I could not bear anything to happen to you, Diana, you must know that. And now we must leave, I fear, with so many things yet to be discussed, because we have been alone together long enough for the gossips to start chattering about us. Come.' And he released her hand in order to stand up, whereupon he took it again in order to lead her back into the busy world.

The door to the ballroom opened even as they reached it, and there was Henry Latimer, walking towards them an ugly expression on his face as though he no longer cared to dissemble in front of them.

'So that's where you were. The paintings must be enormously interesting for you to have spent so long admiring them.' It was a tacit admission that he had been watching them from the moment they had left the dance floor.

'True,' returned Diana, 'and Sir Neville has been giving me a most interesting talk about them and the gods of Olympus who so frequently appear in them.'

'One can always depend on Sir Neville to play the pedant, I find,' was Latimer's mocking answer to that.

Neville found it difficult to control his anger at this sneering dismissal of him, but he thought it politic, for Diana's sake, to make a noncommittal reply. 'At least it has the advantage of being a relatively harmless one.'

'Which, I suppose—' this time Latimer's sideways glance at Diana was little less than a leer '—is because it's the only kind of game you can play.'

That he was trying to provoke him was plain, but Neville was still not prepared to satisfy him with a hot reply although the devil of it was that if he simply walked away from Latimer he would spread it abroad that Sir Neville Fortescue was such a cur that he was prepared to swallow any insult.

Instead, he smiled, and took Diana gently by the elbow. 'Oh, I do know other games, innocent ones, which cause no hurt to others who might play them with me, but this is neither the time nor the place to discuss them. Besides, I am thirsty as, I am sure, is the Duchess, so I suggest that she repairs with me to the supper room before we both say something in front of her that we might regret.'

Once they had reached the supper room, Diana turned to Neville and said simply, 'Thank you for not creating a scene—although he dearly wished that you would.'

Neville's answer was a shrug. 'The last thing we need is a public scandal—and if he thinks me a coward so much the better. He'll be inclined to be a little more rash when he next insults me.'

Diana nodded. She was debating whether to tell Neville that she had employed Dobbins to investigate Henry Latimer, but thought that under the circumstances it might be tactful not to. If the man came up with nothing, then nothing need be said, but if he were successful, then and only then would she need to make a decision.

The rest of the evening was uneventful. They agreed to part to silence the gossips who were eyeing them avidly. Isabella pouted at Diana, but was wise enough to say nothing. Neville spoke to Lord Burnside who, it turned out, had recently visited his mother.

'I hope that you don't object to me renewing my acquaintance with her, but I was pleased that I did. She seemed most happy to see me, particularly when I told her that you were a credit to her upbringing of you. We agreed to be friends again.'

Well, that was one way of putting it, Neville thought, but all the same his mother led a lonely life and having her old beau in it again might cheer her up a little.

'I think it very sensible of you both.'

'And that other business,' his father said. 'Are you still pursuing it?'

'Yes, but with very little success. Since no rumours have been started about you, my mother and myself, I am hoping that my enemies have had the decency not to publish the truth, which would be embarrassing for us all if publicly revealed.'

'No need to worry overmuch,' said m'lord robustly. 'I am too old to be shamed by something that happened so many years ago, and your mother agrees with me. Speak the truth and shame the devil, I say. The whole business was no fault of yours.'

'My fault, though, if it looks as though I am getting near to the truth and my enemies think to revive it.'

'True, but let us not anticipate events that may never happen.'

So that was that and Neville went home comforted by having spent an evening that had brought him closer to Diana as a result of his having solved the enigma which she presented to him. He wondered how many secrets like Diana's and Lord Burnside and his mother's lay behind the serene face that many in society presented to the world!

Diana discovered that having told Neville of her virginity had brought her a new-found peace of mind, whereas before she had always worried about what his—and her—reaction might be if she were to confess the truth about her marriage to Charles.

She became much kinder to poor Isabella and the hot temper that she had been suffering recently cooled down a great deal. She was at peace with the world. Consequently, when at the end of the week after the Templestowes' ball she received an urgent summon to visit her solicitors, she supposed that Dobbins had something to report about Henry Latimer.

She entered Courtney Jenkinson's office to find him wearing a most grave face.

'Pray sit down, your Grace, I have some sad news to impart to you.'

Diana wondered what it might be. She was to find out immediately.

'You may remember that when you were last here I told you that I would employ a man named Dobbins to investigate one Henry Latimer for you.'

'Indeed.'

'He made his first visit to me after forty-eight hours, saying that he had found someone who had promised to give him as much information as he could about Mr Latimer's conduct and concerns. He was to meet him that evening and he would report back the next morning.

'The next morning came, however, but no Dobbins. I thought little of it, until yesterday afternoon a woman visited me in a most distressed state. It was Dobbins's wife. She told me that he had been missing since the day on which he had promised to report to me. A policeman had visited her that morning and asked her to accompany him to the mortuary to inspect a body that had been found near London Bridge. They believed it to be that of her husband.

'It was his. He had been murdered, they said. They asked her if she knew who might have done it, but since he told her nothing of his work she could not help them. Her husband had also told her never to speak of his connection with us to anyone, particularly the police, but she thought it only right to inform us of his death.'

He paused. Diana's face was the colour of ash. 'Murdered,' she whispered, 'murdered when he was carrying out an errand for me.'

'I fear so, but you must not reproach yourself. His tasks were not usually dangerous, but this one seems to have been and you could not have known that.'

Oh, but I could, she thought numbly. *Neville told me that it might be but I didn't take any notice of him, nor did I warn Mr Jenkinson.*

She was so pale and silent that Mr Jenkinson murmured, 'Would you care for a glass of water? I fear that this news has distressed you.'

'Water, please, and yes, I am distressed. This woman is his widow, you say. Does she have children?'

'Two, I believe.'

'How will she live, now that her husband is dead?'

Mr Jenkinson had not thought of that. 'I expect it will be difficult for her since he was the breadwinner.'

'No!' Diana exclaimed. 'He died carrying out an errand for me, so I feel responsible. Give me the details of her address and the arrangements made for his burial. I will create a trust and settle a sum on her, not only to pay for that but also to ensure for her a weekly income, which will take care of her and her children for the future, or until she marries again.'

'That is most kind of you, your Grace—'

'Not kind at all, it is my duty and my responsibility. You will inform her that the money comes from a trust that looks after distressed poor people like herself.'

He warned me, Neville warned me, I took no notice of him and because of that a man is now dead. I must tell Neville and what will he think of me then?

This thought filled Diana's mind all the way home. She arrived there in a state of distress. Isabella was waiting for her and knew immediately that something was wrong. She had seldom seen Diana look so wan and cheerless.

'Are you ill, my dear?' she asked, considerate for the first time in weeks. 'Have you had some bad news?'

'Yes,' Diana said, 'but forgive me if I do not wish to speak of it to you. It does not directly concern either of us.' Which was, of course, true so far as it went.

'Shall I ring for something to drink? It might make you feel a little better. While you are waiting for it, you might like to look at this letter for you, which arrived here by a special messenger and is marked urgent.'

'Very well…' Diana sank into an armchair '…a drink would be most welcome. Not tea, coffee would be better.' She took the letter from Isabella, wondering whether it was a message from Neville and, if so, what it could be that he needed to write to her so urgently?

It was not his elegant script on the envelope, but that

proved nothing. The seal was anonymous, too, and she tore the letter open, wondering what it might contain.

The message inside was brutally brief, and she later thought that it was a good thing that she was already ashy pale as a result of the news of Dobbins's murder or Isabella might have feared for her when she had finished reading it, so shocked was she.

It said, 'If you don't stop poking your pretty little nose into other people's business you will lose it—and your life, too.'

For one horrible moment she thought that she was going to faint before anger followed fear and made her determined to show no weakness. How dare they! On the way home she had decided that she would make Neville happy by withdrawing from any further involvement with his campaign, but not now. She would not be cowed into submission by the vile curs who traded in the bodies of poor young girls.

If, as she suspected, it came from Henry Latimer, then all that he had achieved was to make her even more determined to continue to help Neville. Not only that, by assisting him she might be able to achieve revenge for poor Dobbins's murder as some assuagement for her share of guilt in it.

Once she had recovered her usual calm self she would visit Neville and tell him everything.

Neville, seated at his desk in his study, unaware that Diana had been directly threatened, was staring at the anonymous letter that had arrived that morning and which warned him that if he did not end his campaign it would be the worse not only for him and Jackson, but also for Diana—particularly Diana.

It was the last bit that frightened him the most. It became more and more imperative that not only must she stop trying to help him, but she must also agree that they would meet as little as possible and when they did, they would behave as though they had quarrelled and were no longer interested in one another.

It would break his heart to lose her company, even for a short time, but her safety was paramount, and he could only hope that it would not be too long before they might be together again.

He had just made this sad decision when the butler entered and informed him that he had a visitor—her Grace, the Duchess of Medbourne was asking to see him on a matter of some urgency.

'Show her in here,' he said, for the sooner he broke the news to her, the better. He wondered how she would receive it, but it was up to him, in the light of this letter, to do his utmost to prevail on her to retreat into private life.

Diana knew, the moment she entered, that something was wrong. Neville's drawn face when he walked to greet her told her everything.

'What is it?' she asked. 'Has something horrid happened?'

'Very horrid,' he said, his voice low. 'Sit down and I will tell you.'

'Only if you sit down, too. I, also, have something to tell you, but perhaps, since you are my host, you ought to go first. I wonder which of us has the more horrid tale to tell.'

She tried to make her tone as light as possible, but she could not deceive him.

'No, you must speak first,' Neville said, for although she was putting on a brave face he knew her well enough to be aware that, beneath it, she was greatly troubled.

'Yes, and your horrid cannot be worse than mine, so let me be the first to speak since they say that confession is good for the soul and my soul needs good doing to it.' She drew her letter from her reticule.

She was usually ready-tongued, but this afternoon she was strangely hesitant and when she spoke all the lightness had disappeared from her voice and her face and manner could not have been more sombre.

'I have something to confess to you, Neville. When you told me not to assist you in the matter of the girls I went home and decided that I would not be told by you, or any man, how I ought to behave. Accordingly, after much thought, I visited my lawyers and asked them to employ an investigator, to find out as much as he could about Henry Latimer and Frank Hollis whom I believed were engaged in breaking the law.

'Dobbins had done some work for me before, through my lawyers; in fact, they had recommended him to me when I needed someone to look into the background of the many young men who were trying to marry me—and very useful his information turned out to be.'

So far her voice had been steady and controlled but suddenly, to Neville's surprise, her whole manner changed. Tears sprang into her eyes and rolled down and she began to sob uncontrollably, fumbling in her reticule to bring out a minute handkerchief with which she began, ineffectually, to dab her eyes.

Neville, pulling a spotlessly clean, and large, handkerchief from his breeches' pocket, said, 'Allow me,' and pressed it into her hand.

'Forgive me,' she whispered when she could speak again. 'I have not cried over this before, but, oh, Neville, how I wish that I had obeyed you when you asked me not to meddle before I hired poor Dobbins.

'This morning I learned that he had been found dead, murdered in my service, leaving behind him a young wife and two small children. You have no notion how guilty I feel. I have arranged for his widow and children to be looked after financially, but that does not bring back to life a dead husband and father. I cannot forgive myself for sending him to his death, and how can *you* forgive *me* for not heeding your advice?'

She began to cry again. Neville rose from his chair to kneel beside her, and try to comfort her.

'Hush, my love, do not blame yourself overmuch. From what you have told me, this was his way of life and he must have known the risks he was taking. Yes, you will feel guilty, particularly over not heeding me, but I understand why you behaved as you did, and I should not have been so severe, so domineering with you.'

Diana murmured brokenly, 'But that is not all. On the way home I decided to do as you had asked, and would come today to so inform you. However, when I reached home, I found this letter waiting for me,' and she handed it to Neville for him to read.

He walked back to his desk to read it, his face changing while he read each threatening word.

'Oh, my darling, how dreadful for you, and to receive it after hearing of Dobbins's death, too. You must cease to help me.'

'Oh, no, Neville. After reading it I changed my mind.' She went on to tell him of the conclusions she had reached and that, whatever the cost, she would do her best to bring not only those who exploited the girls to justice, but also, those who had caused Dobbins to be murdered.

'I will not let them cow me. How dare they threaten me? I will not crawl away to hide, my honour will not let me. I will not be threatened. What they did not know was that, if they had left me alone, I would have done as they wished.'

She had stopped crying and her eyes were wild.

'You must not put yourself at risk,' he said.

'It is they who have put me at risk—by their threats.'

Neville thought a moment before replying, 'Yes, in a way you are right. Now that they have threatened you directly— twice—the game has changed because they have brought you into it.' He handed her his letter, which threatened both of them.

She read it and then said, 'They are using me to prevent you from carrying on.'

'Indeed, and if you wish me to stop—and I can well understand why you might—then, however much it grieves me, I will obey you.'

'No. Have you not listened to what I was saying?'

'You really wish me to continue?'

'Yes, yes, and yes.'

'Then I will, and I will also try to protect you, as best I can.' He told her of his scheme: that they should pretend to have quarrelled and parted, but at the same time they would secretly continue their crusade. 'It will be dangerous, for both of us. Before we put anything in hand, though, we must meet with Jackson—as secretly as possible—tell him our news and ask him for his opinion.'

And so it was settled. By first killing Dobbins and then by threatening Diana—twice—they had provoked him into changing his mind about her assistance.

'I must see them hanged,' she told him before returning to Medbourne House, 'in order to gain my revenge for the murder of Dobbins.'

Neville looked at her determined face. In her present mood she reminded him of another Diana: the goddess who was not only a virgin but also a huntress, determined to destroy those who had offended her.

Chapter Thirteen

Jackson approved of Neville's stratagem, though, once he had heard their news, and bearing in mind the threats that had been made against them, he told them that they both ought to withdraw and leave it to him to track down the criminals.

It was Diana who answered him, and passionately. 'Indeed, not, you must understand that it has now become a point of honour to me—and to Sir Neville—that we must do all that we can to expose the hypocrites who are using their power and position to commit great crimes. Besides, if they do try to attack us, they may make mistakes that we could use against them.'

This mad piece of optimism set Jackson frowning. 'You really must not put yourself in danger, your Grace.'

Diana interrupted him to say, 'Mrs Rothwell here, if you please. I'm beginning to be very tired of all the bowing and scraping which goes with being a Duchess.'

'Mrs Rothwell, then. But don't underestimate the determination and ruthlessness of those against whom we are fighting. I say fighting because it is indeed a battle in which we are now engaged—and a battle in which the other side will show no quarter.'

His manner was so sombre that, for once, it silenced Diana.

'Nevertheless,' Neville said. 'We are equally determined and the right is on our side. Evil can only triumph if good men do nothing.'

He was quoting Edmund Burke, the late great statesman who, alone out of all the philosophers, had seen that the French Revolution would end in the rise of a monster such as Napoleon had proved to be, even though he had died before Napoleon rose to power.

'That may be true,' Jackson said, 'but I must warn you that there will always be those who become martyrs before the final triumph of good over evil is achieved.'

After that they discussed ways and means, but more and more it seemed to the three of them that they might have reached *point non plus,* where they knew who some of the villains were but had no proof of their villainy that could be used against them.

'The truth is, though,' Diana told Neville when they were alone again in his Chelsea home, 'that we shall only be able to scotch them if they do make a move against us and we can somehow corner them.'

Neville said, aghast that she had taken so little heed of Jackson's warning, 'I must insist again that you are to undertake nothing that might run you into danger. Indeed, if we make it plain that we have quarrelled and parted, it is likely that they will not attack you, that is, if you do nothing untoward—such as trying to hire another informer.'

'I promise you that I will not do that again, but remember that *you* will still be their target.'

'Indeed, I cannot forget, but I shall go carefully, you may be sure of that.'

Except, of course, that he had no notion of who the most powerful of their enemies might be and by what means they would try to silence him permanently.

* * *

Sir Stanford Markham was talking urgently to Henry Latimer. 'Yes,' he told him. 'I am being badgered from on high over this business, if it were discovered and it was thought that I had done nothing to stop the consequent scandal I should undoubtedly be sacrificed. You may do as you wish now that you have discovered that the Duchess, Fortescue and Jackson are still after us. The Duchess is their weak point, of course.

'We should have acted against Fortescue earlier, using the scandal of his birth, but my superior was too soft hearted and it is now too late to use it. If anything were to happen to her, however, it would surely be enough to stop either Fortescue or Jackson from further interference lest they too end up in the Thames one evening.'

'Have you heard that, after all their public demonstrations of affection, Duchess Diana and Neville Fortescue have quarrelled and are no longer on speaking terms? Why, only yesterday when he walked up to her at my soirée she cut him dead. You have never seen such a Friday face on anyone before. He has taken it very badly and no mistake!'

Emily Cowper was, as usual, excitedly retailing the latest piece of scandal to a group of women in Almack's rooms where everyone who was anyone in society gathered in the evening to dance, eat, drink, gamble and, above all else, engage in titillating gossip.

Lady Leominster remarked, thoughtfully for her, 'It seems very strange to me, particularly since she appears to be more triumphant than sorry—something which I would not have expected of her.'

'They say that she has taken up with Henry Latimer.'

'Now that I will not believe,' riposted Lady Leominster. 'Yes, it is strange indeed.'

Determined to discover the truth, she cornered Diana, who was present as the guest of George Alford, and quizzed her with the words, 'What game are you and Neville Fortescue playing? I would lay odds that you are both busy bamming us all, but why, I cannot imagine.'

To Diana's horror, she said this in her best Town Crier's voice so that quite a number of people around them, including Sir Stanford Markham, could hear her every word. For once the wretched woman had got hold of the right end of the stick and, as usual, she would not let go of it.

'No bamming,' returned Diana. 'We differed strongly on a number of things and I thought it best for us to end our friendship. I am afraid that Sir Neville took it very badly, but that is his worry, not mine.'

If she had believed that this would silence Lady Leominster, she was quite mistaken.

'Nonsense,' she bellowed. 'I think that you are playing a pretty game with us all, but never mind. When, in the future, I am proved to be right I shall expect a suitably contrite apology from the pair of you. In the meantime, believe that you may be deceiving others, but not me.'

Diana's distress was increased by the fact that Sir Stanford was now listening avidly to every word and would doubtless be wondering whether the wretched woman was correct in her assumption. If he believed that she was speaking the truth, then all the trouble that she and Neville were taking to persuade people they were now at loggerheads was being wasted.

She also wondered how they could possibly have given themselves away to her lunatic Ladyship, but that was the least of her worries.

She said, as icily as she could, 'I can only inform you how happy I am that he is not present tonight. I have heard that he has been haunting Renton Nicholson's dubious establishments and, if so, I am even more happy that we have ended our friendship—for that is all it was. And now may we converse on other matters, since I find this one tiresome.'

Her ladyship tossed her head, and said no more about her

and Neville until, as she left to badger other victims, she leaned forward and whispered, 'You don't bam me, Duchess, even if you have succeeded in bamming others.'

Among whom it was possible that she might now no longer count Sir Stanford Markham—with all that that might imply. Even as Diana thought this the man himself approached her, bowing low when he reached her.

'I can only congratulate you on your break with Sir Neville Fortescue. The man is a naïve fool, not worthy to consort with one who has been trained so well by your late—and remarkable—husband, who was anything but naïve as, of course, you must have been well aware.'

'Very true.' Diana tried to sound cool and distant, even though she was being racked by inner turbulence. 'I had not known that you were acquainted with him.'

'Many years ago, I fear, long before he married you. I always thought it a pity that he was such a recluse—he would have made a remarkable Prime Minister.'

As these unctuous compliments to her late husband were cascaded over her, Diana scarcely knew how to reply other than to bow in return, and thank God that George Alford was arriving to escort her to the supper room away from the greasy hypocrite whose very presence she found offensive, knowing what she did of the life he lived behind his mask of virtue.

'Thought you'd like to be rescued from him,' George told her in the supper room. 'Prosy old bore, ain't he? Some champagne wouldn't come amiss after your having to endure first her mad ladyship and then that pestilential old fool.'

She accepted the champagne offered to her, and talked engaging nonsense to George, who immediately decided that he would be a fool not to take his place in the queue of suitors who were lining themselves up now that Diana and Neville had parted.

But later, when he spoke of his ambition to Henry Latimer, that gentleman surprised him by saying curtly, 'Nonsense. For once I believe that Lady Leominster had the right of the matter: they are bamming us all—or trying to.'

'She thought that we were bamming everyone, as indeed we are, but why should she think that?' Neville was incredulous.

They were talking in Neville's refuge in Chelsea. Diana had driven herself there, alone, dressed in her boy's clothes, without giving her grooms any notion of where she was going. She could only imagine the scandal that would follow if her secret excursions became public knowledge.

'I've no notion. I was under the impression that we were both fit for auditions at Drury Lane since we were acting so well, particularly after I snubbed you so heartily at Emily Cowper's soirée. The devil of it was that this came out in high alt immediately in front of Sir Stanford, who then approached me and talked rubbish about your naïveté.'

'So, in a few badly chosen words, she demolished our little pantomime, you think?'

'I fear that may be true.'

'I think,' Neville said slowly, for Diana's presence was having its usual strong effect on him, 'that we ought to stop these meetings. You might be followed.'

She was silent. It was hard enough for her not to be able to meet Neville in public without pretending that she hated him, but not to meet him at all in private would be even worse.

They looked at one another. Wisdom told them both that they ought not to continue, but wisdom had little to do with what they were feeling for each other. Neville could not stop himself. His eyes fixed on Diana's, he moved forward, took her in his arms and kissed her, not gently on the cheek, but firmly on the lips.

Diana did not resist him. She gave a little moan and kissed him back, fiercely. For several delirious minutes they surren-

dered to their mutual passion. A shared danger had only succeeded in making it the more powerful. His hands roamed her
body, slipped her short jacket off her shoulders, and it was
only when he began to unbutton her shirt that Diana grasped
that if she did not stop him now, she would not be able to if
their lovemaking went any further. The possible consequences
of that, both physical and moral, shocked her—the fate of
those who were openly caught breaking society's rules was
never far from her mind.

'No! We must not. It is bad enough that we are meeting in
secret. How much worse will it be if I become your light of
love?'

Neville murmured hoarsely, 'Never my light of love—but
always my true love.'

'If you really mean that, then you will release me.'

Reluctantly he let her go. 'I'm sorry,' he told her, 'but when
we are together you overwhelm me.'

They stared at one another for a moment before Diana, not
acknowledging his last statement because she did not know
how to answer it, said, 'We shall have to continue this stupid
masquerade for the time being. Sir Stanford might not suspect
it is a masquerade. Besides, it's possible that either we or
Jackson might yet discover some evidence, which will mean
that we can go to the Home Office and abandon all pretence.'

'True,' Neville muttered, his frustrated body still aching
from what they had so briefly shared, wondering whether he
was glad or sorry that she had stopped him from making love
to her. On balance, glad won. Suppose that they had consummated their mutual passion and she had become pregnant as
a result? It did not bear thinking of.

'We'll pin our hopes on Jackson,' he finally said.

'Excellent. I'll visit you tomorrow morning, in case Jackson
has some news for us. I refuse to be cowed by our enemies.
We may pretend to be at outs in public, but not in private.'

He could not deny her, only said, 'But not alone or in boy's clothes, I beg of you.'

'It shall be as you wish.'

The next morning Jackson arrived back from the Home Office where the final measures designed to trap Knighton at the very moment when he started his proposed uprising had been determined on.

He found a man waiting for him in his rooms, a stranger plainly dressed who said without preamble, 'Your landlady admitted me because I told her the matter was urgent.'

'And is it?' Jackson asked.

'Yes. My name is William Dobbins. I am the brother of a man who was murdered recently. Before his death he told me that he was working for a firm of solicitors on a very important matter for an unnamed client. He told me that he thought that he might be in danger because from what he had already discovered certain highly placed people would like to see him abandon his enquiries. Indeed, he had been threatened that it was not safe for him to continue them.

'He told me the names of the men whose activities he had been investigating and what he had already discovered about them, and I was to come to you if aught happened to him and to ask for your assistance in catching those who were threatening him.

'Two days later his body was hauled out of the Thames. He had, the police say, been murdered before he was thrown in, so I have come to you as he bade me.'

'I take it that you are not in his line of business,' Jackson asked.

'Far from it. I am a clerk in a solicitor's office, as he was for some few years, but he found the work tedious. His employers discovered that they needed someone at short notice to carry out secret investigations for them, he offered to take the work over and has been so employed ever since.'

He paused. 'I don't think that he believed that those who threatened him would go so far as to kill him.'

'But they did,' finished Jackson.

'Yes, so will you help me? He was only trying to trap bad men, who finally trapped him.'

'I will help you,' Jackson said. 'Tell me all that you know, but I cannot promise you that I may be able to find them and bring them to justice.'

He did not inform the distressed man before him of Neville and Diana's involvement and that his brother had been working, indirectly, for Diana; the less anyone knew of that the better.

'He had been following two people. One of them, Henry Latimer, is supposed to be a moneyed gentleman, although my brother doubted that. The other, Frank Hollis, is another dubious character who, like Latimer, will do anything for money. He was beginning to amass evidence that Latimer was engaged by certain persons of importance to kidnap young women, supposedly virgins, and sell them to a brothel that supplied them to rich clients who would pay the Madame good money for them. Some of it went to Latimer, who was also earning a great deal of money by cheating at cards.

'He told me that he had discovered that Latimer had plans to kidnap a wealthy lady of title whom he knew to be suspicious of their activities. Once he had had his fun with her, he proposed to sell her to Madame Josette so that she might, unwillingly of course, entertain her clients. Hollis seems to be a lesser player in the game.

'My brother did not know who she was, but he thought that it was possible she might be the client of his employers. He was shortly to meet an informer who was ready to give him her name so that he could warn her.'

Jackson knew very well that Dobbins's unknown lady was Diana Medbourne and that Neville's fear for her was fully justified. Both she and Neville ought to learn of this latest development.

'I will do all in my power,' he told Dobbins before sending him away, 'to try to find and punish the men who murdered your brother. No, do not speak to me of payment until I succeed in avenging him. This is a duty I must undertake. I will send word to you immediately if I discover anything useful. Do not come to me again, since someone might be following you.'

Time and tide wait for no man was one of Jackson's favourite maxims so he decided that he would not waste any in sending letters to Diana and Neville. Instead he immediately called a cab and was driven to Neville's Chelsea home to suggest to him that they ought to visit Diana as soon as possible and arrange for her to be guarded day and night. His journey was a difficult one for Knighton's followers were already beginning to fill the streets.

He arrived at last, to be told by Lem that he had just brought Neville's carriage 'round in order to drive him to Medbourne House. The Duchess had arranged to visit his master early that morning with some further information, but she had never arrived. She was now some hours late and Sir Neville had begun to worry that something might be amiss. He was upstairs readying himself for the journey.

After his interview with William Dobbins, this news also worried Jackson. He remembered that he had recently told Neville that it was commonplace in his line of work for a lengthy period of time in which little, or nothing, would happen, to be followed by one in which so much occurred that it was difficult to keep up. Whether that was for good or ill, they could never know. As Neville said, once he had come downstairs to find Jackson, as well as a carriage, waiting for him, the sooner they reached Medbourne House, the better to find out why she had been delayed.

'Indeed,' replied Jackson, 'particularly since the information that I received this morning from Dobbins's brother about Henry Latimer and possibly Frank Hollis means that her life may be at risk.'

'He said that!' Neville exclaimed when Jackson had finished his story. 'By God, I'll kill him if he as much as touches her!'

'Before that,' returned Jackson prosaically. 'We must be on our way as soon as possible to find out whether she is in trouble, or whether she has simply been delayed by Knighton and his followers.'

Neville could scarce contain himself on the journey, his fear for his beloved was so strong. The moment the carriage stopped he jumped out on to the gravel sweep and, trying not to sound too agitated, ran up the steps to ask the butler, 'Is the Duchess at home? I need to speak to her at once.'

Instead of leading him to the drawing room, the butler stared at him, remarking stiffly, 'She is not in at the moment, Sir Neville, and I have no notion where she might be. She left, at half past nine of the clock, in the small chaise with one of the grooms driving, and without Mrs Marchmont in attendance, saying that she would be back in about an hour and a half. That time has long gone and Miss Marchmont is very worried. I will take you to her immediately.'

He had no time to do any such thing before the drawing-room door was flung open, and Mrs Marchmont, who had, from her post by the window, seen Neville's carriage arrive, walked into the hall, also in a state of great agitation.

'Pray come in at once, Sir Neville,' she exclaimed. 'I trust that you might have some suggestion as to where in the world Diana might be. It is most unkind of her to disappear like this and for such a great length of time—it is almost nuncheon!'

Her face was white and, for all her fussy ways, it was apparent that she really cared for Diana since she had omitted all the formal courtesies that Neville's visit would usually have had her performing.

He took her hand in his, bade her sit down, and said gently, 'We must hope that there is nothing for us to worry about, but I have to tell you that she had arranged to visit me this morning around ten of the clock, but that she never arrived.'

Isabella was so distressed by this that she began to wring her hands. Jackson, who had so far remained quiet, said in as kind a voice as he could muster so as not to distress her further, 'I take it that you did not know that she was visiting Sir Neville?'

'No, indeed,' she said. 'She knew quite well that, begging your pardon, Sir Neville, I would not have approved of such a visit. Why are you asking me that, Mr...?' And she raised her eyebrows at him.

'Because someone in this household might have known in which direction she would be driving—which might be useful if we have to start looking for her. Did she always take a groom with her?'

'No, and that was another thing I thought unwise, for her to drive herself anywhere, quite alone. I reproached her about it several times, saying that she was running needless risks, so I was happy to learn that one of the grooms was driving her this morning.'

Jackson looked at Neville, 'I think that we ought to visit the stables,' he said, 'without making too great a fuss about her apparent disappearance.'

'Who is this man, Sir Neville,' Isabella shrilled at him, 'that he should be asking me questions and giving you instructions?'

To inform her that he was an ex-Bow Street Runner might make her shriller and more worried than ever—and to no purpose—so Neville said instead something which was almost the truth.

'He is an official from the Home Office, Mrs Marchmont,

who was visiting me on another matter. I was worried about the Duchess's failure to arrive this morning, she usually being so punctual. Given the unhappy temper of the times, we came here straight away to discover whether she had left home.'

This satisfied Isabella somewhat and she grudgingly ordered the butler to escort Neville and Jackson to the stables to interview the head groom, Corbin.

Unfortunately they learned little of use to them since they were trying not to give too much away, but it turned out that he, too, was worried that the Duchess had not yet returned, and even more so when Neville told him that she had never arrived at her destination.

'A steady fellow, Gilbert,' he said, shaking his head. 'He has a really safe pair of hands and knows London well. I'd trust him not to do anything stupid—so he's the one I allus pick to drive her. They should certainly be back home by now. Worrying, that.'

'Yes,' Jackson said, 'but I gather that there has been a mob with banners out on the streets since dawn, making their way into central London, so it is likely that they may have been delayed. Sir Neville's driver had heard wind of it and as a precaution took a different—and longer—route from Chelsea.'

'Aye, and here I was rather pleased that she was being driven there in the chaise, for once, like the great lady she is. She often dresses in lad's clothes to drive herself in the phaeton that the old Duke had given her. He said that she was better with horses and carriages than most men and wearing breeches made it easier for her. I can't say that I approved of such goings on, especially in London, but today she most particularly asked for Gilbert to drive her to Chelsea in the chaise, instead.'

Because, both Jackson and Neville privately thought, we told her to take care and not wander around on her own. So she listened to us and now there are two people missing, not one. We ought to have insisted that she did not leave Medbourne House for the time being.

'We might,' Jackson told Corbin before they left, 'be making a great to-do about nothing, but whether she is safe or sorry we must try to find out where she is. It is even possible that she might not be in any danger, but that Gilbert has been caught in the crowd and has had to take a roundabout route.'

'I wish I could believe that,' Neville said when they were back in his carriage again.

'Aye,' said Jackson. 'My advice is that we ought to pay a visit to first Frank Hollis and then Henry Latimer. In the present state of the streets it's pointless to wander round London looking for her. From what I have heard of Hollis, I think that we might be able to persuade him to tell us what he knows—if he knows anything, that is. We seem to be chasing shadows.'

Neville could not but agree—only Diana was not a shadow, but the flesh-and-blood woman whom he loved, of whom he constantly thought and whom he hoped to persuade to marry him. He uttered a silent prayer for her on the way to Hollis's home, not far from the Albany.

Afterwards Diana was to think that everything went awry that morning from the moment when they were first slowed down, not long after she had left home, by the marchers, organised by Captain Knighton, who were demonstrating against the government. They were carrying banners and placards on which were written in large letters demands for the right to vote, decent wages and cheap food. The harvest had been poor for the last two years largely owing to the dreadful cold and rainy summer weather that had swept across Europe and was causing similar demonstrations there, too.

Many of the banners also had painted on them in red, 'Remember 1789,' when similar conditions in France had been bad enough for the Parisians to storm the Bastille and set the French Revolution in motion.

The marchers were being led by several men, some of whom had travelled to London from the new industrial towns of the Midlands and the North, to make their wishes for social change known by informing the government of their grievances in the most dramatic way possible.

The press of people in the narrow streets was so overwhelming that the carriages trapped among them were only able to move very slowly and, when the crowd turned towards Westminster, perforce had to go with them.

Occasionally the chaise was halted for minutes on end when the crowd grew so great that no one could move. As a result, hairy and gaunt-faced men and haggard women, some of them dressed in rags, banged on the doors and windows of Diana's chaise, shouting and shaking their fists at her. One of them took a knife from his belt and began to deface the Medbourne arms painted on the chaise door nearest to him.

A group of men armed with pitchforks howled at Gilbert to abandon her and the chaise in order to join them and, when he refused, shook their rusty weaponry at him and threatened to pull him down anyway.

Just as their situation was becoming increasingly desperate, the crowd reached a large square in an area quite unknown to Diana, which, fortunately for her, had a number of streets empty of marchers leading out of it. The press around them loosened and Gilbert, seizing his opportunity, whipped his horses into action and, caring little whether any in the crowd were injured—the man with the knife was thrown to the ground—galloped at speed towards a half-empty side street on his left, which led towards the King's Road and their destination.

As the crowd scattered before him he tore down it. Inside the chaise Diana was thrown from side to side until Gilbert slackened his pace. Safe at last, she thought, when they finally resumed their journey towards Neville's home at a level pace.

Despite now travelling through the familiar streets that she had come to know since she had lived in London Diana could not easily forget the haggard and hating faces of the people who had surrounded her. The one that haunted her the most had been that of a woman clad in rags who had held a pitiful baby up for her to inspect. Its thin face had been pale, not rosy, and its little hands and arms were not chubby but skeletal.

She could not help recalling what Neville had once told her of the many whose lives were so unlike their own and of how he wished that it were possible to do more for them and how difficult it might prove to be.

'Unless we reform our government and way of life,' he had concluded, 'we risk revolution. Change might be gradual, but change we must lest worse befall.'

Diana was still thinking about this and wondering whether, in the future, she might be able to join him in helping some of the poor unfortunates whom she had seen that morning, when she saw that they were now near Neville's home, and had only a short side road to negotiate before they reached it.

Suddenly, without any warning, the chaise stopped and the horses pulling it began to neigh, whinny and prance so violently that Diana was thrown from side to side again. Once they had quietened down a little, she flung open the right-hand door, and stepped down into the road in order to ask Gilbert what was wrong.

Once there she saw that it was not the horses that were in trouble but Gilbert, who had been dragged from his seat and was being carried towards an alleyway by two large and rough-looking men. On reaching the alleyway, the two ruffians flung him, apparently unconscious, into it, where he lay unmoving. His place as driver of the chaise had been taken by another, smaller man, whom she had never seen before and was having difficulty controlling the horses.

Diana, deciding that the better part of valour was flight since she was so near Neville's home, began to run towards it, holding her skirts well above her ankles in order to reach the safety of Neville's home as soon as possible where they might be able summon help for poor Gilbert.

To no avail. The bigger of the two men caught up with her immediately, swung her off her feet and carried her back to the chaise.

She tried to scream, but the large smelly hand that he firmly clamped over her mouth stopped that, too, and in a trice he had flung her back into her seat and slammed the door on her. He shouted to the new driver and the chaise drove on for about a quarter of a mile, past the gates to Neville's house and round the next corner, where it stopped once more.

Diana decided to make one last desperate dash for freedom by flinging the door open and jumping down again—to see before her, standing on the pavement, the face of salvation, a familiar face, the face of someone who would surely help her.

Instead, like the large man earlier, he scooped her up and flung her back into the chaise, which he then entered to sit beside her.

'Now, now,' he told her reprovingly. 'Behave yourself and I shan't have to tie you up and gag you.'

No, her mind screamed at him, no, for he wasn't one of the men whom she had thought might wish to harm her, but someone whom she believed to be her friend. How in the world would Neville and Jackson be able to rescue her now?

Chapter Fourteen

'Are we going to visit Frank Hollis?' Neville asked Jackson when they were being driven to Frank's rooms in the Albany.

'Yes, and I go in first,' Jackson said with a grin. 'Dobbins's brother thought that he's on his hands and knees, stony broke. He's for the Marshalsea any day now, for the rest of his life—and so I shall warn him.'

Neville had never particularly liked Frank, but he shivered a little at the prospect of him being confined in a debtor's prison until he died. Something, though, struck him as odd about this story. 'If he's being paid for helping to trap virgins, why is he so penniless?'

Jackson shrugged. 'Probably spends it all as soon as he gets it. Put the frighteners on him and he may sing like a canary.'

'What is my part in this?'

'You'll wait in your carriage around the corner before that inn we passed a little while ago. After about five minutes pay him a friendly call—be a little surprised to find me there. You can be his kind adviser and I'll be his cruel one. Between us we might be able to persuade him to sing if he hasn't offered me an aria by then.'

'How shall I know what to say when I do arrive?'

'You'll take your cue from me, I'm sure.'

Neville began to laugh ruefully and hoped that he could practise successfully some of the trickery that Jackson constantly engaged in. His new life was asking strange things of him and at the same time he was gaining a greater insight into the darker behaviour of his fellow men and women than he had ever been aware of while he had been so busily concentrating on his own virtue! He must not, however, lose all of that virtue, lest he end up by being as depraved as the men whom he was trying to trap.

Jackson was ushered into Frank Hollis's drawing room to find him slumped in an armchair, smoking a cigar, with a half-full bottle of port and an empty glass on a table before him. Despite the early hour he gazed drunkenly at Jackson, saying, 'I only asked my man to admit you because I hadn't the devil of a notion why someone answering to the name of Jackson, of whom I have never heard before, should be asking to see me and I needed something to cheer up my day besides that.' He gestured at the bottle of port. 'Like some?'

Jackson shook his head. 'No, thank you. I never drink when I'm engaged in matters of business.'

Frank puffed smoke in his direction, before carelessly flinging the cigar into the fireplace.

'What in the world does any business *you* might be engaged in have to do with me? Tell me as quickly as you can, I might find it amusing.'

'I doubt that, sir, very much. I am here on two errands. The first is on behalf of the bailiffs who will shortly arrive to distrain on your property, arrest you and take you to the Marshalsea to hold you there until you pay all of your debts—which I believe to be impossible since you are already bankrupt.

'On the other hand, if you could help me over a rather difficult matter, it might be possible for me to arrange for your debts to be overlooked.'

Frank stared bemusedly at him. 'Are you bamming me?' he asked at last.

'Indeed not, sir, far from it. I have never been more serious. The second errand relates to whether or not you can give me any information relating to those of your friends who are engaged in a singularly vile conspiracy involving the kidnapping of young women. I see by your change of colour that you know whereof I speak.'

'If so, you'll know why I can't tell you a dam'd thing— too dangerous.'

'Dangerous not to, perhaps,' offered Jackson, 'and I could arrange for you to be protected—that is, if you're not too involved yourself.'

His face as white as paper, Frank stared at him. He picked up the bottle of port and drank straight from it. He rubbed his hand across his mouth and said, 'God forgive me, I was once, but though I needed the tin I couldn't stomach it and gave up months ago. I told them I wouldn't take any more part in it. I was threatened with this, that and the other if I acted as an informer, and since I knew what had been done to those who had tried to go to the authorities I've kept quiet—and that's that. It's months since I left off.'

'So, you admit that you helped to kidnap young girls and women who were virgins,' was Jackson's stern response. 'Therefore I have no alternative but to arrest you—unless, of course, you give me the names of your accomplices.'

Frank began to whimper. Between drink and fear he scarcely knew what he was doing and it was at this point that Neville strode into the room, followed by a complaining man-servant.

'I tried to stop him, sir, I told him that you were engaged, but he wouldn't take no for an answer and pushed by me.'

Frank's stare was now for Neville. 'What the devil are you doing here, Fortescue? You come at a most inconvenient time.'

Neville improvised rapidly. 'Why's that, Frank? Is it about your debts? The rumour is that you'll soon be dragged to the Marshalsea. I thought I might be able to help you.'

Frank clasped his hands round his head and bent down until it was between his legs. He moaned before lifting it, wailing, 'I'm being overwhelmed with unwanted help this afternoon, what with him—' pointing at Jackson '—and now you.'

'You'd do very well to follow his advice.' Neville was firm, hoping that he was saying the right thing.

'You know him?'

'Jackson? Of course, very reliable fellow. Gave evidence over some wretched business to do with chimney sweeps at a Parliamentary committee I was on. Why is he offering to help you? Not usually his line of business at all.'

He turned to Jackson and said, 'Could I help, too? Frank's by way of being an old friend.'

'It's rather delicate, Sir Neville, but I can inform you that I shall have to arrest Mr Hollis if he doesn't give me some information about an unpleasant enquiry I'm engaged on.'

'Oh, whatever's that, Frank? You've not got yourself into trouble with the law, have you?' He turned to Jackson. 'What unpleasant business? And are you bound and determined to arrest him?'

'Unless he gives me the information I require from him, yes.'

'Oh, that would never do. Best tell me what this is all about, Frank, and I might be able to help you.'

Frank stared at the pair of them. Kind, upright Neville and stern Jackson, both determined, it seemed, to save him from himself.

'You said that you'd protect me if I cooperated with you,' he quavered at Jackson, 'and that you'd arrest me if I refused—will you protect me if I give you the only names I know?'

'Of course, sir. My word is my bond. No one will know of your part in this horrid affair.'

'What horrid affair?' asked Neville apparently artlessly.

'That must remain a secret between Mr Hollis and myself.' Jackson was following Neville's example and lying like truth. 'I cannot inform an outsider like yourself of any of the details. I'm sure that you understand me, Sir Neville.'

'Of course, of course. You would do well, Frank, to trust Mr Jackson. Be a sensible fellow, name names, and all will be well. Not until after I have left, of course. As for your debts, I can't pay them, but I might be able to do something for you.'

He bade them both adieu and went to wait for Jackson in his carriage, smiling to himself. Good God, he must be fit to appear on stage anywhere after that little scene.

It was some time before Jackson returned, a grim expression on his face. He found Neville sitting in the sun on one of the benches before the inn, reading a newspaper. Lem had driven the chaise into the inn's yard for the horses to be fed and watered while they waited for his return.

He said nothing until they were back in the chaise away from prying ears—if ears could be said to pry, that was. Neville also remained silent and finally asked the equally mumchance Jackson, 'Is something wrong? Have you bad news for me? Was questioning Frank all in vain?'

Jackson shook his head. 'Not at all. But I think that you are going to be very unhappy when you learn who Henry Latimer's right-hand man is. Hollis was never that and I believe him when he claimed to have withdrawn from the conspiracy after a short time because he hadn't the stomach for what he was expected to carry out. The other news is that Sir Stanford Markham is now desperately trying to keep his part in the conspiracy from becoming public since he stands to lose everything if his part in it is ever revealed.'

Neville said brusquely, 'If I'm to be made unhappy, then so be it—as long as it is done quickly. I don't want any beating about the bush. My sensibilities are not so tender as you might suppose.'

'They're going to be tested pretty severely when I tell you that Latimer's chief aide is none other than your cousin and friend, George Alford.'

The expression on Neville's face was a wonder. It was a mixture of shock and disbelief.

'George? George Alford! Are you sure? I've always thought him to be nothing more than a decent, good-natured fribble.'

'Quite sure, and fribble he might seem but, according to Hollis, he has been helping to organise the kidnapping of the girls since the game began a few years ago.'

'I wish we were back at the inn,' exclaimed Neville fervently. 'I could do with a good strong drink of something or other. It's not so much that my sensibilities are affected, but George has spent much of his time lately hovering around Diana and being kind to her.

'It is that that troubles me the most because he must know of her involvement in this wretched business and be behind the threats made about her safety. It does explain, however, why he never seems to be short of money, even though he was left very little and has no real occupation, other than winning occasionally at cards.'

He paused. 'And now Diana seems to be missing, and that is the most worrying thing of all. By God, if George Alford so much as harms a hair of her head I'll kill him myself if I get the chance.'

Afterwards he was to think how much he must have changed in the few months since the taunts about his priggish dullness, made by both George and Frank Hollis, had stirred his temper and his blood, to have uttered such an outspoken threat.

Jackson said mildly, 'I have no wish to arrest you for murder, so I would advise you to take care, Sir Neville. Let the law catch your cousin for you and punish him is my advice.'

'The law had better,' replied Neville savagely, 'because, if not, I'll be compelled to call him out myself and exercise Jedwood justice.'

Jackson said, half-amused, 'A duel is a form of execution before trial, but the trouble is that he might kill *you* in a duel.'

'Unlikely,' snarled Neville. 'He's a dam'd poor shot and a worse fencer. His boxing is non-existent, as mine is, but I suppose he could challenge me to a duel with bladders on sticks if I called him out, but propriety wouldn't allow that. I always thought him to be a decent sort, if a trifle frivolous. The present question, though, is what is our next move? I suggest that I order Lem to drive us to Chelsea to discover whether Diana has arrived there after all.'

Jackson nodded agreement. 'Best to do so before we take any action against Latimer. It's still a possibility that she might have been delayed by today's riots and we don't want to go off half-cock by making false accusations about him or anyone. That would dish us completely.'

So back to Chelsea it was—to find that Diana was not there.

Diana was looking out of her chaise's side window to try to discover where she was being taken until George, Lord Alford leaned over and pulled the blind down. She promptly pulled it up again, whereupon he, equally promptly, pulled it down again.

'Do that once more,' he warned her savagely, 'and I'll tie your hands together. You wouldn't like that, would you?'

Pointless to defy him further, so she said, as calmly as she could, 'Where are we going?' She had already noticed that they were being driven back to central London.

'That would be telling,' he smiled at her, as charming now as though they were chatting together in a ballroom.

'Why are you doing this, George? Kidnapping me, I mean? If you're caught it's either the hangman's noose or transportation—neither of which you would like.'

'You know perfectly well why I am disposing of you, my dear Duchess, and the next on the list will be your paramour, Sir Neville Fortescue, and that damned ex-Runner you've hired. Besides, I have no intention of being caught, I do assure you, since I have powerful friends.'

'So I believe and, for your information, Sir Neville is not my paramour.'

'Then he's an even bigger priggish fool than I thought him to be. Now be quiet or I *will* gag you.'

Whether this was an empty threat or not Diana had no wish for him to as much as touch her, let alone gag her, so she remained silent, trying not to think about what was going to happen to her, and to Neville whom she might never see again.

It was only then that she realised how much she had come to love him with a passion that was quite different from the calm and—admit it, Diana—daughterly affection which she had felt for her late husband. So much so that the memory of him and his kindness was growing dimmer and dimmer. Immediately after his death, whenever she was confronted by any problem, however large or small, she had constantly asked herself, *What would Charles wish me to do in this situation?*

These days it was Neville who was always in her thoughts, not her former mentor, and it was he whose judgement she was beginning to rely on. Where was he? Was he still alive and well? Was he distressed when she failed to arrive at the time she had promised? Did he think that she had been trapped by the marchers and had continued to wait for her until it became plain that she must have changed her mind?

If he thought that some harm might have come to her, however, as the consequence of their campaign, how could he

possibly save her? It was most unlikely that he would ever
suspect that it might be his cousin George who had her in his
power, for his name had never once been mentioned as one
of those involved in the trade in girls.

Diana had only just reached this mournful conclusion when
for the second time that day the chaise suddenly stopped, but
unlike the previous occasion it did not remain standing in the
road. Immediately afterwards there was a loud and dreadful
noise of whinnying horses when the chaise was suddenly
struck with such force that their horses and carriage were
knocked sideways on to the road, throwing George and Diana
on to the floor.

It was a heavy brewer's dray whose horses had bolted, having been made frisky by the unusually heavy traffic. Their
driver had lost control of them and had been unable to prevent
them careering into the chaise's offside horse.

The dreadful noise was followed by silence. The chaise had
been dragged along for a little way on its side, and had then
stopped again. Diana had fortunately not been injured when
she had been thrown about, other than having suffered some
heavy bruising and a sprained left wrist. It was some minutes
before she could look about her to find that George had not
been so fortunate. He had not only taken the brunt of the
collision but, ironically, had also broken her own fall.

He was lying unconscious on the floor, his head was bleeding and his right arm and leg were at an odd angle. Had he
not recently been her gloating captor Diana would have seen
it as her first duty to assist him. Instead, she had only one
idea in her head—was it possible, if she were not too badly
hurt, for her whole body was aching, that she might still be
able to escape?

The voices of both men and women could be heard outside.
The window in the door had been shattered and a burly man
put his head through the large hole it had created.

'Anyone there still alive?' he shouted. 'If so, we'll try to get you out of the chaise.'

'Yes, I am unhurt, but my companion is unconscious and needs to be seen by a doctor.'

'Can you move, missis?'

'Yes, a little.'

'Then we'll try to force open the carriage door and pull you out. Hang on for a minute.'

His voice was kind and when he had finally opened the door he took her hands and helped her into a standing position before he and another man lifted her out. Once she had recovered enough to stand up on her own after she had been lowered on to the carriageway, everything swam about her so much so that she started to sway and was in danger of falling.

Her rescuer, a burly fellow, on seeing her distress, said encouragingly, 'Now, now, missis, you've had a right nasty shock, lean on me, there's a low garden wall over there that you can sit on,' and he led her across to it.

After a few moments' rest Diana stopped shivering and was able to look about her without feeling faint. For the first time, too, she could see, in all its horrid detail, the shocking consequences of the accident in which she had been involved. Not only was her left-side horse dead, but the right-side one was lying in the gutter with its leg broken, whinnying constantly in its agony.

The brewer's dray, after colliding with her chaise, had careered on to the pavement and straight into a high brick wall. Its driver, after being hurled from his seat on to the carriageway, was lying there badly injured. Several passers-by had stopped to look after him. Many of the dray's barrels had also fallen off the dray. Several of them had been smashed by the force of the collision and ale was running along the cobbles and into the gutters.

On hearing the noise of the accident, people seemed to have sprung out of the ground, for a large number of men and women had suddenly appeared. Some of them were just idle spectators, while others were doing their best to help the injured. One group was easing the unconscious George Alford out of the chaise and another was looking after the brewer's boy who, like his master, had also been thrown from the dray. He was sitting up on the pavement and had been lucky enough to receive only minor injuries.

Beside him, quite still, his head twisted to one side, lay the small man who had replaced Gilbert as the driver of Diana's chaise. He had been pulled from beneath the left-hand horse, which had fallen on him, and was being examined by a doctor who had just arrived and was shaking his head.

A woman servant came out of one of the houses, followed by a footman who was carrying blankets and sheets. The doctor asked for one of the sheets and covered the driver's body with it. He seemed to be the only person to have been immediately killed in the accident, although Diana guessed that George Alford, whom the doctor had begun to examine, was also in a bad way.

She refused one of the sheets, for she had stopped feeling quite so dreadfully cold and was wondering how she might disappear, without anyone noticing that she had gone. She could then walk to Neville's home, which she knew was only a few streets away. If she remained here too long, someone would be sure to question her as to who she and George were and that would never do.

Not only that, some of the more kindly spectators kept coming over to ask her anxiously whether she needed the doctor. She was able to reply quite truthfully that although she was bruised and her right wrist was a little painful she had been most fortunate in escaping serious injury.

She *must* disappear—or risk being the subject of scandal once it was known that she and George Alford had been alone together in her chaise. It had been damaged so much that the Medbourne arms on its door were unidentifiable owing to the vandalism of the marchers and the consequence of the accident.

If she were now able to vanish and George remained unconscious for any length of time—which looked increasingly likely by the doctor's behaviour—it would never be known that the Duchess of Medbourne had been involved in the accident.

Her fears of being identified increased when a police officer and a self-important beadle arrived to try to discover the accident's cause, but her wish to leave without attracting attention grew when a platoon of soldiers led by a cavalry officer on horseback suddenly appeared around the corner of the street, escorting a number of men in irons.

They were the leaders of the first group of marchers, including Captain Knighton, who had been surrounded in Parliament Square, arrested and were on their way to Chelsea Barracks before being transferred to Newgate prison to await trial; Newgate being full of those marchers who had been arrested before they had reached the Square.

Their presence served to add an extra dimension to the confusion that already existed. The narrow street was blocked by the dead and dying horses, the dray, its fallen barrels, the chaise, the dead and injured men and a plethora of idle spectators, making it necessary for the platoon's officers to turn back and attempt to find another accessible route to the Barracks. The presence of the growing crowd made this difficult and matters were not helped by the arrival of another group of marchers who had never reached Parliament Square, but had lost their way in the rabbit warren of London's unfamiliar streets and suburbs and were now in retreat.

In the middle of the noisy mêlée which followed, Diana was able to slip away unseen, knowing that George was being cared for since, despite everything, she did not want his death on her conscience, making for the nearest side road in order to try to reach Neville and safety.

Her progress was slow because she was not dressed for walking, her shoes were too light and she was still in a state of shock. More than one passer-by stopped to stare at her, at her dusty clothing and limping walk, her bruised face, and her dishevelled hair—she had lost her bonnet in the accident. Nevertheless, ignoring them, she plodded stoically on, determined that she would reach Neville before some busybody tried to detain her and make it necessary for her to concoct some story for her strange presence in these respectable streets.

It was her iron will, forged by her late husband, which refused to allow her weariness to overcome her, particularly since she was sure that by now Neville and Jackson would be very worried by her failure to arrive in Chelsea that morning. The other thing that drove her relentlessly onward was that she must, as soon as she possibly could, tell them of George Alford's unexpected part in the hateful conspiracy that they were investigating.

Neville and Jackson were busy debating what stratagem they might employ in order to try to find Diana when there was a knock on the door and Lem entered, looking excited.

'Her Grace has just arrived...but—'

Neville did not allow him to finish. He leaped to his feet, pushed past Lem and ran into the entrance hall. *Diana! Diana was here! At last!*

Yes, it *was* his Diana, seated on the chair to which Lem had helped her and from which she rose to greet him: but it was not a Diana he had ever seen before. Her face was white, a great bruise ran down the left side of her face, her hair was dishevelled, and her disordered dress was torn and dusty. Oddly, although she was so different from the invariably *à point* woman he had always known, there was still something gallant and dauntless about her, even though the smile she offered him was a small and painful one.

She stumbled towards him, swaying slightly, whispering his name, and fell into his waiting arms.

Neville caught her up, lifted her and, regardless of Jackson and Lem, carried her to the drawing room where he gently sat her down on the sofa and began to stroke her cold hands in an effort to warm them.

Oh, this was heaven, was it not? To find that she was still safe and sound, had been in his loving arms, and was now close to his fast beating heart, being cared for. Despite her exhaustion, Diana gave him another smile and said his name again since, for the moment, it was impossible for her to tell him of all that had passed since she had left Medbourne House.

Jackson poured a glass of wine from a decanter on a side table and handed it to Neville, who held it to her lips. She drank it greedily as though it were the reviving nectar of the Greek gods of old and, looking into his anguished eyes—for he had remained silent in order not to overtax her by compelling her to speak—she whispered hoarsely, 'Oh, Neville, I have so much to tell you.'

'Not now, my darling heart, later, when you are a little more revived.'

She moved restlessly against the comforting arm he had put around her shoulders, knowing that it was necessary for him, and Jackson, to know immediately of the full extent of the deceit that surrounded them and had nearly caused her death.

'Oh, no, for all our sakes, I must speak at once. It was George, George Alford—' and then she stopped, the enormity of what she was about to tell them overcoming her. After all, George was his cousin and their friend.

Neville stared at her. Was it possible that she was delirious? No, her great eyes pleaded with him and she gave a choked laugh. 'Forgive me, I have started at the end, not at the beginning. Give me but a moment's pause and I will tell you everything in the right order.'

Slowly, but coherently, her voice fading now and then, she told Neville and Jackson everything which had happened to her since she had left Medbourne House that morning. 'And Gilbert,' she ended, 'he must be found and driven to a doctor or a hospital if he is still alive. I can take you to the place where they threw him down.'

During her long narrative Jackson watched the growing fury on Neville's face when Diana told him of her kidnapping and his threats. He opened his mouth to speak once, but Jackson put his hand on his arm and shook his head. When she reached the end of her sad story, he said, 'You are sure that Lord Alford was unconscious, and possibly dying when you made your escape?'

Diana nodded.

'Then that gives us a little time to make our plans. But first of all, I must try to find your driver who may also be in a bad way. I think, that for the moment, you ought to rest, so could you give me directions to the alley into which he was thrown?

'Sooner or later we must take you home after concocting a convincing explanation of where you have been since your chaise was stopped and Gilbert was attacked. It will, of course, leave out Lord Alford and his attempt to kidnap you. Perhaps you could both put your heads together and think of a likely story while I go to look for Gilbert.'

So it was arranged. Diana told Jackson where she had last seen Gilbert, and once he had gone Neville arranged for Lem to bring her tea. 'And something to eat,' he added.

'No,' she told him. The very idea of food made her feel faint. All that she really needed was to sleep, preferably in Neville's arms, and forget everything before the time came for her to be driven back to Medbourne House. But she and Neville had each been left with a duty and Charles had emphasised to her more than once that duty always took precedence over pleasure and the fulfilment of one's own desires.

Consequently while drinking their tea she and Neville constructed a plausible explanation of what had happened to her after her chaise had been commandeered and Gilbert attacked not far from Neville's Chelsea home. In this version of events, George was omitted and the chaise had been stolen by a group of marchers who had been trying to escape from London as quickly as possible in order to avoid arrest. This would place her quite a long way away from the collision with the brewer's dray which had shattered her carriage, killed her horses and left George Alford in a coma.

'So then,' she finished, when, between them, they had concocted this mixture of truth and falsehood, 'shaken and shocked, I walked the short distance to your home in Chelsea, and if I can tidy my dress a little and restore my hair to its usual neat condition, I can claim that the bruises on my face were caused when the marchers dragged me from the chaise and I tried to resist them. Does that sound believable?'

'Yes, indeed. It will prevent any scandal that might have followed if it became known that you had been alone in the wrecked chaise with George. Instead, you will receive only pity for your mistreatment. Yes, I think that will do and now we must wait for Jackson.'

'The only thing that I don't like about this story,' admitted Diana sadly, 'is that it transfers the blame to the poor wretches who were demonstrating about their unfortunate condition, and were innocent of any wrongdoing so far as I am concerned. But since it will be impossible to find them, because they never existed, I can't feel too exercised about blackguarding them.'

'It does depend a little, though, on what Gilbert may remember if Jackson finds him,' Neville offered thoughtfully.

'Fortunately, George was not present when his bruisers attacked our chaise. He was waiting for me around the next corner—possibly so that Gilbert would not know who had run off with me—and if he recovers he is hardly likely to confess that he had attacked and kidnapped me.'

At this point Jackson arrived back, with news which he said was both good and bad.

'The good news is that Gilbert was found by some passers-by and carried to an apothecary's house nearby where I found him. He has no memory of anything after the chaise was stopped by two men and he was dragged from his seat. I know this to be a common occurrence after a blow to the head. I think that it would be better if you appeared to know as little as possible about what happened this afternoon—apart, of course, from the Duchess's experiences. Best not to volunteer anything. When in doubt, look puzzled and shake your head.'

For the first time in the course of that dreadful day Neville and Diana both laughed.

Neville's riposte was a wry one. 'Difficult, I fear, for both of us since neither of us ever cares to look puzzled or in doubt, but I'm sure we'll try our best—a little practice might come in useful.'

The occasion thus lightened they made ready to be driven to Medbourne House where their reception by Isabella Marchmont was exactly what might have been expected. It was she, rather than the poor victim, who swooned when she saw Diana's bruised face and, on recovering, peppered them with questions such as, 'What in the world has happened to you, my dear?' before anyone could so much as get a word in edgeways.

'If you will allow one of us to speak,' retorted Diana, who was well on the way to resuming her usual lively state after the rigours of the day, 'then we might be able to enlighten you. Pray sit down and try to compose yourself and I will tell you what happened to me on the way to Chelsea.'

Neville was fascinated by her resilience, as was Jackson when she gave Isabella a brief account of her adventures, ending with, 'I believe Mr Jackson ought more properly to inform you of what happened to poor Gilbert after the chaise was stopped.'

'Gilbert?' Isabella was bewildered.

'My driver.'

'Oh, the driver.' Isabella was now dismissive, and Neville could not but contrast her indifferent attitude to Gilbert and his fate compared with Diana's solicitude.

Jackson duly told her that all was well with him, but all that she said was, 'My dear Diana, I think that you ought to go to your room immediately, drink a tisane which will help you to sleep, and try to rest until tomorrow morning so that you might the better recover from your sufferings.'

'By no means,' retorted Diana. 'I must go to the stables and inform Corbin that Gilbert, although injured, is safe and well and not like to die and that our chaise and the two horses have been stolen and are probably many miles away from London by now.'

Having delivered herself of yet another thundering lie, she set off for the stables after turning at the door and hurling a final dart at Isabella. 'All things considered,' she advised, 'it might be better if you ordered the tisane for yourself.'

How Neville and Jackson stopped themselves from laughing at the sight of Isabella's offended face they never knew. They both excused themselves by begging her pardon but they needed to leave straight away, Jackson to the Home Office to report on Diana's misadventure and the consequences of Captain Knighton's arrest. Neville was accompanying him as a useful witness.

'Provided,' Jackson reminded him, 'that you remember what I told you earlier about not volunteering anything.'

To Neville's surprise, and that of the secretary who escorted them to his office, it was Lord Sidmouth, the Home Secretary himself, who received them. He welcomed them both, immediately offering them armchairs, and treating Jackson after a fashion that was a reproach to Isabella Marchmont's behaviour towards those whom she thought her inferiors.

'I understand that you may have news for me,' he began, 'and I certainly have news for you. Perhaps Mr Jackson could begin by giving me his.'

Jackson launched into the Duchess of Medbourne's loss of driver, chaise and horses to a group of marchers who were trying to flee London, and of her bravery in finding her way to Sir Neville Fortescue's Chelsea home on foot after her dreadful experiences. The Home Secretary listened gravely to him.

'I trust all is now well with her, Sir Neville,' was his only comment on that. 'I shall ask for a watch to be kept for her chaise and horses, but I am not hopeful that she will ever see them again. You did well to inform me, though. I am also grateful to you, as well as to Mr Jackson, for your information about the activities of the so-called Captain Knighton. It enabled us to keep a close watch on him and also be prepared to scotch any attempt of his to start a revolution here. I understand that he has already been arrested and his destination will most certainly be the block on Tower Hill or the gallows. For that I thank you both.

'Now I have a piece of news that I am sure you will both be relieved to hear. Prince Adalbert of Eckstein Halsbach has been informed that his presence in our kingdom is no longer wanted. A passage home has been booked for him so that he may leave us as soon as possible. Further to that, we are preparing to try to put a stop to the activities of his undesirable associates. It is most unfortunate that some of them, not all, remain unknown and we can make no open search to discover their identity.

'The problem that we in authority face is that it is most important that everything must be done *sub rosa,* that is, without the public knowing, lest such radical scandal sheets as Mr Leigh Hunt's get wind of the more unsavoury details of their behaviour. I cannot emphasise too greatly the damage that this might do to our country and our constitution were this to happen. We must never forget that the public airing of reports about the supposedly scandalous behaviour of Queen Marie Antoinette—all of which were untrue—contributed in part to the onset of the French Revolution in 1789.

'That the scandalous behaviour of which *we* speak is unfortunately only too true renders it even more necessary for us to practise caution in punishing the guilty in a manner that escapes public comment. I am sure you understand me.'

Both Neville and Jackson offered him mute assent. As Jackson had advised Neville earlier, the less said the better. One thing was quite plain, either through Jackson or some other informers, Lord Sidmouth had been fully briefed about the trade in virgins for the benefit of diseased members of the *ton*.

Lord Sidmouth smiled at them and rang a small bell that stood on his desk. The Under-Secretary ghosted in from an office off Sidmouth's and was instructed to furnish him and his visitors with a couple of bottles of the best port as soon as possible.

'There is one piece of news of which I am sorry to inform you,' he told them while waiting for the port to arrive. 'My colleague, Sir Stanford Markham, was set upon this morning by a group of bravos who left him dead on the pavement before his home. It is supposed that his upright life in defence of the law had caused them grave offence.

'Ah, here comes the port. Let us toast the King, the Prince Regent and our Constitution, which is the envy of the world.'

And our discretion, too, thought Neville drily, for he could scarcely think of anything more convenient than Sir Stanford's sudden death, which successfully avoided the need to do anything about his undoubted association with the disgraceful conspiracy originally set in train by Prince Adalbert and his debauched friends.

Once they were outside again, on the way back to Neville's chaise, and could not be overheard, Neville turned to Jackson and asked him, 'Does that mean that they have no real evidence implicating Henry Latimer and Lord Alford? Are they going to suffer unfortunate deaths, too?'

'Who knows? One thing is certain, there hasn't yet been time for Lord Sidmouth to be informed of Lord Alford's accident. It's also quite possible that his identity is still unknown, and that we may know more about the pair of them than the Home Secretary himself.'

'I noticed that you never gave him either of their names.'

Jackson smiled and put his finger beside his nose. 'As for discretion, two can play at that game. He might not know everything about the conspiracy yet. Sir Stanford was almost certainly the sacrificial goat, paying the price of his failure to control the Prince's activities—possibly because he was involved in them himself. The problem for Lord Sidmouth is what to do about the ones he does not know of.

'Our problem is that we cannot tell him of Lord Alford's involvement because the only proof we have is his attempt to kidnap the Duchess, and we dare not risk her good name by telling him of it, even though her evidence would implicate Alfred as a member of the conspiracy. Imagine the sniggers of the *ton* if it turned out that she was alone with him when the accident occurred—let alone what Leigh Hunt and the rest of the radical press would make of it!

'It's likely that Sidmouth will want me to look, most discreetly, into the accident in which Lord Alford was injured. Latimer needs further investigation because we have nothing that directly implicates him yet—only suspicions. Once he learns of the Prince's disgrace, Sir Stanford's death and Lord Alford's failure to dispose of the Duchess, he's likely to be a loose cannon, flailing about him, looking for revenge, and not knowing what to do next.'

'So it's not over yet,' sighed Neville.

'No, and by the guarded way in which he spoke, I believe that Lord Sidmouth expects us to do some of his work for him.'

Neville's response to that was a wry one. 'I am happy to accept that commission so long as he does not expect us to act as Latimer's executioners.'

'Amen to that,' was Jackson's answer.

After the drama of the day before it seemed strange to Diana to be spending the next afternoon with her canvas work while she listened to Isabella reading aloud Miss Jane Austen's *Emma*. Oddly enough Isabella's own choice would have been for a lurid Gothic novel with plenty of death and suspense in it, but after her recent adventures Diana had asked for the quiet, if witty, chronicle of life in provincial England to soothe her ravaged soul.

Isabella had just ended the first chapter when the butler entered and announced, 'Sir Neville Fortescue has arrived and is asking if her Grace will receive him.'

'Certainly,' replied Diana, 'you may show him in.'

Isabella rose, saying drily, 'I am sure that you would prefer to speak to him on your own.'

'If you will be so good,' said Diana, smiling when Isabella made her slow and stately way out of the room moments before Neville was ushered in—to be astonished all over again by the speed with which she had regained her normal composure.

What a remarkable creature she was! There she sat as if nothing in the world had happened to her, as though she had spent the previous day chatting or tatting, or doing whatever mild and genteel great ladies did, with nothing but her bruised cheek to betray her recent agony. Neville's heart almost burst with love and admiration for her and he had the greatest difficulty in not taking her into his arms immediately in order to reward her for her fortitude.

Instead he bowed and said, 'I see that you are much recovered.'

'Yes, but I must tell you, now we are alone that, during my recent ordeal, two things troubled me the most and they were that I had no idea whether poor Gilbert was alive or dead, or whether you might be in danger, too.'

'As you see,' he said, 'I am well and here to give you some news that I learned from the Home Office, so that it will not be too great a shock to you if I leave it to others to inform you of it. First of all, while you were being kidnapped, Sir Stanford Markham was murdered, supposedly by some bravos who might, or might not, be a group of Knighton's marchers who were demonstrating yesterday. The other news is that Prince Adalbert will be leaving England shortly at the request of the Home Office.'

'Thank God for your last piece of news,' exclaimed Diana fervently. 'I had grown weary of his greasy overtures, and since it seemed that he was linked with George and the rest, he at least, will no longer trouble us. As for Sir Stanford, I must say that, given everything, his death seems most convenient, but now we shall never know whether our suspicions about him were justified. Is there any further news of George?'

'Only that Jackson, whom I drove home yesterday evening, found when he reached it that a messenger on horseback had arrived and was waiting anxiously for his return. It seems that he is being asked to discover the identity of the unknown man who was seriously injured in a collision between his chaise and a brewer's dray earlier today. He is still unconscious and, since his driver was killed in the accident and his lady passenger has disappeared, there are no witnesses who can help them to notify his family. He has been carried to the home of a nearby doctor.

'Jackson will inform us later of George's condition and, if

he has recovered consciousness, what he has to say about his accident.'

Diana paled a little. 'And if he asserts that I was with him, what then?'

'That is in the lap of the gods, I am afraid.'

'So we are still not yet out of the woods.'

Neville offered her a somewhat grim smile. 'Do not worry overmuch, my darling heart. I doubt whether cousin George will wish to explain why a strange driver had replaced Gilbert, who was found, knocked on the head, well over a mile away, and why he was in the Medbourne chaise at all—if its arms are still identifiable, that is—with an unknown woman.'

'That is true, but I shall not be completely happy until everything is settled satisfactorily.'

Neville rose to sit by her. 'Fret not, my love. I know Jackson, and now that I have met Lord Sidmouth I know, too, that the last thing which they would want is for it to become known that you have played any part in this whole hateful brouhaha. The government will do all in its power to prevent any scandal surrounding George's accident reaching the radical newspapers and pamphlets.'

'I will try to be brave,' she announced suddenly, her great sorrowful eyes firm on his, 'but I do wish that this was over and that we might live in peace again.'

She had said 'we,' associating herself with him yet again. Neville leaned forward and kissed her gently on her undamaged cheek. 'You have been very brave already by walking to my home in a state of great distress after the accident. Particularly when I know that your first thought was for Gilbert and the need to find him as soon as possible.'

'It was the least I could do.'

'Not at all. You could have carried on like Isabella Marchmont, swooning and demanding to be looked after, instead of making your difficult journey to tell Jackson and me your vital information about George, as well as caring for Gilbert's welfare.'

The thought of what she had endured made Neville unable to restrain himself now that she was so near and dear to him, instead of being lost forever. He was so overwhelmed by her delicate floral scent that he kissed her full on the lips with all the passionate intensity of a man who was truly in love for the first time in his life.

Diana, clinging to him and returning his kiss with the same fierce pleasure, was experiencing something that she had never known before: the strange bond that unites a woman with the man whom she loves even before they have fully consummated their mutual passion. She had felt for her husband only daughterly love and gratitude and not the all-consuming desire of a woman to be at one with the man with whom she wishes to mate.

Consequently she offered Neville no resistance when he kissed her face and neck and began to explore her body with his urgent hands, both of them mentally cursing their clothing, which denied them full access to each others' treasures. So strong was their mutual joy that Neville, lost to everything, began to lower her to the carpet to bring their lovemaking to its final, natural conclusion.

It was only when Diana exclaimed, 'Oh, yes, Neville. Oh, yes, oh, please, Neville,' when he lifted her skirts, that he was suddenly stricken with the knowledge that to go any further would not be an act of genuine love, but one of lust, since only a cur of the first water would take advantage of a virgin who could not resist him, nay, was even encouraging him, knowing that they might both feel the deepest regret afterwards.

It was one of the hardest things he had ever done. His whole body aching with all the pains of thwarted desire, he lifted her back on to the sofa.

'No, my darling, not now. It would be wrong.'

Wild-eyed, her senses roused as they had never been before, she cried, 'Why not? Do we not love one another?'

'Yes, and that is exactly why we should deny ourselves. You have been in danger and I wish to comfort you, my love, in the most time-honoured way, and were we but a man and a woman in a forest we might mate here and now without guilt, but we are not. We are bound by the laws and customs of our own time, which insist that we must marry before we mate—and you are virgin, which would make our sin worse.'

'Oh, that.' She was contemptuous. 'Charles said—'

He let her go no further, putting a gentle hand over her mouth. 'It is the woman who always pays the sad price of illicit love, never the man. Let me say to you, here and now, something that I wanted to delay speaking of until this whole wretched business was over. My darling Diana, will you do me the honour of marrying me as soon as possible and make me the happiest man alive?'

Diana's reply to him was typical of her whole approach to life. 'Oh, Neville, I thought that you'd never ask me! I was beginning to believe that *I* might have to propose to *you*— and what would Isabella have thought of me then?'

She had nearly undone him all over again by the wicked look she gave him, when she offered him this, quite unintentionally, for she was truly innocent.

'Witch,' he said thickly. 'I have only to look at you and I am lost. No, do not tempt me, for I might not be able to resist you and we should both then fall.'

'But if we are to marry?'

Neville had suddenly recovered his old self again, the upright man who had always wished to do what was right and true.

'Then it becomes even more important that we behave ourselves and that we wait until after the ceremony is over to fulfil our love.'

'Then I can only hope that we shall not have long to wait,

for I am sure that my patience will be strained. The very thought makes me feel quite ill.'

Her lovely face was so earnest when she came out with this that Neville began to laugh. After a somewhat baffled moment Diana murmured, 'What have I just said that was so amusing?'

'Nothing,' he choked, 'everything. I see that I am to marry a nonpareil. One thing is certain. When we are finally married I shall never be bored, for you are sure to come out with something lively which no other woman would have dreamed of saying and dull care will fly away immediately.'

'Really, Neville, really?' And her voice became more teasing than ever. 'I only wish that we could fly away immediately, to Arcadia, or, failing that, fairyland, somewhere quite unlike the wicked world in which we are living.'

She had dished him again, if only by revealing that behind her apparently carefree nonchalance she was well aware of the realities of the world around her. In this she was quite different from Lady Caroline Lamb, with whom some compared her, because Lady Caroline lived perpetually in a universe of her own making and was thus constantly surprised when she had to deal with those outside it.

'You have, my love,' he told her tenderly, 'what the late Dr Johnson called a bottom of sound common sense, which saves you from the worst excesses of those who do not possess it. You have been teasing me, have you not?'

'True, because I love you and I can say to you those things that I would not say to anyone else. And if I do possess common sense, then that is due to Charles also. He always told me that most women are without it because they have been brought up to believe that they do not need it—that it is something which most men will look after for them. He even taught me bookkeeping to prove that women, given the same training and opportunities, could be as practical as men.'

'Bookkeeping!' Now *he* began to tease *her*. 'Does that

mean that I will not need a secretary or an agent to run my estates?'

'If you like.'

Who knew how long this banter might have lasted, for Diana had begun to enjoy herself so much, and Neville, too, that without meaning it they were on the edge of physical, not mental, love again, and they both knew how dangerous that might be. Fortunately a knock on the door brought them out of the fairyland—to use Diana's word—in which they had both begun to live.

Neville was also finding that true love, as opposed to the immediate and selfish satisfaction of the body and not the whole mind and soul, had delights of which he could not have previously imagined. For Diana everything was so new and strange that each time that she met Neville she was surprised to find that the pull of the body was allied to the pull of the mind. She was also clever enough to know intuitively that this was something that only a minority of lovers shared and that it added another dimension to life, like an extra sense, to those which she and Neville already possessed.

Regretfully, for she had been enjoying herself, she cried, 'Enter,' and the butler came in to announce that a Mr Jackson had arrived and was asking to speak most urgently to Sir Neville, whom he understood was visiting her Grace.

'Very well,' she told him. 'You may admit him at once. I would wish to speak to him also.'

Jackson's face when he arrived was inscrutable. Diana warmly welcomed him. 'And,' she ended, 'if you wish to speak to Sir Neville alone, I will leave you at once.'

'No need for that, your Grace. Since you have been involved in this wretched business from the beginning, you may as well hear what I have to tell Sir Neville. It is this: Lord Alford has recovered consciousness, although it is not yet known whether he will survive his injuries. He wishes to speak to his cousin Neville and to no one else. Consequently

I am here to ask you, Sir Neville, to accompany me to the home of the surgeon who is caring for him, since trying to move him might cause his immediate death.'

He was at his most formal, quite unlike the jovial man Neville had come to know in the last few weeks. Neville was a trifle puzzled. 'He wishes to speak to me? I find that surprising.'

'I think—' and Jackson was being careful again '—that he may be about to confess to you what he does not wish to confess to anyone else. In a court of law, when a trial is being held, a dying man's last words are regarded as one of the most powerful pieces of evidence that may come before it. Now while it is true that Lord Sidmouth does not wish this scandal to become public, it may yet be impossible to keep it private. Therefore, if Lord Alford wishes to inform you of anything that might incriminate others, it is essential that you obey what may be his dying wishes. A priest has been sent for because he wishes to revert to the Catholic faith in which he was brought up, but which he has long abandoned.'

'In that case,' Neville agreed, 'I am sure that the Duchess will allow me to leave at once.'

'Indeed.'

Diana, although exceedingly curious about what his cousin might be ready to confess to Neville, had learned over the last few weeks that it would be wise for her to keep quiet rather than bombard him with questions and advice. If he wished her to know of anything that George might confess to him, he would be sure to tell her of it when next they met.

And if Neville thought that her silence, given her previous demands to know of everything he did, was most unlike her, he did not say so.

The surgeon's house to which Jackson took him was not far from where George Alford had suffered the injuries that were slowly killing him. He was lying in bed in a ground-floor room, which was next to the office where the surgeon, a Mr Andrew Long, saw his patients. Jackson had earlier told him that George wished to confess first to his cousin and then to a priest.

A fat, old woman who was acting as his nurse sat by him. 'You may leave us,' Mr Long told her brusquely, 'and I shall accompany you, to return only if Sir Neville believes that my medical skills are needed.'

George offered Neville something of a wry smile when he saw him. 'So you came,' he muttered in a low voice quite unlike his old carelessly confident one.

'You sent for me—so it was my duty,' was Neville's answer. He had not meant to say the last five words, but they had flown out of him, quite unintended.

'Ah, your duty.' And George's smile grew even more wry. 'Your damned duty that involved you in sitting on committees to save climbing boys from sweeping chimneys, and mourning over the wrongs of the handloom weavers in the company of Lord Byron—and now I have joined that sorry number of those who need to be saved.'

He gave a hoarse laugh before speaking again. 'And it is my duty to tell you what you, and the law, wish to know— if God gives me strength, that is. I have many other sins to confess to the priest who is waiting, but I shall tell you only of the greatest of them all.'

Neville said, since George had made no mention of Diana, not even to ask whether she had been injured in the accident, 'You will be relieved, I am sure, to learn that the Duchess of Medbourne escaped unhurt from the collision that so gravely injured you. It was only after making sure that you were being cared for that she left to walk to my home in Chelsea so that you might both escape the scandal which would have followed if it had become known that you were alone together. Her driver was found alive, but wounded, not far from the place where you kidnapped her. Your driver was not so lucky as you and was killed instantly, I fear.'

After Neville had finished speaking, George closed his eyes for a moment so that Neville and Jackson feared that he was about to die before he could give them the news for which he so urgently summoned Neville. Presently he looked up at Neville only, not wishing to acknowledge the silent Jackson's presence.

When he finally spoke his voice had recovered some of its former strength. 'You may remember that when we were boys together we were not only cousins, we were friends, but as we grew older I came to resent you because you were everything that I knew I was not. What was the worst thing of all was that our fathers were spendthrifts and boon companions, something that affected me but not you. My father threw our family fortune away on the gaming tables and the horses, but when yours did the same it did not make you penniless because he could not touch your mother's inheritance since it had been remaindered to you.

'Consequently, when we reached twenty-one you became rich and I remained poor, and on my father's death I inherited a bankrupt estate. Oh, no one knew that, but his and my debts were so large that I could not even afford to buy a commission during the late wars. I gambled even more heavily to try to recoup my losses and in the end committal to a debtors' prison for life was staring me in the face.

'It was at this point that I met Henry Latimer, to whom I had frequently lost large sums at cards, so that when he told me of a way to make money by joining him in the many disgraceful enterprises that were keeping him afloat, I was only too happy to oblige him. They ranged from being taught how to cheat young innocents when they were playing cards, chess or backgammon against me, to those darker ones that have led me to this pass.

'Of course, a percentage of all my winnings went back to

Latimer towards clearing my debts with him; finally, when one of his associates, for so he called us, died of the pox, he persuaded me to take over his post as the provider of virgins for those roués who thought that lying with them would cure them of the pox. It had evidently not cured the fellow whose place I took.'

Every now and then Neville had to wait for George to pause to allow his faltering voice a rest. At this point he stopped speaking altogether, lying silent for several minutes. When he resumed his speech was so weak that Neville and Jackson moved nearer to him so that they might hear every syllable of his painful confession.

'You must understand that I did not know our clients, or any of our superiors except for Prince Adalbert—I was only a go-between, helping Latimer. Thus when it seemed that we were in danger of being unmasked, the horror of the scandal that would be created if the public learned that young virgins were being kidnapped by men in high positions was enough to ensure that every effort was made to keep our dreadful secret. So much so that killing those who might try to betray us was undertaken as a matter of course.

'It was at this point, Neville, that you began your campaign against us, and refused to be stopped even after you had been disgraced. To make matters worse, the damnable Duchess, as Latimer called her, also took a hand in the game, as well as Sidmouth's pet spy, Jackson. Latimer decided that the only way out of this impasse was to dispose of the three of you, Diana being the first to go, and that I should be the one to snare her.

'God forgive me, I agreed to that, too. And the end of it is that I am the one who has been snared and is now dying. She, and you, have had the luck of the devil, while I, who served Satan as my master, have had none at all. I am telling you this so that Latimer will go down with me, for neither he nor

I can ever wash from our hands the blood of the innocents whom we betrayed.

'I am prepared to sign an affidavit testifying to this and after that you may send me the priest to whom I will confess my other sins, which have nothing to do with this matter.'

He paused again, turned his face away from his cousin and ground out, 'Now do your damned duty, Neville, so that I may rest in peace.'

His duty, George had said, and that he was confessing because he was ashamed of what he had done and wanted Henry Latimer punished for organising such a dreadful trade in innocent human beings. Later, Neville came to think that it was more likely that George's main desire was to be revenged on Latimer for having led him into such a quicksand of wickedness and deceit.

In the great sum of things George's motives for confessing were unimportant. After the priest had given him absolution and departed, he signed, in a faltering hand, the affidavit that had been drawn up and Neville and Jackson also signed it as a true and faithful record before leaving him to Mr Long's ministrations.

'What next?' Neville asked.

Jackson shrugged his shoulders. 'I shall give this to Lord Sidmouth—and then, who knows? I ought, perhaps, to warn you that if Latimer thinks that you have been instrumental in stopping his profitable game he may set about you next.'

It was Neville's turn to shrug. 'He may do as he wishes so far as I am concerned, if it means that he keeps his dirty hands off Diana.'

'So long as you are prepared for what he might try next,' were Jackson's last words before they parted. 'A thwarted villain is the most dangerous villain of all.'

Chapter Fifteen

'Just like old George to be half-killed in an accident in the middle of an afternoon *affaire*—he was never the luckiest of men.'

This comment from one of Lord Alford's oldest friends, Henry Latimer, was typical of many made in the aftermath of the failure of Captain Knighton's attempt at revolution. It was commonly assumed that George had come to grief as a result of the confusion that had followed when the marching protesters had become mixed up with the heavy traffic on the roads. The same villains, it was reported, had also stopped the Duchess of Medbourne's chaise, injured her driver and made off with the chaise to parts unknown.

The news that a woman had been with George Alford but had disappeared before the authorities had arrived on the scene was also greeted with lewd amusement by many of those whom George had considered his friends. Her identity was unknown and it rapidly became the subject of further unpleasant conjecture. Some sympathy, however, was expressed when it was learned that he was not likely to recover from his injuries.

The only person to say very little about who the mysterious and missing woman might be was Henry Latimer, something that surprised most of his boon companions who knew of his close friendship with George. He had no doubt that she was Diana Medbourne, but he was too busy seething with rage at the failure of that idiot, Lord Alford, to succeed in his attempt to kidnap the damnable Duchess to exchange chatty inanities with fools.

He also had no doubt, either, as to the identity of the others who had destroyed the profitable trade in virgins that he had been running for some years and if he could do little about Jackson, Sidmouth's spy, he intended to make short work of that self-righteous prig, Neville Fortescue.

It was only a question of cornering him in such a way that he would have the choice of weapons, not Fortescue. The polite world knew that Latimer was a crack shot with duelling pistols, having seen him in action at Manton's rooms. As for Fortescue, however, the whole world also knew that he had never engaged in any of the sports in which the foremost dandies of the day excelled.

Yes, he would pay, and pay dearly, for his interference in matters that were no business of his...

It was in this vengeful mood that he arrived at a reception given by Lord and Lady Cowper, where he had had the dubious pleasure of seeing his enemy and the damnable Duchess dancing the waltz as though neither of them had a care in the world. Well, he would make sure that both he and the Duchess would have a few after this night was over.

He saw Bobus Ventress yawning in a corner of the room, only present because the heiress he was uselessly pursuing was also there. The very man, he thought, whom I can easily control, and strolled, apparently lazily, over to him.

His prey, for that was what Bobus was, owed him a great deal of money, some of which he had won by cheating the stupid fool at cards and the rest of which he had lent to Bobus so that he might gain a hold over him that might prove useful in future.

Bobus had been promising to pay back both sets of losses for some months, but he always had an excuse as to why it was impossible—'But you'll have it next week, old chum,' he always ended, even though next week never saw the money handed over.

Now the time had come when he could use Bobus's debts to force the wretch to help him to destroy Neville Fortescue.

'You owe me a favour, Bob,' he told the fellow brusquely.

'Oh, and what can I do for you?'

'I'm off to Watier's shortly and I need to have a word or two with Neville Fortescue where I can say what I please to him without upsetting all the male and female tabbies who are present here. Persuade him to join you in paying a visit there instead of going home early.'

'Now how the devil do I do that? He never visits gambling clubs like Watier's as you well know.'

'Tell him that if he accompanies you he will certainly learn something to his advantage there and I guarantee you he'll agree like a shot.'

Bobus was dubious. 'If you say so, Latimer.'

'I do say so.'

'Well, I can but try.'

They were alone in a small cabinet off the main rooms so Latimer did not scruple to seize Bobus by his cravat and snarl in his face, 'Oh, I tell you again, I do say so, and if you don't oblige me I'll set the bailiffs on you for the money you owe me and your next lodging will be in the Marshalsea—permanently.'

'Very well, then, if I must, I must.' And Bobus strolled away, cursing the day when he'd let that swine Latimer talk him into betting more money at cards than he could afford and, after he had lost it, talk him into trying to recoup it, to no avail. After that he had played the kind friend who helped him to pay back many of his other debts, which, not being debts of honour, meant that he would end up in a debtor's prison if his creditors cared to take such a drastic action against him.

And now Latimer was using his debts to him to make him carry out a distasteful errand. What might he wish him to do next?

Diana and Neville were enjoying their evening much more than Henry Latimer had enjoyed his. So much so that more than one spectator, surprised by their apparent reconciliation, wondered how much longer they might have to wait before Fortescue declared himself since they were so obviously *épris* with one another again. Even Isabella Marchmont was smiling at them, for if Neville were to marry Diana then it would be wise not to antagonise him overmuch.

Neville had told her that the conspiracy involving the girls had collapsed, but that Sidmouth did not want to move against Henry Latimer openly because of the scandal that might be caused.

'But now that it's over,' Diana had said to him when they were briefly alone together, 'he cannot be a threat to anyone, now that Sir Stanford is dead, the Prince has been forced into exile and George has made his confession, which means that all the principals have been disposed of. He's like a general without an army.'

'True, but he may, after a short time, try to recoup his losses and start again.'

Diana nodded a thoughtful agreement because they had just reached the corner where Isabella was sitting and further confidential conversation was thus at an end.

Neville had not told her that Jackson thought that he might be in danger from Latimer, partly so as not to worry her overmuch and partly because he thought that Jackson might be exaggerating Latimer's response to his defeat. There was also the problem that there might be others involved who had not been identified, and who, if found, needed to be watched to discover whether or not the whole business might be starting again.

It was in this mood that, having left Diana, who had accepted an offer to dance the cotillion with Frank Hollis, he retreated to the supper room to collect food and drink for her and Miss Marchmont after the dance was over. Once inside he was stopped by Bobus Ventress who exclaimed cheerfully, 'Enjoying yourself with Duchess Di, old fellow?'

'You might say so,' murmured Neville shortly. Bobus was not a person whom he particularly liked.

'So much so that you might not wish to go with me to Watier's once the crowd here thins off a little?'

Neville shook his head as though to try to rid himself of this troublesome fly, but Bobus, remembering what Henry Latimer had said, leaned forward and whispered confidentially, 'Not if I told you that if you came with me you might learn something to your advantage there?'

Henry Latimer had told him the truth, for Neville said slowly, 'What am I to make of that, Bobus?'

'Whatever you will. You might as well come with me and find out.'

Neville had earlier seen Bobus and Henry Latimer talking together before they had disappeared from the reception room and wondered whether this had anything to do with Bobus's somewhat surprising offer. Jackson had warned him to be careful, which might mean that he ought not to accept this invitation. On the other hand, if Latimer *was* indirectly behind it, then he probably ought to visit Watier's, however much he disliked the place.

'Very well, then, but not yet. I am at present looking after the Duchess and her companion. Come for me later.'

'Midnight?' Bobus suggested happily. His happiness arose from the knowledge that he had, yet again, postponed the evil

day when he would have to settle his debts with Henry Latimer.

'Midnight it is,' agreed Neville, 'and now I must leave you,
the music has stopped and the Duchess and her companion
will be arriving to join me.'

He knew that Diana always left before midnight—'One of
my few good habits,' she had once told him. 'Charles always
claimed that an hour's sleep before midnight was worth more
than two after it.'

Midnight saw him bidding farewell to Diana. He had told
her nothing of his projected visit to Watier's, for he still had
no notion of whether Henry Latimer had proposed it nor why,
if he had, he should have done so.

Nevertheless his parting words to her were, without him
meaning them to be, so solemn, that they surprised her a little.
He seemed to have become again the rather severe man he
had been when she had first met him. Afterwards, she was to
discover why he had been so reticent, but at the time she
assumed that it was tiredness that was afflicting him, and with
Isabella by her side was constrained to be equally cool with
him.

She was not to know that Neville was already regretting
accepting Bobus's proposal, but could think of no way of
avoiding it. He was, however, a little surprised by the almost
pitiful eagerness that Bobus displayed on their way to Watier's, unaware that it was only his acceptance of Bobus's
invitation that had saved that sorry wretch from the Marshalsea and ruin.

As usual, Watier's was crowded, and the air was thick with
the fumes of drink and tobacco. Neville knew few of those
present and refused Bobus's suggestion that they find someone to make up a four at whist. He was on the point of asking
him about the information that might prove advantageous to
him when he saw Henry Latimer approaching him, a glass of
port in his hand.

He offered Neville a drunken leer and said, loudly enough for half the room to hear each sneering word, 'Thought you never came to these places, Nev. Duchess Di not obliging you in bed tonight, eh? Was the other afternoon enough for her?' and he turned to laugh at the grinning cronies who surrounded him. It was the laugh, as much as the vile reference to Diana, and the chorus of mocking appreciation, that roused Neville to a pitch of fury which he had never felt before. Later, he grasped that that was not strictly true. He had felt the same profound anger when he had shot the man who had tried to kill Jackson.

Thus a red, almost berserker, rage had him clenching his left hand and striking Latimer so hard in the face with it that he was sent flying backwards and was only saved from falling to the floor by being caught by those around him. Neville's own knuckles were scarlet from the force of the blow.

Silence fell. Pleased that his stratagem had worked and that he had succeeded in baiting Neville so successfully that he had gained the advantage he had sought in provoking a duel, Latimer said thickly, 'Since you apparently can't take a joke, Fortescue, neither can I. I take that to be an invitation to a meeting on Putney Heath tomorrow morning. You may name your seconds and my choice of weapons is pistols.'

Half of those present, being those least affected by drink, were shocked by Latimer's insult to a lady: the other half, barely able to stand, were amused by the whole affair. They thought that a prig like Fortescue, who had been found dead drunk in the street and was now being accused of rogering a woman of quality, ought to be unmasked as the hypocrite he was.

No one was more surprised by his immediate and violent response to Latimer's unpleasant lie about Diana than Neville himself. He was equally astonished at his reaction on finding himself involved in a duel. He discovered that he was too busy looking around him trying to find two possible seconds to worry about being afraid.

Frank Hollis was looking timorously at him, but he owed Neville a favour so that when Neville asked him if he would be his second, replied, 'Of course, Nev, only too happy.' And what a blatant lie that was! The very thought of merely being present, even without having to fire a pistol, had him inwardly quaking. The sight of blood had always set him shivering and shuddering: but it wouldn't do to look like a coward.

Neville's second supporter was a surprising one. One of those visiting Watier's was an unwilling Lord Burnside who had, of necessity, to accompany some of his fellow peers when they had decided after a short meeting spent discussing how they would vote on a coming bill in the House of Lords, that they deserved some light relief after a hard evening's work.

He strode forward to stand by Neville, saying, 'If you have difficulty in finding another second, Fortescue, then I will stand as one. First, however—' and he looked severely towards Henry Latimer, who was conferring with Bobus Ventress and another of his cronies, Lucas Courtney, who had promised to be his second '—it is possible that you might avoid a duel altogether if the two principals agreed to apologise to one another for their recent conduct, and shake hands.'

To his surprise, Neville, as well as Henry Latimer, said loudly and decidedly, 'No, certainly not!' He was not surprised by Latimer's rejection, but he had not expected that of his unacknowledged son since he had always thought him to be a reasonable and peaceable man.

There was nothing for it. The duel would go ahead and, knowing of Henry Latimer's prowess at Manton's rooms, he had put himself in the way of seeing his only child killed.

Neville, sensing his true father's distress, said, 'If you wish to withdraw as my second, m'lord, I would quite understand.

I have several friends who are not present tonight, but who would, I believe, act for me instead.'

Lord Burnside knew that he could not, in honour, withdraw. He slowly shook his head. 'Very well, then. We shall all meet on Putney Heath at six of the clock tomorrow morning when this sad affair will be settled. Agreed, gentlemen?'

Principals and seconds both nodded, and withdrew. Lord Burnside said to Neville when they were well away from Henry Latimer and his supporters, 'If you wish to come home with me, I shall be only too happy to accommodate you— and Mr Hollis, too.'

'I thank you, but I have another duty to perform, so I must refuse your kind offer.'

'So be it, then,' said his father sadly. Neville did not wish to tell him, or Frank, that his duty was to Jackson, who must immediately be informed of this latest development.

Neville drove himself to Jackson's lodgings in the hope that he might still be up. He was relieved to see a light on in one of his windows and hammered at the door until a rather cross landlady appeared, wearing a voluminous nightgown and cap, and carrying a candle.

'Oh, it's you,' she said ungraciously. 'You ought to ask him to give you a key if you're proposing to wake me at this hour very often.'

'It's an emergency,' offered Neville, which was, after all, the truth.

'Very well.' And she led him up the stairs, grumbling all the way.

Jackson, sporting a tartan dressing gown, was seated at his desk, writing in a large ledger. However impassive Neville had tried to keep his face, Jackson knew at once that something was wrong, either because of Neville's wry expression or the odd hour of the night at which he had called.

'What is it?'

Neville was brief. 'I am to fight a duel with Henry Latimer on Putney Heath at six of the clock tomorrow morning.'

'I warned you,' was all that Jackson had to say to that.

'I know. I wouldn't have lost my temper, only he publicly besmirched Diana's name at Watier's.'

Jackson did not say, 'What in the world were you doing there?' but instead went, as usual, straight to the point. 'I suppose he managed it so that he was the one who had the choice of weapons so that he might use his skill with duelling pistols.'

'Unfortunately, yes, he's a devil with them, I understand.'

'Hmm.'

'Is that all? Hmm?'

'Yes. You see it's one thing to be able to hit the centre of the target again and again at Manton's, but it's quite another to do the same thing in a duel.'

'Meaning?'

'Meaning that Latimer has never fought a duel—in other words, he's never been blooded, but you have.'

'But I've never fought a duel, either.'

'Come, come, Sir Neville Fortescue, have you forgotten that you saved my life when that villain tried to kill me? You never hesitated, and your aim was true. That is your advantage over him.'

Neville's laugh was as wry as his face. 'And that's all you have to tell me. I must say that you have a profound faith in me, I only wish that I shared it.'

Jackson did not answer him. He knew that Neville had always underestimated himself, but having seen how well he had behaved in a dangerous situation he knew that behind his quiet exterior he possessed greater courage and passion than many a more flashy and noisy man.

'Does the Duchess know of this?' he asked.

'No, and you are not to tell her.'

'But you are telling me.'

'Because we have been in this together.'

'As has the Duchess.'

'But there is a difference. Through your connections with the Home Office you could, if you wished, stop the duel by using any sort of excuse you could conjure up. Not that I am asking you to do such a thing. If I am killed, Latimer gains nothing but revenge, but if I kill him, then he, at least, cannot start his filthy trade in girls again.'

'Is that why you engaged in this duel with him?'

'No, I lost a temper which, until this wretched business began, I did not know I possessed. Now I must leave you to try to get some sleep.'

Jackson said nothing more, other than to wish Neville good luck, but he had already decided that he would be present at Putney Heath, regardless of whoever else was there.

Chapter Sixteen

Diana could not sleep. Neville had seemed most unlike himself when they had parted and she was sure that he was worried about something—and she thought that she might know what that something—or rather that somebody—was. It could not be other than Henry Latimer.

He had always been so adamant that she should be protected from any form of danger and, furthermore, she must never know when he was putting himself in the way of it, that she was quite certain that her instincts about the reason for his changed and reserved behaviour were correct. She could not, however, try to find out what he was up to until the morning.

It was also quite useless to try to question him about it because, if she did, he would be at his most nobly protective and evasive. She would have to visit Jackson who, in his downright fashion, had long ago recognised that while women needed to be cared for, one need not go to extremes while doing so. More, by his manner to her, Jackson knew that she was not one of those silly females who would swoon and whine and wail, but who would, if spoken to reasonably, respond with rational behaviour.

So be it. When morning came she would call on Jackson and try to find out why Neville was behaving so oddly.

On his drive back to Chelsea Neville had thought that he might not be able to sleep. It was not merely that he was facing the possibility of death in the morning that troubled him, but whether he could behave himself with dignity when the time came for him, a pistol in his hand, to face Henry Latimer. After all, when he had shot Jackson's assailant he had had no time to think, no time at all, whereas now there was the night to get through, and then those last fatal moments on Putney Heath before the handkerchief was dropped that would give the duellists permission to fire.

In any case, neither he nor his seconds would have much time for sleep since they would be calling for him at four forty-five of the clock in the morning to be sure that they would make the journey from Chelsea to reach the Heath after crossing Putney Bridge in time for a rendezvous at six of the clock.

Once he had reached home he fetched the case containing his supposed father's duelling pistols from his study and checked that they were in good working condition. For the first time in his life he remembered him with some little affection. Furious that the son whom Burnside had unintentionally blessed him with was a quiet creature and not the rowdy boy whom he might have fathered, Sir Carlton had taught Neville to shoot, and he had proved to be an apt pupil. It was, he remembered, the only occasion on which Sir Carlton had ever taken any interest in him or shown him anything other than dislike.

The result of this one piece of kindness was, ironically, that he had given Neville a talent that he had never needed to use until he had found himself the subject of Henry Latimer's revenge. The other irony was that his true father, Lord Burn-

side, might be present at his unacknowledged son's death if
Henry Latimer were to kill him.

The final irony, however, was that when, at last, he reached
his bed, expecting to spend the rest of the night wide awake,
he fell at once into a deep sleep, only to be roused when the
faithful Lem arrived at four of the clock to prepare him for
the day—and the duel.

Not long afterwards Lord Burnside and Frank Hollis arrived. Lord Burnside had brought with him a case of pistols,
which he and Neville examined to see whether they were
better than Neville's. Frank was bemused by the knowledge
of their use that Neville displayed.

'Thought you weren't interested in sporting matters, Nev,'
he offered. Lord Burnside looked sharply at him.

Neville's answer was brief, but, as always, courteous. 'It
was the one thing Sir Carlton taught me, how to shoot with
anything you please. His only other bequest to me was his
collection of small arms, rifles and fowling pieces.' He did
not tell Frank and Lord Burnside of the little breech-loading
pistol with which he had killed Jackson's attacker.

Nor did he tell either of them that he had informed Jackson
that the duel was taking place. That was his business, not
theirs, and they had enough to worry them without their wondering what the consequences of that might be. He had already noticed that Frank was looking very green about the
gills—apparently even being a second in a duel was worrying
him almost as much as though he were one of the principals!

It was, fortunately or unfortunately, Neville wasn't quite
sure which, a very fine morning when he was driven to Putney
Heath in Lord Burnside's carriage. It had long been a favourite place for duellists to meet. He remembered the excitement in 1809 when George Canning and Lord Castlereagh,
both members of the Cabinet, had met on the Heath. It was
rumoured that Castlereagh and his second had sung arias from

a popular opera of the time on the way to the encounter, while Canning had never fired a pistol before! Fortunately both of them had survived the encounter, although Canning had been wounded in the thigh.

Well, he knew how to use a pistol, but whether it would help him or not was uncertain. Henry Latimer's party had not yet arrived and Lord Burnside, who, as the senior in rank of all the seconds, would be giving the order to fire by dropping a handkerchief, pulled out his hunter in a pointed fashion when the time drew nearer and nearer to the hour of six and there was no sign of it.

It lacked only two minutes of the hour when Henry and his seconds arrived, driving furiously before leaving their carriages on the road at the edge of the Heath. Bobus Ventress leaped out of his, exclaiming breathlessly, 'Our apologies, m'lord and gentlemen. We were caught in the damned market traffic coming into the City and nearly missed arriving here before six o clock.'

Henry Latimer's support of this was an anxious nod and Neville drew some hope from the fact that his colour was nearly as bad as poor Frank Hollis's. His own feelings were mixed; mostly he wanted the whole damned business over as quickly as possible.

Lord Burnside was obviously in full agreement. He again asked both principals whether they wished to jointly apologise, thus doing away with the need for a duel to take place at all. Henry Latimer would have dearly liked to, but he knew by Neville's expression and stance that he would refuse. To withdraw now would make him a laughing stock: he would be branded a coward who had impugned a lady's honour and refused to defend himself, so his 'No,' was muttered, unlike Neville's sure and certain one.

Next the examination of pistols and balls took place, only one pair of which would be used to ensure that their weaponry would be the same. Neville's pair was chosen. After that Lord

Burnside laid down the rules of combat. The duellists would stand back to back and walk forward ten paces. They would then turn to face each other, their arms extended and their pistols at the ready. The order to fire would be given when he dropped a handkerchief.

'You have understood what I have told you, gentlemen?' he asked when he had finished.

Neville's reply was a firm, 'Yes, m'lord.' Henry Latimer merely nodded his head.

Lord Burnside's answer to that was a straightforward, 'That will not do, sir. I require a formal verbal answer.' In return he received from Latimer, who was now wondering why in the world he had embarked on this deadly piece of nonsense, a muttered repetition of Neville's response, before ordering them both to stand back to back.

The final stage of the duel had begun.

Diana, after a fitful night's sleep, in which she became more and more certain that Neville was in danger, decided that she could not rest until she found out what the danger consisted of. It was useless appealing to Neville, he would fob her off with some gentlemanly pretence that he was preventing her from falling into danger again.

Well, pooh to that. She knew that there was one person to whom she might appeal and that was Jackson. He did not love her, but he had made it plain that he admired her courage and straightforward attitude to life. She also knew, because Charles had told her, that in the world in which Jackson lived women were able to carry out many hard tasks and duties of a kind forbidden to the ladies of the aristocracy and gentry because they were believed to be either unwomanly or impossible for women to perform.

Underground, in the coal pits, he had told her, women dragged along wagons filled with coal. Outside, in the fields, they helped to load other wagons full of hay and produce.

They balanced baskets filled with fruit and vegetables on their heads and on their shoulders a yoke carrying two full buckets of milk. In the factories they were hired to do both dangerous and dirty tasks for as many as ten hours a day.

Yes, she would visit Jackson as soon as possible, if only to ease her troubled mind. At five thirty of the clock, with the sun streaming into her bedroom, she rose, put on her boy's clothes, and went down into the stables where the grooms, like the indoor servants, were already up and about their work and ordered Corbin to make her phaeton ready.

'Now?' he exclaimed. 'Forgive me, your Grace, but have you mistook the time?'

'Now,' she ordered him. 'Which means at once.'

'Which of the grooms do you wish to accompany you?'

'None,' she told him.

'But, you will be alone, on the streets of London in the early morning? Is that wise?'

'How many other women are on the streets of London at this hour without a single person to protect them?' she told him sternly. When he continued to demur and time was beginning to waste, she said, wearily, 'Very well, since Gilbert has not yet recovered, order your best groom to accompany me.' Off she soon was, her stable hands all shaking their heads and wondering what mad thing she would do next. She reached Jackson's lodgings at half past five, to find a light on in the entrance hall, and rapped smartly on the front door.

It was opened by his landlady, who stared at her.

'Mrs Rothwell! Whatever can you want from me at this hour?'

'Mr Jackson. I need to see him most urgently.'

'Well, you can't. He left some time ago. In a great hurry he was.'

'Have you any notion of where he was going?'

The landlady's face took on a sly expression. 'He didn't

tell me where, but I heard him order the hackney cab driver who called for him to take him to Putney Heath.'

Every bit of colour in Diana's cheeks disappeared. Putney Heath!—the favourite duelling ground of the men in high society. So that was why Neville was being so odd and so mysterious. He was going to fight a duel with Henry Latimer, which she was sure, knowing them both, Latimer had provoked, most probably by making some slanderous remark about herself. Hence Neville's refusal to confide in her.

Well, he would not fob her off anymore. After she had offered the landlady some brisk thanks and a guinea, she set off at once to the infamous Heath, hoping that Neville was still in the land of the living.

His right arm at his side, his pistol pointing at the ground, Neville walked his ten paces. He could see that they already had an audience. Word had travelled round among those on their way to work that 'they' were at their tricks again, and with a bit of luck they might even see some real blood, not that funny stuff that was used in theatres. Someone might even be killed!

The ten paces performed, he prepared to face Latimer, remembering that he must turn sideways, extend his right arm and wait to see Lord Burnside's handkerchief drop. Before that happened, however, Latimer, now firmly in the grip of terror inadvertently tightened his finger on the hair trigger of his pistol so that it fired even before he had completed his turn. The ball thus flew sideways, missing Neville, and hit, instead, Frank Hollis, who fell to the ground bleeding from a wound in the chest.

Henry Latimer stared at him. He was three ways doomed. Neville had the right to fire and might, or might not, fire his pistol into the air. He was dead if Neville chose to fire, and dead if he didn't because, having hit Frank Hollis instead of his opponent, he would find himself in court on a charge of either murder or attempted murder and his destination would be the gallows. At the very least he was socially dead.

He let out a howl, and, throwing his pistol down just before Neville fired into the air, he began to run, as fast as he could, towards his carriage on the edge of the Heath. He had only one idea in his head: to get out of England before he could be caught by the law.

Fortunately for him, Neville and the seconds were too worried over poor Frank's possible death to stop Latimer from escaping. Neville, indeed, knowing that Latimer might try to escape to France, was quite content to let him disappear into the distance, no longer a threat to the peace and stability of his country.

Jackson, meanwhile, who had wanted to be present at the end of the duel rather than its beginning, had reached Putney Heath in time to see Latimer running towards his waiting carriage. Once arrived there, he shoved his driver out of his way, jumped into it and drove in the direction of London. Like Neville and the others, Jackson made no effort to detain him, although he was left wondering what the devil had been going on.

After telling his cab driver to wait, he rapidly made his way up the slight incline to where the remainder of the party, including Neville, were looking after Frank Hollis. Neville was shirtless; he had used his to try to stanch the flow of blood from Frank's wound, and, on seeing him, exclaimed, 'Just the man to help us. We need to get Frank to a surgeon, he's bleeding very heavily—or perhaps bringing a surgeon to him here first might be better. Unfortunately we did not have one with us.'

Frank, who had just returned to consciousness, on hearing the word bleeding and finding that he was surrounded by blood, moaned and lapsed into unconsciousness again.

'I've a cab waiting,' Jackson told him. 'I thought one or the other of you might be in this desperate case. Its driver might know of a surgeon nearby, but before I run to ask him, perhaps someone could tell me how Mr Hollis came to be wounded, seeing that he wasn't one of the principals.'

Lord Burnside, who had met Jackson before and knew of his sterling reputation, replied, 'That idiot Latimer—I trust it was idiocy and not malice—fired on the turn and Mr Hollis had the misfortune to be in the bullet's path, whereupon Sir Neville fired into the air. Perhaps you might like to take a look at poor Hollis and give us your opinion of his wound before you go for help.'

'Deloped, did he?' Jackson smiled, before examining Frank and assuring them that he had been fortunate; although he was losing a lot of blood, since the wound had now been stanched it might not prove fatal.

He returned to his cab to discover that yet another carriage had drawn up to join it and the others. Of course, it was Diana Medbourne's and how she knew of this meeting was yet another mystery to be solved!

'Is he safe?' she called to him, her face anxious.

Jackson did not need to ask who *he* was, but finished his task of asking the his cab driver to fetch the nearest surgeon to them before answering her.

'Yes, but Mr Latimer played the fool and, by what we may charitably describe as an accident, shot Mr Frank Hollis instead.'

'Is *he* safe, then?'

'If the driver returns soon with a surgeon he may live.'

'And Sir Neville is with the rest of the party?'

'Yes.'

'Ought I to leave?'

Jackson thought for a moment, before saying, 'I wouldn't join them on the Heath, if I were you, but it might be a good idea for you to wait here for Sir Neville. It might reassure him to have you with him on the way home. He may, knowing him, feel some responsibility for poor Mr Hollis being shot, and you could reassure him by saying, ''Pooh'' and ''Nonsense'' every now and then.'

This brought a wry smile to her worried face and, soon, the return of the hackney cab whose driver had known of a surgeon nearby. She watched him and Jackson make their way to the wounded man. Yes, she would wait, but not where she could be easily seen, so she instructed her driver to move a little way away.

Some time later, Frank, who had lapsed into unconsciousness again, was driven to the surgeon's home, leaving the rest of the party to make their own way from Putney through streets crowded with workmen's carts and those of the market gardens and farms around London and its suburbs carrying their produce to Covent Garden.

Lord Burnside had given Neville his long, old-fashioned jacket to wear, and congratulated him on his coolness throughout the whole wretched business. Jackson took Neville on one side, saying, 'I gather that you behaved well today.'

'Don't over-refine on that,' Neville riposted. 'I wasn't, fortunately, required to kill Latimer, and was relieved that I didn't need to, but had it been necessary, I would have done. I was extremely happy that, after a fashion, he shot himself.'

'Don't underestimate yourself. You had already proved your courage when you turned up trumps and saved me that night when you had never before fired a shot in anger. That blooded you and gave you an advantage over your opponent, who had only played with pistols, and had never used them for the purpose for which they had been made. I have no doubt that after this morning's disaster Mr Henry Latimer is following the path which many broken men have taken before him and is making for France. Good riddance to him, I say. He can threaten no one now. Please allow me to accompany you to your carriage.'

Neville stared at him. 'I haven't a carriage. Lord Burnside's coachman drove me here so that I might be fresh when the time came for the duel.'

'Your mistake. There is one waiting for you.'

Even Neville could not have believed that his daring Duchess would be waiting for him, so the sight of her when Jackson led him to where she was hiding was not only a surprise, but balm to his weary soul. He might have known that, somehow, she would be there waiting for him. Her boy's clothing was a true reflection of her gallant spirit. Her usual female trappings served only to enhance her beauty: they did not portray the inward Diana.

'What in the world are you doing here?' he asked her, a wry smile on his face. 'How did you find out about the duel?'

'I'll explain later.' She smiled at him. 'It's not easy to deceive me, Sir Neville Fortescue, when I know you so well. I've been waiting to drive you to your grand home in London, or to your less remarkable one in Chelsea. Which shall it be? You may have my groom's seat—Jackson is taking him back to Medbourne House in his cab with a message that I shall be along shortly.'

Neville could not but agree. Damn all conventions, let the gossips say what they might; he knew, without ever having taken her to his bed that Diana, for all her daring, was like her namesake: virgin and chaste. He climbed stiffly into the phaeton, the events of the last two days having finally taken their toll of his strength and spirit.

'Do what you will with me,' he muttered when he was finally beside her.

'You may be sure of that,' she returned merrily, 'and I think, for your sake and mine, that I shall drive you to Chelsea before going home, in the faint hope that we shall both avoid further scandal.'

She didn't need to say 'Pooh' or 'Nonsense' to him because Neville was too tired to talk and her only worry was that he might fall asleep by her, which would be dangerous. He had, however, retained enough of his hard-won self-control to remain awake until he reached Chelsea, where the faithful Lem was waiting for him.

Before he climbed out of the phaeton he said his first words to Diana since he had joined her in it. 'Latimer's disappearance almost certainly means that all the exploited girls have been avenged and you are safe at last from his plotting. Tomorrow, therefore, I shall visit you to make you a proposition that you cannot refuse.'

'Really. Neville, are you so sure of me?'

Now that she knew that he was safe she could not resist teasing him. Only a short time ago she had been fearful that she might never see him alive again; now that he was here beside her, relief was making her light-headed.

'Only of myself,' was his drowsy reply. 'After a good day's sleep, I am certain that I shall be sure of everything. My last request will be that you will allow Lem to act as your groom on your way home. Do not deny me that.'

'At the moment,' she riposted, 'I could not deny you anything, but here is neither the time nor the place where I might oblige you, so my answer is yes.'

Regardless of whoever might be watching them, he left her with a passionate kiss on the lips, before entering his home to be received by an ecstatic Lem.

'I knew you'd win, master,' were his first words to Neville.

'Only after a fashion, and now I will ask a favour of you. That is, that you drive the Duchess home to Medbourne House so that she has a groom with her on her journey into London.'

'Certainly,' and he bounded happily away. Part of his happiness was that Neville had promised him that when all danger for them was over, Belinda would return to London. They would then be able to marry and join Neville's household.

The memory of Neville's kiss left Diana in a fever of excitement and a burning desire to experience more of them.

Tired though she had been, that one short touch of his lips had been enough to set her whole body on fire and she could barely wait for the following day to come when she could see him again.

Alas, tomorrow brought not Neville, but Lem with a letter for her. It informed her that he and Jackson had been most urgently summoned to attend on Lord Sidmouth in his office that very morning and after that to appear before a small private committee in mid-afternoon.

It was, Jackson had told him, extremely unlikely that he would be able to visit her as he had promised and in sending his apologies he assured her that he would call on her on the following day. Diana's disappointment that she would have to wait another day for him was lessened a little by the second page of the letter, which told her of his own disappointment before assuring her of his undying love and admiration.

It was the first love-letter that she had ever received and the most exciting thing of all was that as the letter grew more impassioned, so Neville's usually careful handwriting grew wilder and wilder.

Nothing for it but to send him one back by his faithful servant in which she returned his passion with interest. 'Yes, you must do your duty,' she wrote at the end, 'but, your duty done, you must come to me as soon as possible to obtain your reward, my own darling heart.'

That afternoon Isabella came to her in the drawing room where she sat reading David Hume's philosophical treatise, *An Inquiry Concerning Human Nature,* in the hope that it might be so difficult to understand that puzzling over it would make her forget about having to wait to see Neville until the next day.

Isabella, at her most excitable, immediately began to pour gossip over her. 'My dear, have you heard the latest news about Sir Neville and Mr Latimer? It seems that they quarrelled the other night at Watier's, not long after they had been at the Cowpers' reception, with the result that they fought a duel the very next morning!'

She paused for breath. Diana looked up from her book but, fortunately, before she was required to speak Isabella was off again. 'It appears that when they fought Mr Latimer fired on the turn before the handkerchief was dropped and hit poor Mr Hollis, who is in a bad way, but like to live—unlike Lord Alford, who expired last night. He then ran away.'

Diana refrained from asking which *he* it was, but waited for Isabella to get her breath back again. 'Sir Neville then deloped. The *on dit* is that Mr Latimer is ruined and has fled to France. I was surprised that Sir Neville did not visit you today, he has been such an attentive suitor, but I am sure that he is feeling too overcome to attend on you.'

Diana replied, 'Dear, dear, I haven't heard from him, but I am certain that when he is ready to visit me he will tell me all about it.'

It was as much as she dare say. Fortunately for her, gossip had not placed her on the scene and she had to hope that her grooms would keep quiet about her early morning visit to Putney Heath.

Far from feeling overcome, Neville, driving to Medbourne House on the following morning, was happier than he had been for years. His mission, to destroy those who had been mistreating innocent young women, had succeeded. More than that, the cloud that had hung over him all his life, until he had discovered that Lord Burnside was his father and not the debauched Sir Carlton, had served to uncover in himself reserves of strength, spirit and raw courage that he had never known he possessed.

Oh, he had always been determined to do his duty, to wipe out the stain of his supposed inheritance, but his life had been essentially joyless and severe. And then he had overheard

Frank Hollis and Henry Latimer jeering at his priggishness and comparing him unfavourably with George Alford. Their unkind mockery had made him examine his own behaviour—and find it wanting. The irony of that was that their mockery of him had set in train the change in him that had led them both ultimately to Putney Heath and its consequences, after Lem's appeal to him to rescue his lost Belinda had resulted in his beginning the campaign that had just ended in success.

His encounter with danger in his many adventures with Jackson had also shown him that, whatever else he lacked, it was not courage when he was in a tight corner. Without that he might never have been able to face Henry Latimer calmly when he was on the duelling field at Putney Heath and give a public demonstration of his courage in outfacing him, which had made him society's latest hero.

It was his meeting with Diana, however, with whom he had fallen in love—a woman so different from any of those whom he might once have hoped to make his wife—who best symbolised his journey towards his true self. It was that man who loved her so dearly who was driving to his daring Duchess to propose to her, the strong woman who would complement his own new-found strength, and not the outwardly timid, self-effacing prig he had once been.

So it was that he strode confidently into Medbourne House to find Diana there, alone, waiting for him, dressed not in all her society glory, flaunting her jewellery, but in the simple clothes which, to him, most enhanced her true beauty and which made him love and adore her the more and, as usual, served to overset him.

She rose from her seat on the sofa, her face aglow. She saw at once that Neville was dressed simply and soberly, too. He wore no brocaded waistcoat, no fancy cravat, or over-tight breeches and, like her, he sported no jewellery. His plain attire was that of a gentleman not wishing to stun those around him with a display of wealth and rank.

Diana thought that his face had changed since she had first met him. There were new lines on it, but it also displayed a strength and power that had previously been missing. She did not resent that new-found strength, and she was compelled to acknowledge that he would always wish to protect her, and that, too, was why she loved him.

'May I congratulate you, Sir Neville, on the successful outcome of your recent campaign.'

'Indeed you may, Duchess, and may I thank you for all the help and support which you have given me during it. In my meeting with Lord Sidmouth yesterday, I gave you full credit for your assistance. I will, if you will so allow, delay telling you the rest of what occurred yesterday until after I have dealt with the more important business which I have come here to conclude.'

Why was he being so formal and distant with her? Were they not already betrothed—or had he forgotten that in all the recent excitements? It was time that she reminded him how matters truly stood between them.

She moved forward to throw herself on to Neville's breast, to kiss his right cheek as his arms closed around her, and then to withdraw a little to exclaim, 'For heaven's sake, Neville, if you have come here to discuss with me the due date of our marriage, do so—before I expire with unsatisfied longing!'

'Unsatisfied longing!' he snorted. 'For heaven's sake also, I am so afraid of losing all my hard-won self-control since, without it, I might carry you to the sofa and have my way with you instanter. To be formal will allow me to make our arrangements in due form.'

'Due form! Who wants that? Just tell me plainly that you love me and that you will rush off immediately to obtain a special licence, and then we may do as we please.'

'Oh, my dearest love, I have anticipated you. I took out a special licence a week ago in the hope that once all other considerations were over and done with we could be married at once, without pomp and ceremony—unless you wish it!'

'Pomp and ceremony indeed! All I want is you.'

'As I want you—and now let us put your sofa to some use. Hard though it might be for both of us, I think, that in honour, we should keep to our previous decision to delay the last rites of love until after the marriage ceremony.'

The smile that she offered him was particularly sweet. 'Since the knot will be tied so soon I am compelled to agree with you. But first I must tell you a small secret—I hope that when I have finished you will not immediately flee Medbourne House.'

'A secret? Not too horrid a one, I trust.'

'Not horrid at all, but when I first came to London and was besieged by fortune hunters I consulted my solicitors and they hired poor Dobbins to investigate their finances for me. That's why I knew that Henry Latimer and George Alford's pockets were to let—and now I come to my confession. I hired them to check yours, not long after we first met. Fortunately you were as rich as they were poor.'

Neville began to laugh. 'Fortunately for whom?' he enquired when he could speak clearly again. 'You, or me? Do you marry me for my money, you minx?'

'No more than you marry me for mine,' she riposted.

'So, take your punishment now for ever doubting me,' he exclaimed, and, sweeping her up, carried her over to the sofa to engage in a little love in the afternoon, which only by the exercise of great control by them both, did not turn into a lot of love. Indeed, only a sudden unexpected knock on the door saved them from performing the last rites before the marriage.

If Diana's butler thought that the lengthy period before his mistress cried, 'Enter,' and their somewhat rosy and slightly dishevelled appearance when he did so, told an interesting story, nothing in his expression gave anything away. He was carrying a silver salver on which reposed a letter bearing a most grandiose seal.

'Forgive me for interrupting you, madam,' he announced, 'but a despatch from the Prime Minister, Lord Liverpool, marked extremely urgent, has arrived for Sir Neville. The messenger has already visited his home where he was referred to Medbourne House,' and he offered Neville the salver.

Neville took the letter from it—he knew exactly what it contained—and the butler retired downstairs to tell the housekeeper and the kitchen staff that 'by the looks of it there might soon be wedding bells for the Duchess and Sir Neville, and a good thing, too. She needs a strong man to keep up with her.'

The assembled staff gave a cheer, before continuing to prepare the light early evening meal that Diana had ordered instead of a nuncheon.

Upstairs, Neville said to her, after he had asked for her permission to open and read his letter, 'Not only was your butler's arrival most fortunate for we were both in danger of forgetting ourselves, but this letter will probably save me a great deal of explanation. When I visited the Home Office yesterday to confer with Lord Sidmouth about Henry Latimer's fortunate disappearance into France, he congratulated Jackson and myself for our part in ending the conspiracy in which Latimer had been involved without creating any undue publicity. Not only that, he thanked us for passing on to the Home Office the early news of Captain Knighton's attempt at revolution, which had enabled him to nip it in the bud.

'We were both then brought before a House of Commons committee to receive the formal thanks of the government. Jackson was given a large sum of money as a reward, but mine was somewhat different. I am, and this letter confirms it, to be created Viscount Fortescue in the next Honours list, ostensibly for my work on various committees, but actually as a measure of thanks for the services that I have so recently performed for my country and of which there can be no public mention.

'I know that you will lose your title of Dowager Duchess to become Viscountess Fortescue, but I hope that you will agree that gaining a husband who loves you will make up for that, particularly since without your assistance and encouragement the result of my and Jackson's endeavours might not have been so successful.'

Diana's eyes were shining. 'Ever and always. I shall not mind losing my title, for neither my late husband nor myself acquired ours as a consequence of anything we did, but received them because of the exploits of his ancestors. You, however, have been elevated in rank because of your courage and discretion in carrying out what you saw as your duty—so becoming your Lady wife will be a greater honour.'

'I trust, seeing that we require no great fuss to be made, that we can be married as soon as possible in the chapel, here at Medbourne House, so that we can work together in future as we have done in the past.'

'With Jackson as my best man at the wedding,' Neville suggested.

Diana began to laugh. 'A choice that only a man who married the Daring Duchess would himself dare to make.'

'So be it,' Neville replied, and so it was.

The Daring Duchess had met her match in a man who had learned in a bitter school to find his true self and was rewarded, not only with his title, but with a woman who could match and meet everything that he asked of her—including the love that lasted until the end of their long lives.

A Regency Invitation

to the House Party of the Season

Nicola Cornick, Joanna Maitland,
Elizabeth Rolls

On sale 3rd December 2004

*Available at most branches of WHSmith, Tesco, ASDA, Martins,
Borders, Eason, Sainsbury's and all good paperback bookshops.*

MILLS & BOON®

Live the emotion

Regency Brides

A wonderful six-book Regency collection

Two sparkling Regency romances in each volume

Volume 6 on sale from 3rd December 2004

*Available at most branches of WHSmith, Tesco, Martins, Borders,
Eason, Sainsbury's, and all good paperback bookshops.*

REG-BRIDES/RTL/6

MILLS & BOON

Stroke of **Midnight**

Three gorgeous
men…one sexy
New Year Party!

Jamie Denton   Carrie Alexander   Nancy Warren

On sale 7th January 2005

*Available at most branches of WHSmith, Tesco, ASDA, Martins,
Borders, Eason, Sainsbury's and all good paperback bookshops.*

WE VALUE YOUR OPINION!

YOUR CHANCE TO WIN A ONE YEAR SUPPLY OF YOUR FAVOURITE BOOKS.

If you are a regular UK reader of Mills & Boon® Historical Romance™ and have always wanted to share your thoughts on the books you read—here's your chance:

Join the Reader Panel today!

This is your opportunity to let us know exactly what you think of the books you love.

And there's another great reason to join:

Each month, all members of the Reader Panel have a chance of winning four of their favourite Mills & Boon romance books EVERY month for a whole year!

If you would like to be considered for the Reader Panel, please complete and return the following application. Unfortunately, as we have limited spaces, we cannot guarantee that everyone will be selected.

Name: _____

Address: _____

_____ Post Code: _____

Home Telephone: _____ Email Address: _____

Where do you normally get your Mills & Boon Historical Romance books (please tick one of the following)?

Shops ❏ Library/Borrowed ❏

Reader Service™ ❏ If so, please give us your subscription no. _____

Please indicate which age group you are in:

16 – 24 ❏ 25 – 34 ❏

35 – 49 ❏ 50 – 64 ❏ 65 + ❏

If you would like to apply by telephone, please call our friendly Customer Relations line on **020 8288 2886**, or get in touch by email to readerpanel@hmb.co.uk

Don't delay, apply to join the Reader Panel today and help ensure the range and quality of the books you enjoy.

Send your application to:

**The Reader Service, Reader Panel Questionnaire,
FREEPOST NAT1098, Richmond, TW9 1BR**

If you do not wish to receive any additional marketing material from us, please contact the Data Manager at the address above.

FREE

2 BOOKS AND A SURPRISE GIFT!

We would like to take this opportunity to thank you for reading this Mills & Boon® book by offering you the chance to take TWO more specially selected titles from the Historical Romance™ series absolutely FREE! We're also making this offer to introduce you to the benefits of the Reader Service™—

- ★ **FREE home delivery**
- ★ **FREE gifts and competitions**
- ★ **FREE monthly Newsletter**
- ★ **Books available before they're in the shops**
- ★ **Exclusive Reader Service offers**

Accepting these FREE books and gift places you under no obligation to buy; you may cancel at any time, even after receiving your free shipment. Simply complete your details below and return the entire page to the address below. You don't even need a stamp!

YES! Please send me 2 free Historical Romance books and a surprise gift. I understand that unless you hear from me, I will receive 4 superb new titles every month for just £3.59 each, postage and packing free. I am under no obligation to purchase any books and may cancel my subscription at any time. The free books and gift will be mine to keep in any case.

H4ZEE

Ms/Mrs/Miss/Mr...Initials ....
BLOCK CAPITALS PLEASE

Surname ....

Address ....

....

....Postcode ....

Send this whole page to:
The Reader Service, FREEPOST CN81, Croydon, CR9 3WZ

Offer valid in UK only and is not available to current Reader Service™subscribers to this series. Overseas and Eire please write for details. We reserve the right to refuse an application and applicants must be aged 18 years or over. Only one application per household. Terms and prices subject to change without notice. Offer expires 27th February 2005. As a result of this application, you may receive offers from Harlequin Mills & Boon and other carefully selected companies. If you would prefer not to share in this opportunity please write to The Data Manager at PO Box 676, Richmond, TW9 1WU.

Mills & Boon® is a registered trademark owned by Harlequin Mills & Boon Limited.
Historical Romance™ is being used as a trademark. The Reader Service™ is being used as a trademark.